TROUBLƎMAKERS

TROUBLE

MAKERS

CATHERINE BARTER

carolrhoda LAB

MINNEAPOLIS

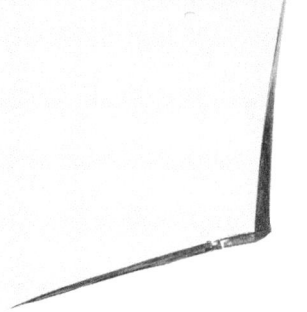

Carolrhoda Lab™
An imprint of Carolrhoda Books
A division of Lerner Publishing Group, Inc.
241 First Avenue North
Minneapolis, MN 55401 USA

For reading levels and more information, look up this title at www.lernerbooks.com.

Cover and interior images: Homer Sykes Archive/Alamy Stock Photo (people);
iStock.com/Hayri Er (glass); iStock.com/Anagramm (barbed wire fence).

Main body text set in Janson Text LT Std 10.5/15. Typeface provided by Linotype AG.

Library of Congress Cataloging-in-Publication Data

Names: Barter, Catherine, 1983– author.
Title: Troublemakers / Catherine Barter.
Description: Minneapolis : Carolrhoda Lab, [2018] | Summary: When east London
  is targeted by a bomber, fifteen-year-old Alena, raised by her half-brother and his
  boyfriend, becomes increasingly rebellious and insistent on learning about her
  long-dead activist mother.
Identifiers: LCCN 2017009176 (print) | LCCN 2017034586 (ebook) |
  ISBN 9781512494235 (eb pdf) | ISBN 9781512475494 (th : alk. paper)
Subjects: | CYAC: Coming of age—Fiction. | Conduct of life—Fiction. | Brothers
  and sisters—Fiction. | Gay fathers—Fiction. | Mothers and daughters—Fiction. |
  Bombings—Fiction. | London (England)—Fiction. | England—Fiction.
Classification: LCC PZ7.1.B3728 (ebook) | LCC PZ7.1.B3728 Tro 2018 (print) |
  DDC [Fic]—dc23

LC record available at https://lccn.loc.gov/2017009176

Manufactured in the United States of America
1-43244-33074-11/7/2017

PART ONE

1

So I went to live with Danny. And that's the end of a story. But it's a story I don't remember because I was three years old. I probably cried for my mother a lot but I don't remember it. I don't remember anything about that time except for when I try and think about it sometimes and I'll remember a blue carpet. That's it, a blue carpet—and then there's nothing else, and then there was Danny. I was three, and he was twenty-two. It was twelve years ago.

"Your brother is amazing," my friend Teagan says to me sometimes. "Don't you think he's amazing?"

I think he's OK. I don't think he ever had much choice in anything. I know there were long conversations with social workers and relatives and who knows who else, including the one where my aunt and uncle told Danny that I should live with them in Australia, and then he threw them out and then they called the police: *that's* a pretty good story, even though Danny never wants to tell it. Apart from them, there probably wasn't a line of people down the street wanting to adopt me. So in one blurred memory there was a blue carpet, and next and always after that there was the apartment in Hackney: wooden floorboards and the big, gray sofa and the elevator up to the fourth floor where we lived; and there was Nick as well, who apparently liked my brother enough that he didn't complain that Danny now came with a three-year-old. He must have really liked him.

This is what I write for my English homework one day: the assignment title is "Family Portrait." I get an A, and my teacher writes, *Very experimental!* and draws a smiley face.

I don't know if she means my writing or what.

2

When I was five or six or something my brother used to hold both my hands and let me run up his legs and I'd use the balance of his weight to do a backwards somersault through this arms. Then I'd hit the floor and say, *Again, again, again.*

Teagan is doing cartwheels outside the school gates. That's what makes me think of this. I'm sitting on a bench with her violin case propped against my knees, waiting for her to stop. We had hockey last period, and Teagan hasn't bothered to change out of her gym clothes, so she's cartwheeling over the cold concrete pavement in her tracksuit. Teagan's the shortest girl in our class and I think this is why she's good at cartwheels, which I haven't been able to do for years. I'm too gangly, all flailing limbs and no balance. Also, I don't like being watched.

Oliver Cohen, sitting next to me, tells her, "I think you should stop, Teagan. You're going to break your arm or something."

"All right, thanks, Dad," says Teagan. She stands up, face flushed, and starts brushing the gravel off her palms. "How many was that?" she says to me, slightly out of breath. "The first one doesn't count. I didn't land properly."

"Six, I think," I say. "Here." I give her violin back as she sits down, and I start searching for my gloves, which are balled up somewhere in my bag beneath all my overdue library books. The sun's out but it's the end of January and still cold, dirty slush on the ground from when it snowed last week, and I came to school without my coat.

Ollie's looking at some guy across the road who's sitting on a bench like ours, all on his own, just watching everybody leaving school. He's got one of those bland, familiar faces, and Ollie says, under his breath, "That guy looks a *lot* like the East End Bomber, if anyone's interested."

"Every old, white guy looks like the East End Bomber," Teagan says. "That's the whole point. That's why they can't find him."

This is true. They have one grainy photo of the East End Bomber. ("I wish they'd call him something else," my brother keeps saying. "What if he decides to branch out?") It's from the CCTV outside a Tesco's supermarket in Shoreditch where last week he left a brown paper bag, the kind they give you if you buy coffee and a sandwich to take away, but with a bomb inside, or an *improvised explosive*, or whatever you want to call it. Some homemade thing with a bunch of wires. Three of them so far, all left lying around supermarkets in East London, like litter. They say there's no technical reason why the bombs don't work. They say the next one probably will. Everybody's wringing their hands because they can't find him and and nobody knows why he's doing it . . .

"That's it," Danny will say, watching the news. "We're leaving. We're moving somewhere safe. Everybody make a list of the safest places they can think of."

Nick and I ignore him. We are not moving.

Ollie starts picking at his nail varnish and then sighs and

leans back and folds his arms and looks sad, which is his default expression. He wears these canvas shoes to school and they're soaking wet from the snow. So no wonder he's sad, I guess.

Ollie got transferred into our class last week. He got into a fight with another boy in our year, supposedly, although it's honestly hard to imagine Ollie fighting anybody. He spends most of his time on his own in the art room or the IT lab, looking sensitive and complicated and drawing pictures of birds. Or now, since he's switched classes, hanging out with me and Teagan, since nobody else wants to talk to him. He's mostly silent, so this is fine with us. Teagan likes the stuff he draws. He did a perfect sketch of her violin, in black and white with colors radiating out of it, and gave it to her. She has it taped on the inside of her locker.

I find my gloves—green with little embroidered stars, a birthday present from Nick's mum, whose presents are always related to keeping me warm—and pull them on.

I'm waiting for Nick to pick me up, which happens basically never, because he hates driving and only takes the car into the city so he can complain about it.

"You don't have to wait," I say to Teagan, but I know she will, because lately she has developed some weird sort of crush on Nick and will take any opportunity to catch sight of him.

She shakes her head. "I'm not. I've got violin. I'm waiting for that." And she digs her hands into the pockets of her tracksuit top and squints up the road.

× × × × ×

It was my birthday two weeks ago. A card from my aunt Niamh turned up yesterday. Her cards are always late, but then who knows how long it takes for mail to get here from Australia.

Even though she hasn't seen me since I was three, she still sends me birthday cards and Christmas presents every year. She writes things like:

Dear Alena,
We wish you a very Happy Birthday and hope we will be able to see you soon. Even though we are far away, if you ever need somebody to talk to, or if you are ever having problems at home, please email us or even phone. We are not in touch with your brother, so you can talk to us in confidence.
With lots of love from Niamh and Drew

Nick says that Niamh and my mother didn't get along and I believe him. Something about the way she never mentions her in the cards she sends. Still, there are probably things she could tell me about her, stories about them growing up, stuff nobody else knows. I think about this sometimes, when the cards turn up.

I actually remember meeting Niamh. Apart from the blue carpet, it's the only memory I've still got from being that young, the only thing that stayed in my brain, stubborn as a weed, when all the memories of my mother just disappeared, emptied out of my head like they weren't important. Honestly, I'm pretty angry with three-year-old-me about this. Stupid little kid not paying attention to the important stuff, not remembering the right things.

So that my first proper memory is this.

Danny crouching down, telling me not to be shy. We are in a bright room with pictures on the walls. I guess it's a play-school or something. Niamh is there. It must be the time she came to visit after my mother died. I've never met her before.

She is coming toward me, holding her arms out, and I start screaming and try to hide behind Danny's leg. She's a total stranger and I have the idea that she wants to take me away.

Probably the only reason I remember this is because that fear used to come back to me a lot, in weird nightmares or sometimes just when I was playing on my own or waiting for my brother to pick me up from school: this anxious, awful feeling that somebody I didn't know was coming to take me away.

Since it turned out that Niamh *did* want to take me away—all the way to Australia, in fact—I obviously had good instincts back then. She'd never even met me until she turned up for the funeral, Danny says, and she was nice at first, trying to be helpful, and then after a few days she started talking about their home in Melbourne and how her husband Drew had a good job and how there was a yard and it was a good place for a child. Thanks but no thanks, Danny said. Then she turned up at the apartment with a lawyer.

Danny makes her sound terrible. They're both crazy, her and her husband, he'll say. Both completely batshit. And Drew's a racist.

Fine. Except every time I get a card from Niamh I feel a little bad about it because after all, her sister had just died and it probably hurt her feelings that I was frightened of her. I never put the cards in the living room or on the fridge where all the others go, or anywhere that Danny will see them, but he knows she sends them. And I've never written or phoned because it seems disloyal and I never have anything to say anyway.

Still. I've kept all the cards. So maybe one day.

3

"Who's the kid in the eyeliner?" says Nick as I get in the car, throwing my bag on the back seat. My bag is brown and it's real leather, but old and scratched and very soft, with red lining that's covered in ink stains from where pens have leaked. I found it in Camden Market last year and persuaded my brother to buy it for me if I cleaned the whole apartment including the inside of the fridge. Which I never did, so it was a pretty good deal.

"Oliver Cohen. He's like that."

"Is he allowed to wear that at school?"

"No. But he makes all the teachers uncomfortable, so they never ask him to take it off."

"I see."

"His older brother got expelled for selling pot at school."

"That's—good to know."

"He wasn't selling it to me."

"Also good to know."

"And if he was, I wouldn't have been able to afford it."

Nick runs a fair-trade coffee shop around the corner from our house and I've been trying to get him to employ me.

"I'm not giving you a job so you'll have money to buy drugs, Alena."

"Fine." I turn the radio on and then off again. "Danny called me twice at lunchtime today. For no reason. Just like, *Hey, I'm just checking in.*"

Nick sighs. "I know. Me too."

"He's having some kind of breakdown."

"No, he's fine. He's just stressed."

"He's making *me* stressed."

"I know. We just have to try and be nice to him."

"I am nice to him."

"I know you are."

Danny's a little obsessed with the East End Bomber. He sits around reading about it all the time. He hasn't been working, or he hasn't been working enough hours that he doesn't have time to sit around reading conspiracy theories online and sending me text messages giving me random safety tips—*don't get in an unlicensed minicab!*—as if there's ever been an occasion in my life where I've gone anywhere in a minicab. I will text him back: *OK!* He'll text back: *Just read an article. anyway have a good day.* So, thanks.

My brother has had a lot of jobs. He used to write for the *Hackney Standard.* Then he worked for a charity, researching and writing long reports that went up on their website. For a while he did something in local television. Then he worked for a local politician. He wrote long reports for her as well. But nobody ever voted for her, and eventually she gave up. That was a few months ago. Then he went back to the *Standard.* Freelance, he said. I don't know what that means, other than that he seems to be at home a lot in the middle of the day.

Nick has been running the coffee shop the whole time. The apartment is always full of coffee samples. I can't smell coffee without smelling home.

There's a lot of ways that Nick and Danny are totally different. Like that Nick gets up at six a.m. and wears nice shirts and does complicated things with his hair, whereas Danny rolls out of bed five minutes before he has to be somewhere and his morning grooming routine basically involves trying not to spill coffee on his shirt. And Danny gets stressed out all the time and always thinks terrible things are going to happen, whereas a word people like to use about Nick is that he's *unflappable*. But then Danny is one of the only people who can make Nick laugh, and he can do it whenever he wants: like if Nick is in the middle of some super-serious speech over dinner about sustainable agriculture, Danny can still catch his eye and get him to crack up. Which is important, I think.

When we get back to the apartment, Danny's sitting on one of the high stools at the kitchen counter, with paperwork spread out in front of him, Bob Dylan playing on the kitchen stereo. Danny loves Bob Dylan. More than is probably normal. He has all of his music and about twenty hardback books about him, lined up on the shelves behind the TV.

The minute we walk in, he shuts his laptop and starts tidying the counter, gathering all his papers together and shoving them into his bag. "Lena, your coat has been lying on the back of the sofa all day," he says to me. "And I've had to look at it all day and think, she's going to freeze to death, and everybody at her school is going to say that it's because I let her go to school without a coat."

I dump my bag on the kitchen counter and roll my eyes at him. "Are you more worried about me freezing to death or about what people would say about it?"

He gives me a very serious look. "I'm more worried about what people would say about it, obviously."

"Are you doing more stuff for Mike?" Nick says, glancing at Danny's paperwork. "You shouldn't do that unless he's actually going to pay you properly."

Mike is the editor of the *Hackney Standard*. We have known him forever.

"He does pay me properly," says Danny. "And no, anyway. I'm working on something else."

"What?" says Nick.

"Since when does Mike not pay me? Mike, our friend, who always gets me work when—you know, he's not just some random—"

"So what are you working on?"

"Nothing," Danny says. "Nothing. Just work. I'll tell you later. Nothing. Anyone hungry? I'll make dinner."

4

"So this is interesting," Danny says. "You'll find this interesting."

We're in the middle of dinner, and I'm trying to pick mushrooms out of my pasta sauce, but it's too hot and I burn my fingertips.

Nick looks up. "Find what interesting?"

"Yeah. I mean, it's funny, actually."

"All right," says Nick, and then there's a long pause.

Danny glances over at me. "I thought you liked mushrooms."

"I don't like it when there's this many of them."

"You liked them yesterday."

"I still like them. I just don't want to eat a meal entirely made of mushrooms."

"So far this isn't interesting or funny," says Nick.

Danny looks between us, wipes his hands on his jeans, leans back in his chair and folds his arms. "Yeah," he says. "So, Nick, do you remember my friend Leonie?"

"Not really."

"My friend Leonie that I went to school with. I ran into her the other day. She's actually—it's interesting. She's something like Chief Executive of Southwark Council now. Or

Deputy Chief Executive, or something like that. Something pretty high up."

"That's interesting," says Nick, which it isn't.

"Yeah. And I mentioned to her that I was looking for work—"

"Why would you—"

"I mentioned that I was looking for work, and she was talking to somebody she knew, and—anyway, so, it's interesting, but I actually ended up getting offered a job."

Nick frowns. "With Southwark Council?"

"No. With someone else. It's on a campaign." Danny very carefully starts twirling a strand of spaghetti around his fork. "I suppose you probably remember Jacob Carlisle."

I don't know who Jacob Carlisle is, although if Danny has started working for him he's probably going to lose whatever it is he's running for. But Nick has gone stone-cold silent and they are having some kind of intense staring match.

"Yes," Nick says, very slowly.

"I know how you're going to feel about this, but it's working with Jacob Carlisle."

"Who's Jacob Carlisle?" I say. Nobody answers. "Hello. Who's Jacob Carlisle?"

"He's a politician." Danny goes back to concentrating on his food. "He used to be our local MP. He's running as an independent candidate for mayor. He hired me as a researcher for his campaign. They liked the stuff I did with Sally."

"He's running for *mayor* now?" Nick says. "As a joke?"

"No. For real. I mean, not that he's going to win or anything, he just wants to kind of put himself out there and—"

"Danny—"

"Listen," says Danny. "Before you get on your high horse, just listen. This is going to be full-time for the next four months, and the pay is like—you know, they've offered me an actual salary, proper money, not just—"

"Well, I would *hope* you got a good price, since you've sold your *soul.*"

"Mayor of London?" I say, which is a stupid question but I'm unnerved. Nick and Danny don't fight, not really, at least not in front of me. They bicker all the time, but you can tell they both enjoy it.

What does happen: sometimes—hardly ever, just sometimes, like for a few seconds—it will seem like they forget that I exist; I'll be right there in the room and they'll be talking about something and in this way I can't really explain, I will just know that they've forgotten I'm there: like for a few seconds they think that they have normal lives and no responsibility to anybody but themselves and each other. I notice this sometimes.

Nick is shaking his head. "How long ago did this happen? Why are you just announcing this now?"

"I thought you might have a problem with it, but I obviously shouldn't have worried."

"You thought I *might* have a problem with it. I can't even—*Danny.*"

I hear the elevator ping as it reaches our floor, and footsteps down the corridor. A door opens and closes. Mrs. Segal next door.

"Let's talk about it later," Danny says, his voice gone suddenly quiet.

"Fine," says Nick.

"Look, I need a *job*," Danny says. "I need a *career.* We can't just eternally live off of coffee and hope that maybe next week I'll get some freelance, you know, whatever—we can't. We need to *save*."

"Why is this suddenly—"

"Lena might want to go to college when she's eighteen, which is not, like, a hundred years away—"

"I don't want to go to college," I say.

"Oh, well, problem solved," Danny snaps.

"I do want to learn guitar."

"OK, she wants to learn guitar, so now we have to buy her a guitar."

"I didn't say you had to—"

"You *have* a guitar," says Nick.

"And then we're going to have to pay for—I do *not* have a guitar."

"Yes, you do. It's in the storage locker."

Danny is briefly distracted by this revelation. "Really?"

"Really?" I say. "Can I have it?"

"Of course you can have it," says Nick. He looks at Danny. "Right? I don't know what it sounds like. Probably needs a bit of fixing up."

"I had a guitar when I was about fifteen," says Danny. "And I sold it or gave it to charity or something."

"Nope," says Nick. "You put it in your mother's garage, and then we put it in storage with everything else."

"Which, by the way," says Danny, "renting that damn storage locker is something else we need to pay for."

"Can we go and get it tomorrow?" I say.

"Yes," says Danny. "Let's go and get it tomorrow. And maybe we can find something in there that we can *sell*, since I'm expected to be unemployed for the rest of my life."

"Don't be so dramatic," says Nick.

"I don't think I'm the one being dramatic."

"Everybody knows that he's a shallow, opportunistic, fear-mongering—he doesn't have a single conviction in his—everybody *knows*, Danny. *You* know."

"When you say *everybody* you mean you and your friends at the coffee shop."

"I mean *our* friends at the coffee shop, yes, for starters."

"And hardly anybody else has even heard of him, so there's not exactly a widespread—"

"I haven't heard of him," I say.

"See? Lena hasn't heard of him."

"Lena." Nick turns to me. "Do you remember when the council tried to close the coffee shop down?"

"No."

"Nick, they didn't try to *close*—"

"About five years ago I got into all kinds of trouble because our friend Jacob Carlisle decided that the coffee shop was *harboring extremism* because some animal rights organization held a meeting there once—"

"They held *all* of their meetings there, and it wasn't just the animal rights people; it was those anti-capitalist anarchist whatever—"

"—and left a few leaflets lying around or whatever and all of a sudden I've got some guys from Special Branch accusing me of selling lattes as a cover for all my terrorist activities—"

"That is a *massive* exaggeration of what happened—"

"And it was all part of Jacob Carlisle's *Let's clean up the streets* campaign which basically meant *Let's kick out independent business in favor of*—"

"And you acted like Jacob Carlisle personally supervised

the whole thing when I'm pretty certain he hadn't then and still hasn't even *heard* of the coffee shop, much less developed some personal animosity toward it."

"Well, OK, then, that absolutely absolves you from selling out your community," says Nick.

There's a very hard silence.

"No," I say. "I don't remember that."

Nick starts cutting up his food into little bits. He's looking at his plate when he says—under his breath but loud enough that we can both hear—"God, I'm just trying to imagine what your mother would think."

I freeze, my fork hovering in the air.

My mother died very suddenly. She had a brain hemorrhage. Or an aneurysm. Something like that. Danny doesn't talk about her. Any time I mention her at all it's like a power outage. The lights go out behind his eyes. If I want to know anything about her, I have to ask Nick, and he hardly knew her. He knew her for like a year or maybe even less. Some of the stuff he tells me I think he makes up just to try and make it seem like she was a real person. She isn't, really, not to me. She's more like a photograph, or not even that.

Sometimes I pretend that I remember her but I don't. I say things like, *Oh, I was playing in the kitchen and she was there reading a book* or *Oh, she used to sing this song to me,* when probably she didn't sing at all, that's just a stupid idea I got from somewhere, a film or something. When I was little Danny used to ask me, sometimes, stuff like, *Do you remember this?* and *What can you remember about that?*, almost like a test, and I'd lie and say yes and make things up, because I thought that he wanted me to remember her. I thought it would make him happy, but it didn't, and anyway he must have known that I was lying. And now we never talk about her at all. Like she never existed.

We definitely don't just casually bring her up around the dinner table, and Nick already looks like he knows he's made a mistake, like he's said something really irreparably terrible.

I scoop up some spaghetti and flinch at the sound my fork makes as it scrapes against the plate. I'm trying to think of something to say to break the silence, but I can't think of anything, and Danny is screwing up his napkin and dropping it on the table, shoving back his chair and taking his plate to the kitchen.

"Danny—" Nick says.

"Let's talk about it later," says Danny without looking at us. He dumps his plate in the sink and then walks down the corridor to their bedroom and goes in, slamming the door.

Nick leans his elbows on the table and rubs his eyes.

I don't know if I should just carry on eating or what. "Why are you trying to imagine what our mother would think?" I say, lowering my voice so Danny won't hear.

"I shouldn't have said that," Nick says. "That was a stupid thing to say. Sorry."

"But—"

"It's just, she'd have hated Jacob Carlisle. She'd have just— politicians like him. You know. She just didn't have a lot of time for them. She thought they were all the same. That's all."

"Oh."

"Never mind. Forget it. I'm sorry."

"I've literally never even heard of him."

Nick smiles, a little. His eyes are red where he's rubbed them. "Lucky you," he says.

Lucky me.

5

I look him up, obviously. Jacob Carlisle. After dinner when I'm sitting cross-legged on my bed with my ancient laptop that barely works. On the front page of his website there's a black-and-white photograph of him writing something down in a notebook, with a phone tucked between his ear and his shoulder, like he was too busy working to pose for an actual portrait. He has short silver hair, but he looks young and healthy and serious. Kind of good-looking, if you like that kind of thing.

There's only four sections on the website. *Who I Am and What I Stand For*, *My Vision for London*, *Election News*, and *Get Involved*.

Get Involved is asking for money and people to deliver leaflets.

Election News says, *Coming soon!*

Who I Am and What I Stand For has another black-and-white picture of him—this time he's leaning against a desk with a cup of coffee, laughing. Underneath, it says:

My name is Jacob Carlisle. I'm a lifelong Londoner; I'm a single parent to a teenage son; I'm a marathon runner, a dog lover, and a football fan. I'm a believer in real democracy, and in an era of cynical party politics,

I'm a true independent. You may not have heard of me, and my opponents would like to keep it that way, but I am running for Mayor of London and I propose an alternative to "business as usual." I'll be shutting down the venues that harbor radical and extremist views before they can infect our communities with hatred; making sure that violent crime is swiftly punished, and that chaotic public protests are better controlled. I'll be ensuring that innocent Londoners are never caught in the crossfire of someone else's war.

That's all it says. I start to wonder if nobody on the campaign knows how to run a website, because me and Teagan have done websites for school projects that have more content than this.

I kind of like the idea that the coffee shop might harbor radical views. The walls and windows are covered with flyers and stickers and leaflets campaigning to stop this and start that and vote for that but not for this, and let's meet here to protest whatever. If you stop and read any of them you realize a lot of them don't even agree with each other, but Nick will let anybody put stuff up as long as it's not, quote, "against the general ethos of the shop." There's a feminist book club that meets there once every two weeks, and sometimes people give talks and do book signings for their self-published novels about radical utopias.

But truthfully: the idea that the coffee shop might infect a community with hatred is pretty funny. It sells milkshakes and mango smoothies, and as far as I can tell, nobody at the feminist book club has ever even read the book—they just turn up and drink coffee and laugh a lot. I've spent almost as much of my life at the coffee shop as I have at home and I feel safe there.

I feel calm. If it ever closed down it would be like the end of the world.

If Nick thinks that my mum would have hated this guy then I believe him, but then what do I know? I have no idea what she thought about anything. The idea that she would hate some politician is interesting. Not earth-shattering or anything, but interesting. It's specific and human.

There's a bunch of her old books in the storage locker, but I usually ignore them because I only really like novels, and these all have titles like *Women's Struggle* and *Global Injustice* and *Resisting War*—the kind of thing that Nick reads, in fact. But I think maybe tomorrow when we go looking for the guitar I'll flick through them, maybe take one when Danny isn't paying attention. Look for clues.

Politicians like him, I imagine myself saying sometime, if Jacob Carlisle is ever on the TV. *They're all the same.* Danny looking at me like I'm a ghost.

6

On Saturday morning they find another bomb. That makes four. This one they have to blow up in a controlled explosion. It's in Mile End or somewhere. A tired-looking man in a suit is on the television, saying that the investigation is ongoing and that people should be vigilant. Danny and Nick both watch with serious faces.

"Morning," I say, padding toward the kitchen in my slippers. There was a cup of tea by my bed when I woke up but it was already cold. Danny and Nick both have coffee and they look exhausted, like maybe they were arguing all night.

They spend the morning being carefully nice to each other, and to me, until I remind Danny that he said he'd drive me out to the storage locker to get his old guitar, and then he gets annoyed again and tries to make Nick do it. Danny hates going out there. But Nick has to go in to work, and eventually I persuade my brother that me getting a guitar will lead to the two of us sitting around talking about Bob Dylan all the time, so he sighs and looks at his watch and says, "Fine, all right, fine, but we're making it quick."

The storage locker is like this vault of treasure. Or it's like someone's moldy garage filled with broken furniture and sad old children's toys. They've been renting it for years, ever since our mother died and Danny sold her house, and it's a forty-minute drive, so all the stuff just sits there, unwanted, rotting away in the dark because nobody—because Danny— can't ever commit to getting rid of any of it. It's mostly stuff that belonged to her, and some of his things from when he was a teenager.

Any time we go there I find something, though. As well as broken furniture there's photo albums and birthday cards, old clothes and cushions and books with yellow pages and cracked spines, letters, coffee tins filled with beads and necklaces, tins of paint and comics and tennis racquets and bicycle parts. Last time I came home with an old Pentax camera that still works and a portable record player and a stack of old vinyls by folk singers nobody remembers. My room is strewn with all this stuff: weird, contextless ornaments and photos of people I don't recognize. "How can you ever find anything you're looking for?" Teagan always says to me when she comes to my house. I can't.

We're in the car on the way and Danny is really quiet.

"I read some stuff about Jacob Carlisle last night," I say.

He glances sideways at me. "Where?"

"On the internet."

"Where on the internet?"

"Did he really try and shut the coffee shop down?"

He looks back at the road, hands braced on the steering wheel. "No."

"Then what's Nick's problem?"

"He just doesn't like him."

"Why?"

"Because he's Nick. Because that's what he's like."

"That's not what he's like."

"Yes, it is. Come on. Nick's like, black and white, good versus evil, he's like—"

"Is he evil?"

"Is who evil?"

"Jacob Carlisle."

"Yes, Alena. He's evil. He drowns puppies. Makes children cry. Hates fair-trade coffee."

"But do you think he's OK?"

There's a silence. The traffic is slow, and up ahead you can hear sirens, like maybe there's been an accident.

"It doesn't matter what I think," Danny says eventually.

"It kind of does if you're going to work for him."

"Look, I don't think he's a bad person. I don't think he's going to destroy the world."

"Is that going to be the campaign slogan?"

He grins. "I don't know, what do you think?"

"I'd probably spend a bit longer on it."

"Yeah, maybe."

"There wasn't that much on the internet about him running for mayor," I say.

"Yeah, well," says Danny. "He's only just declared his candidacy. And he's kind of an outsider. He's an underdog."

"So why is he even bothering?"

"Hey, another great campaign slogan," Danny says. "*Jacob Carlisle: why is he even bothering?*"

"Yeah. But really. Why is he bothering? Why are *you* bothering?"

Danny sighs. He goes serious again. "It's complicated."

"I am capable of understanding complicated things."

He sighs again. "I know you are," he says, but he sounds

so tired I give up asking, thinking maybe I don't even want to know. Sometimes you can't talk to Danny at all.

I reach and turn the radio on. "We will not be terrorized," a voice is saying. "The people of this city are stronger than that."

I change the station.

7

We find the guitar; it only has two strings, but when I wipe away the dust with my sleeve, the body is smooth and unscratched, almost like new.

Danny wants to leave as soon as we find it, but I persuade him to let me look around for a bit.

"Ten minutes," he says. "I'm going to go talk to the manager. See if we can get some kind of discount for renting for so long. Don't touch anything that looks dangerous."

"Like what?" I say, but he's already gone.

I prop the guitar up carefully by the door and squint through the gloom at the rest of the stuff. There's an old dressing table with a cracked mirror that's been sitting in the corner for as long as I can remember, and on top of it there's a stack of books. I go over and pick up the top one.

It's an old paperback with a yellow cover and it says in black letters: *A Guide to Disobedience* by Ellen Caffrey. It's tattered and fragile and there's a coffee ring staining the front. I open it, and on the first page someone has written, *To Heather. Thought of you! Happy birthday. With love, Lynn.*

Heather is my mother. I try to think of when her birthday is but I realize I don't know. I don't know if I've ever known.

I stare at some woman called Lynn's loopy, unfamiliar

handwriting for a moment, and then flick through the pages of the book, which are dry and delicate and sun-faded, even though it's been sitting here in the dark for years.

Someone has tucked a postcard into the middle and I take it out. I actually collect old postcards. I used to be organized about it: I have folders at home where they're all categorized by theme. But all my recent ones are just stuck around my mirror or inside my locker and tucked inside books. You can buy whole boxes of them at charity shops and markets, but I'm selective. I like ones with people in them.

I squint at the picture. It's black and white, and there are lots of women lying on the ground with their arms linked together. Some of the women in the middle have their fists raised in the air. I like the expressions: they look angry and joyful at the same time.

No one has written anything on it, but there's a few lines of small printed text on the back.

Published by Sheffield Women Against Pit Closures and Hackney Greenham Women: WOMEN MAKE LINKS. Set of eight postcards. Women blockade the Blue Gate, USAF Greenham Common, in July 1983. L-R: Sue Dines, Lynn Wallace, Heather Kennedy, unknown, DeNel James, unknown.

So I turn it back over and look at the third woman from the left, who has her eyes closed and is shouting something at the sky, and who is, apparently, Heather Kennedy. My mother.

Then I hear Danny coming back, so I tuck the postcard back inside the book and put the book into my bag. There's a pair of glasses with black plastic old-fashioned frames on top of the dressing table, too. I pick them up and turn them over in my hands, and then I put them on and turn to look into one of the dusty mirrors leaning against a wall.

"I can see through these," I say as Danny comes back in. It's true: the glasses are filthy but even through the grimy lenses everything seems a little sharper. Danny comes and stands behind me, and we look in the mirror.

"We should get your eyes tested," Danny says. Then he glances at what I'm wearing, obviously noticing for the first time today. "Lena, are you trying to style yourself as an eccentric character?" he says. "Don't we ever buy you new clothes?"

I can see what he means. I'm wearing a t-shirt that used to be his, and an old cardigan from a charity shop with leather patches on the elbows. My jeans are washed-out and rolled up at the ankles, and my red Converses are scuffed beyond recognition. My hair is getting way too long and my part is crooked. A few weeks ago I tried to dye blue streaks in my hair: it didn't really work because my hair is too dark, but you can still see them, uneven widths and faded indigo, growing out at the roots. The glasses basically complete the look.

He's not much better, in a t-shirt I happen to know he's had since before I was born, and jeans splattered with white paint from when he repainted the bathroom. Which is still basically like formal-wear for him.

"Were these our mum's?" I say, carefully touching the frame of the glasses.

He hesitates, meets my eye in the mirror for a moment. Then he turns away, picks up his jacket from where he's tossed it on the back of an old chair. "I suppose so," he says, flatly. "Come on, let's get out of here. I've got stuff to do."

I take the glasses off and put them in the front pocket of my bag. I don't want them to get broken, but I reckon if they've lasted all this time, they must be hard to break.

8

"Listen," Danny says when we get back in the car, after I balance the guitar carefully on the back seat. "I actually have to swing by my new job, just for ten minutes. It's out of the way but I have to sign some stuff. You can come with me or you can wait in the car, and then we can go and get guitar strings or whatever you need, OK?"

"Whatever I need?"

"Yeah. Do you need something?"

"Yes," I say, although I don't know what. I'll think of something. Then I look at him. "Are you trying to buy my loyalty?"

"Yes," he says. "Will it work?"

I say that yes, it probably will.

× × × × ×

Danny takes us to a tree-lined street of big, white-terraced houses in west London and parks on the street. There's a Jacob Carlisle poster in one of the ground-floor windows.

"Is this his office?" I look down the road, wondering if anybody famous lives in any of the houses.

"Yeah." Danny turns the engine off and sits for a moment as it ticks, cooling down. "But I think it's his house. Or one of his houses. Something like that."

"Oh, right. Just one of his houses."

"Yeah. He's pretty rich. Do you want to come in?"

"Not especially. Do you want me to come in?"

"Not especially, since you're dressed like some orphan I just found in the street."

"You don't want to do your *Hey, everyone, here's my sister who I heroically raised single-handedly, aren't I a great guy* routine for them?"

He grins. "No," he says. "Not today." Getting out of the car, he says, "Ten minutes. Don't get in trouble."

I've never been in trouble a single day in my life, but Danny says this to me probably fifteen times a day. He says it to Nick too. *I'm going to buy some milk. Don't get in trouble.* What trouble he thinks we're going to get into I have no idea.

I watch him as he walks up to the front door. He punches a key-code on the security panel and goes inside.

This isn't the first time he's been here, I realize. And for some reason it's not until then, until I watch the door swing shut behind him, that it occurs to me that he must have been lying to us for a while.

× × × × ×

I decide I need a new set of highlighters for school and somehow Danny ends up buying me twenty-five different colors of the most expensive kind, even though, honestly, I don't highlight that often. Then he finds a music shop for guitar strings and then we stop at a Starbucks for coffee and orange juice. We sit at one of the tables by the window and I watch people going past with their shopping bags and headphones. Across the road there's two policemen standing in front of the subway station with huge guns and blank expressions, neither of which, I think, will help all that much if someone leaves a homemade bomb in a sandwich bag somewhere, but anyway.

There's a weird nervousness everywhere, here included; people looking at each other suspiciously while they drink their coffees. I get a message from Teagan. *I have literally been in that Mile End Tesco's 100s of times it's near where I used to do orchestra*, she says, followed a few seconds later by *!!!!!!!!*

You could be dead right now! I text her back and then feel bad for making a joke.

I could literally be dead!!! she replies.

I send her a photo of myself, looking fake-shocked, and she replies, *You're in Starbucks! I can see the cups! Nick will flip.*

This is true. If he knew we were inside Starbucks he'd go mental: he'd deliver his lecture about protecting independent businesses and make me and Danny both read *A Very Short Guide to Ethical Living* again.

"So," I say, putting my phone down.

"Hm?" Someone's left a newspaper on the table and Danny's trying to do the Sudoku with a blunt pencil. He can't do Sudoku and is therefore obsessed with it even though it's basically for old people who don't want to get Alzheimer's, which I've told him.

"When I'm seventeen, will you teach me to drive?"

He stops what he's doing and looks up, studies me for a moment. "Don't talk to me about you being seventeen," he says. "That makes me feel ancient."

"You've got the Sudoku to keep you young, though."

He looks back at his paper. "Yes, thank you."

Squeezing my hands together under the table, I say in a rush, "So do you know someone called Lynn who was friends with our mum?"

His pencil is pressed against one of the empty boxes but he doesn't write anything. He goes very still and puts the pencil down and I *knew* it. I knew he would do this and I don't even know why I thought it was worth trying because I *knew* it. Power cut, all systems down, you have trespassed into a forbidden area. "I'm sorry?"

"Someone called Lynn."

"Someone called Lynn."

"Yeah."

"No. Why are you asking me that?"

"I think she was a friend of Mum's."

"What are you talking about?"

I reach under the table for my bag, search around inside and find the book, push it toward him, and flip open the first page. He looks at it and I almost snatch it back because, for some reason, I get this idea that he will take it and not give it back. My heart is beating a tiny bit faster than it should. It's weird how you can still sometimes feel nervous with someone you've known every single day of your life.

"What's this?"

"I found it just now. See, it says, *Happy Birthday from Lynn* inside. I wondered if you—"

"Alena, I told you not to go hunting through all that shit, all right? It's not *safe* in there. All that old furniture is dangerous. There's nails and god knows what."

"Nails."

"Yes, *nails*."

"Right," I say. "It's amazing I wasn't killed when I picked up this book, by a *nail*—"

"All right, cut the attitude."

I take the book back, hold it on my lap. "*Happy birthday.*

With love, Lynn. I thought you might know who she was. There was actually—that's not the only thing I found. There was also this postcard—"

"All right, OK. Yeah. Lynn. She had a friend called Lynn, maybe. Yeah."

"I've never heard of her."

"So? She had lots of friends."

"Did she?"

"If you want to call them that. She knew a lot of people. Like anybody does."

Not anybody. I have one friend. Two if you count Ollie. Danny thinks he has friends but they're mostly people he hasn't seen in years. He really only spends time with me and Nick.

"Did you—I mean, you obviously didn't—did you stay in touch with any of them?"

Danny folds his newspaper over and finishes his coffee, puts the mug down in a *let's go* way. "No."

"Didn't you ever want to—"

"Look, not right now, OK?"

"Not what right now?"

"This."

"What?"

"Alena."

"*What?*"

"We need to get going. We should get home. We shouldn't be in Starbucks. Nick can sense it." He sees the expression on my face and says, with what sounds like a lot of effort, "Yes, she had a friend called Lynn. It was a really long time ago. All right? There's nothing else I can say about it."

Greenham Common, *A Guide to Disobedience*, a postcard

with a picture of both of them on it—it seems like there's a lot he could say about it, or *someone* could say about it. She would have hated Jacob Carlisle, Nick reckons.

But I back off. I drop it. We are having a nice day. I have a guitar. And I want him to think of me like a grown-up, not some kid who's always nagging him.

Nick always says you have to be careful with Danny. Whatever that means.

9

This is what it means.

You have to be careful with Danny. In fact, there are lots of people out there that you have to be careful with: treat them like they might be carrying ancient unexploded weapons inside, like those Second World War bombs they find buried in allotments. We had a math teacher once who found one of those at the end of her yard. She had to call a bomb disposal team. *Things that are old are not necessarily inert*, she said. She spoke like that. She was very profound. Sometimes I used to write her sayings down on the inside of my math book. Anyway.

Danny is like this. I never even really knew it for years until this one day when I was twelve—I know I was twelve because it was right after my twelfth birthday and right around the time all the women I know, like Nick's mum, Teagan's mum, and Zahra at the coffee shop, started giving me boxes of tampons and telling me I could talk to them anytime if I ever didn't want to talk to Nick and Danny about *Things*, which Danny found hilarious and Nick was offended by.

The things people think must be difficult about my family are never the same as the things that are actually difficult.

Anyway, I was twelve, and I asked my brother why there was no grave.

I was going through a weird religious phase which they had both been stoically ignoring. We had been learning in school about different religions and their traditions around death. And all of them had seemed beautiful to me, really nice.

And someone had said in class that they didn't know anybody who had died, and without thinking I said, *Me neither*, and a couple of people in the class had whispered to each other behind my back and that's the only reason I remembered that I *did* know somebody who had died.

Isn't that bad? That I forgot? I know. Her not being there was like cars and windows and breakfast. It was every day. I just never thought about it.

"Is it because she was cremated?" I asked him. And then suddenly I wasn't even sure about that. "*Was* she cremated?"

It didn't seem like that serious a question. Like how did Napoleon die, or something.

Danny stopped what he was doing but he didn't look at me. He was standing on a chair. He'd been trying to reattach the fire alarm to the ceiling, and I was holding the back of the chair so it didn't wobble. He'd given up trying to connect it properly and had just been trying to force it to snap back into place. It had been broken for weeks, just the plastic base on the ceiling with a few wires hanging down. But Teagan was coming around later, plus this other girl from school that we were briefly friends with, and Danny obviously wanted their parents to think that their daughters wouldn't die in a fire at my house because he was a competent parent who could fix a fire alarm, which he couldn't.

"Yes," he said eventually in that flat voice that I recognized but hadn't yet worked out was a warning sign. Danger, danger. Abort.

"Oh. But you didn't do a plaque or something?"

"A plaque?"

"Or something."

"No."

"Wouldn't it have been better if there was somewhere to visit?"

"Wouldn't what have been better?"

"For me. Like if there was somewhere to visit. Somewhere I could go and think about her."

He lowered his arms and held the fire alarm in both hands, looking at it.

"Or we could go together. Or we could all go. Every year or something, like at Christmas."

He raised the fire alarm closer to his face and tried to do something with one of the little gold connections where the wires are supposed to attach. Maybe he thought if he ignored me I'd shut up.

"Or we could go on her birthday. Or *my* birthday."

Still not looking at me, Danny said, "What's this about?"

"What's what about?"

"Why are you asking me this?"

"I think it'd be nice if there was somewhere to visit. A grave or something."

"This is the first time you've ever said that to me."

"I know it is."

"So you've just suddenly got this idea, or why are you—"

"I've just been thinking about it."

He whacked the fire alarm pointlessly with the heel of his hand and started speaking monotone. "She wouldn't have wanted anything like that. She was all like, stars and dust and rivers. Returning to the cosmos. The idea of some kind of block of stone—"

"Or a tree. Some people plant trees. There are these special parks—"

"So let's add that to the list of my many failures. I could have planted a tree. I'm sorry. I didn't plant a tree. I didn't think about it. I was twenty-two. I didn't plant a tree."

"You don't have to be like—"

"Why are you suddenly—what is this about?"

"It's not about anything. I was just thinking that—"

"You can plant a tree if that's what you want to do. If you care that much about it, you can plant a tree. Do what you like. Trees take about a hundred years to grow but if that's what you want, then do it. I don't want a tree."

I let go of the back of the chair and took a few steps back.

Danny said, "If you don't hold on to this chair I'm going to break my neck."

If you care that much about it, you can plant a tree. It seemed like such a mean thing to say. It probably doesn't sound that bad. I am a sheltered child. I felt like I'd had a door slammed in my face when I hadn't even known there had been a door there.

This was also around the age I quite often burst into tears for no reason, so I don't suppose either of us was that surprised when my voice shook and I said something like, *Oh my god, you don't have to be like that. I'm just asking—*

"Alena."

"How would you feel if you died and I didn't do anything, I just forgot about you?" I said.

He should have probably gotten down from the chair but he didn't; he just stood there holding the fire alarm and not looking at me. "Nobody's forgotten about anybody," he said, and I said, "Yes, they have: you've forgotten about her," when what I really meant was that I had forgotten about her without even noticing—but his face went very dark.

"I was twenty-two," he said again, like that mattered. "How was I supposed to know—I didn't know what to do. How was I supposed to—you can't just turn around now and go, *Oh, I want a tree, I want a plaque, I want somewhere to go*, when you weren't even—maybe if I hadn't been so busy worrying about *you*, then I might have had *time*—"

I remember he was suddenly like some person I didn't know: some strange, angry person whose voice was rising for no reason—and he was still standing on a chair and in my memory he was actually frightening, with this weird, blank, angry expression—and I was saying, "*Everybody* has *something*; you're supposed to *remember* people—" and he was saying, "I'm the only one who *does* remember—" and then, like a psycho child, because I guess I didn't want to hear what he had to say, I picked up a glass from the kitchen counter and smashed it on the floor. I don't remember doing this but I know it happened, and later on when Nick was sweeping up the glass and I told him I couldn't remember doing it, he said he believed me, which was nice. Honestly, it was like I was possessed for a second. Somebody's ghost came into the kitchen and ran through me.

Danny said, "Jesus *Christ*, what the *hell* are you doing?" and then tried to get down from the chair but he tripped and smacked his knee on the coffee table. And he dropped the fire alarm and when it hit the floor it went off, and when Nick walked in about a minute later, the fire alarm was shrieking and Danny was shouting at me and I was crying and the neighbors were in the hallway about to call the police.

So that was the last time I raised the subject with Danny.

Later that day Nick sat me down and had this watershed *I'm going to talk to you like an adult* conversation with me which, after thinking I wanted it, it turned out I hated and I immediately wanted cuddly toys and bedtime stories again. Nick told me that after she died there was so much stuff to deal with—with me and my aunt and uncle and everything—that Danny never really got a chance to actually grieve, which, Nick says, is a really important process, and that's one of the reasons Danny's basically still walking around all shell-shocked and like he's mortally wounded all these years later. Because he never had a chance to grieve properly. And I just thought when Nick said that, and I still just think: *Well, guess what, neither did I.*

I learned my lesson though. Things that are not safe to talk about. Me and Danny were weird and careful with each other for ages, like we were covered in broken glass and kept finding bits of it on our skin. I never wanted it to happen again. I hate fighting. I still cry easily. You have to be careful with me as well, I guess. Or I break things.

10

Teagan never cries. Almost never. We've been friends nearly six years and the only time I've ever seen her cry was once watching *Finding Nemo*. She used to wear these thick-lensed glasses to school and people used to try and make fun of her and steal them off her and whatever, but within about thirty seconds it would be obvious that she wasn't going to get upset or even respond in any way; she'd just carry on with whatever she was doing and look bored, and there is just no point trying to pick on someone like that. They are immune. This is a good quality to have in a friend, I think.

She wears contact lenses now, anyway. And she has a sheepskin duffel coat that used to be her mum's that every girl in our school is in love with. And I have my leather bag from Camden Market and no one really talks to us but honestly, we sometimes feel invincible.

x x x x x

Monday night, we are in the coffee shop, the same booth at the back where we always sit.

We spend a lot of time at the coffee shop. Teagan even drinks actual coffee, and her parents will let her stay out late if they know that's where we are.

A few months ago somebody turned the empty building on the corner of the street into art studios, and suddenly all these skinny, good-looking people are here all the time, having intense conversations over black coffees and then standing outside to smoke. They never notice us, so we can just watch admiringly. Other kids in our class meet outside the Caffè Nero near our school in the evenings, but no one's got any money to do anything, so they just stand around smoking cigarettes they've stolen off their older sisters or drinking gin and orange squash or whatever weird combination they've smuggled out of their house in a plastic bottle. Me and Teagan joined them once but nobody spoke to us and it was raining and cigarette smoke makes me want to throw up, so we left. We came here.

Tonight it's nearly empty. The radio is playing quietly and Zahra, who works here, is sitting behind the counter reading a law textbook and scribbling in the margins with a pencil. Nick is in the back office doing money.

There's a chalkboard on the wall behind the counter that's supposed to say that day's special offers, and Zahra is artistic, so she's supposed to update it. But there never are any special offers, so it always just says stuff like, *Today's Special: Revolution!* And then a drawing. Tonight it says, *Buy one cup of coffee, get one cup of coffee* and then a picture of a rainbow with a coffee cup at the end.

I have aspirations to write on the chalkboard myself one day.

Outside it's dark and starting to spit rain against the windows. Teagan has her laptop on the table and is pretending to research our joint history project, but really she's reading music on the internet. She likes to do this. Look up the scores for pieces of classical music that she wants to learn on her violin, and then just sit there, reading the screen like it's a book. Teagan is a big classical music geek. She's always going around school with her headphones in, listening to Sibelius or Schoenberg or some other dead composer. I know the names of the composers because she emails me their violin concertos sometimes. I hardly ever listen to them but I think it's nice when people are super enthusiastic about something.

Sometimes I think that I need a weird interest or a hobby or a special skill. Something where people will say, *Oh, yeah, that's Lena Kennedy—she's really into Caribbean cooking*, or *Yeah, that's Alena—she's amazing at gymnastics*.

Instead of what they say now, which is, *Oh, that's Lena Kennedy—she lives with her gay brother and his boyfriend*. Which is not really about me at all.

"Are there any pictures of the assassination of Franz Ferdinand?" I say.

I have written *History Project!* at the top of a blank page in my notebook and highlighted it in purple.

Teagan turns away from the screen and looks at me. "Wow," she says. "I hope not."

"Look it up."

"In a minute." She turns back to the screen, starts twisting a strand of hair around her finger. She got her hair cut right after Christmas, super short with sideswept bangs that she keeps tugging at, like that will make them grow long again. She has two piercings in each ear, which isn't allowed at our school, and now that she's got no hair to hide them with, she knows she's going to get a letter to her parents any day. She doesn't care.

"Because we could do a visual history of the causes of the war," I say. "With pictures."

"Or we could do a *cartoon* history of the causes of the war," Teagan says, turning back to the screen. "Like we could draw it all ourselves and make it really funny."

"I don't think it's supposed to be funny."

"All right, we'll make it really sad, then."

I doodle a little sad face in my notebook. "I don't think Ollie's coming."

She looks at her phone. "He is. He's getting the bus. He's probably on it now."

"I don't think he leaves his house. I think he just stays at home coding and listening to weird electronic music."

"He's not into coding."

"Well, whatever he's into. He just doesn't seem as if he's the most sociable—"

"And he doesn't like his house. He's a home-avoider. Sometimes when I finish violin practice it's like six o'clock and he'll still be in the computer lab on his own. The janitor has to kick him out." Teagan puts her phone down. "Honestly. He was excited we invited him."

"I don't think excited is one of his emotions."

"He was slightly less depressed for about half a second."

We were both kind of reluctant to invite Ollie to hang out here with us, because the coffee shop is our place and is better than most other people's places, and once you've invited someone somewhere they might think they're always invited and just start turning up. Also Ollie gets a weird look on his face when I mention Nick or my brother and you don't know with people, sometimes.

But we invited him anyway, because we are good people.

"So Nick's like—your stepbrother, or your stepdad, or something?" Ollie said when we told him about the coffee shop.

"No," I said. "Not really. He's just Nick."

"What do you call him?"

"I call him Nick."

"What did you call him when you were little?"

"I called him Nick."

"Regardless," said Teagan, which is a word she likes. "If you want to meet up with us there one night—" She glanced at me, and I nodded. "Or whatever. That's fine."

Ollie rubbed one of his eyes and smudged black eyeliner into the crease of his eyelid. "All right," he said. And then, after a while, "Thanks."

By the time he turns up it's nearly closing time and when he sits down he says, "I can't stay long. I have to go home. There's something wrong with the dog. I think she ate something. She was sick on the carpet."

Zahra at the counter is looking at us with her eyebrows raised like she's never seen me with anybody else but Teagan, which she probably hasn't. She briefly disappears into the back office, maybe to tell Nick the news.

"What kind of dog is it?" says Teagan.

"I dunno. Some kind of terrier or something. She's a pain." Ollie's eyes are roaming around the walls of the coffee shop, looking at all the posters.

The way Ollie does his eyeliner is actually beautiful. I have tried wearing eyeliner about four times and even watched a bunch of tutorials on the internet about how to do it properly, and it just looked wobbly and uneven and stupid and made me look old—not sophisticated-old, just old—and so I gave up. But Ollie does it perfect so he just looks like he has naturally black-rimmed eyes, like some sad exotic bird or lizard or something. It's really a skill he should get more credit for.

I get up to get him a drink and when I sit back down he is looking at the chaos that me and Teagan have spread out all over the table: textbooks and notebooks and pens and lip balm and empty glasses. He looks slightly stressed by it. I think Ollie likes things to be neat.

The black-and-white postcard from the storage locker is also on the table. He picks it up.

"See that woman with curly hair, with her fist raised?" says Teagan. "That's Lena's mother."

I always show Teagan the stuff that I find in storage. Her parents are beautifully neat and organized people with photo albums all labeled by date and subject, and her mum did a family history course and produced a family tree with all these black-and-white photos of Victorian relatives who died of consumption. She has all the documents in a special album with protective archive paper. So the near non-existence of my family history has always been interesting to Teagan.

Ollie is staring down at the picture, hair falling in his face. "I thought she died," he says.

"She did," I tell him. "It's an old picture."

"She died after it was taken," adds Teagan helpfully, which makes it sound like she died later that afternoon instead of twenty years later.

He looks at it more closely, then glances back up at me. "Is she protesting Vietnam or something?"

"Uh, no," I say. "It's not *that* old."

"It's about nuclear weapons," says Teagan. We looked it up. "They were all camping out at an army base to protest nuclear weapons. They were there for years. Isn't that a great picture? I love that picture. In a million years my mum would never have—"

"Anyway, give it back," I say, but Ollie has turned the card over and is reading the text.

"Who's Sue Dines, Lynn Wallace, all these other women?"

"Don't know." I reach and snatch it out of his hand, tuck it back inside my notebook. "Lynn Wallace was one of my mum's friends."

"Which one's she?"

"The black woman on the left, in the jacket."

"Do you know her?"

"No. My brother remembered her. I tried looking her up but there's about a thousand Lynn Wallaces."

"Oh." He looks over my shoulder and I can see him reading the chalkboard. Then back at me. "She's dead," he says. "Your mum."

"Very tactful, Oliver," says Teagan.

"Yes," I say. "She died."

"How old were you when she—"

"I was three."

"Oh. How old was your brother?"

"Twenty-two."

I don't know why this is difficult to process but his eyebrows are knitted together like he's thinking really hard. "Why's he so much older than you? He's twenty years older than you."

"Yes," I say, like I'm talking to a child. "It's because he was born twenty years before me."

"But I mean—"

Teagan clears her throat and says, "Ollie, when did *your* dad die?"

Ollie blinks a few times. "He didn't die. He lives in Swansea."

"What?"

"He lives in Swansea. He has another family." He picks up his headphones from the table and loops the wire around his fingers. "They just had a baby."

"I thought he was dead," says Teagan.

"So did I," I say.

"No. My mum wishes he was dead, I think."

"I can't believe this." Teagan is looking at Ollie like he's betrayed her deeply. Honestly, I don't know why we both thought his dad was dead other than that Ollie never mentions him and goes around school with a sort of tragic air about him.

"Sorry," says Ollie, shrugging.

"How often do you see him?" I say.

"I dunno. Not that much. He's got all these other kids now."

Teagan is shaking her head. "I really thought he was dead."

"No. Swansea." Ollie taps his fingers against the table top. He hasn't opened his drink. I gave him a can of the organic apple cola from the fridge next to the counter. It's good. I want him to drink it and acknowledge this.

"So was she some kind of radical or hippie or something?" says Ollie. "Your mum?"

"What?"

"Protesting nuclear weapons."

"Oh," I say. "Yeah. I guess. I don't know."

"How did she die?"

"She had a brain thing," I say. "An aneurysm."

"Like, sudden?"

"Yes. Sudden."

"Oh," Ollie says. And then, "Sorry."

"Ollie, what do you think about Jacob Carlisle?" says Teagan. She nods her head in my direction. "Since you're so interested in her family. Her brother's got a job with him."

"I've never heard of him," says Ollie.

"Yeah. He's running for mayor but nobody knows. Lena, if he wants to win he should probably tell somebody that he's running."

"Good idea," I say. "I'll tell Danny."

"Anyway, I looked him up. I think he's good-looking. He's not even that old. I think he's going on The List."

The List is a piece of paper with *The List* written at the top that she keeps inside her violin case. It's a list of men she's in love with. A lot of them are really old. I'm not totally clear on the purpose of The List and neither is Teagan, but it's been going for a long time. For about five minutes Nick's name was on it but I made her take it off. "Wrong in so many ways," I told her.

"What's the list?" says Ollie, and Teagan says, "You're not ready for that information, Oliver."

× × × × ×

Ollie stays for less than half an hour and he never drinks his apple cola—he takes it with him when he leaves, tucked inside the pocket of the gray hoodie he always wears instead of a coat.

It's nearly nine. The coffee shop usually closes by then. There's a movie on TV and Teagan is supposed to stay over. We've been promised the sofa and the remote.

There was a time when we were little that she wasn't allowed to sleep over at my house. Then she used her parents as a case study of intolerance during Celebrating Diversity Week at our school. She had a poster and everything. *This is Rachel and David Esler and they are intolerant.* This was years ago, but Danny and Nick continue to find it hilarious.

We give up on our history project and I head to the back office to ask to go home, even though I promised to stay out of the way.

I stand in the doorway and wait to be noticed. Nick is on the phone, slouched low in his office chair. On the computer screen in front of him there's a spreadsheet.

"I appreciate that," he's saying. "But we've had a very long relationship with this supplier." He notices me and nods, holds up a finger to tell me to wait. He's been back here doing business stuff for hours. His hair is sticking in all directions like he's been running his hands through it all evening. I don't know if this is intentional; you can't always tell with him.

"Teagan thinks Jacob Carlisle is attractive," I say, as soon as he hangs up.

"Oh yeah," Nick says, swiveling on his chair to face me. "If you're attracted to the vacuous and corrupt and ideologically—"

"Anyway, we want to go home."

"Tough."

"And you've run out of bananas."

"What do you care if—"

"We can't have milkshakes."

"Have something else."

"We can walk home. We'll be fine."

"Nope," says Nick. "Not at night. Is your friend still here?"

"Teagan?"

"Zahra said you had another friend. A boy."

"*A boy.*"

"Yes. A boy." His cell phone starts vibrating on the desk. He picks it up and looks at it.

"Is that Danny?" I say. "I bet I'm psychic and that's Danny."

He puts the phone down and lets it buzz away. "And being *attractive* isn't a good reason to vote for somebody, OK?"

"Well, I can't vote, so it doesn't really—"

"If you want to talk about politics, you know, we can talk about politics. I'm not going to tell you what to think."

"I know that," I say. "I don't want to talk about politics. I want a banana milkshake."

"Hey," he says. "Bananas are political."

He reads the expression on my face and grins. The *bananas are political* lecture is not one of my favorites. "Anyway. Is your *other* friend still here?"

"No. He had to go home."

"Does he live nearby?"

"Yes. You could have come and said hello if you're that interested. It's just Ollie from school."

"I didn't want to embarrass you."

"You wouldn't embarrass me."

His phone buzzes again, once. Danny has probably left him a message.

"We want to go home," I say.

"Twenty minutes, kid," he says, turning back to his spreadsheet.

"We can walk on our own."

"No."

"What do you think will happen?"

He looks serious for a moment. "Nothing will happen," he says. "But just wait for me. This won't take much longer."

"What are you doing? Is it boring?"

"It's extremely boring."

"OK," I say, "we'll wait." As if I'm doing him a favor.

"Thank you," he says.

The reason they never want me to walk home from the coffee shop at night is that Nick got hit by a car once, walking home from work. He has a big scar on his head but you can hardly see it under his hair. It goes from his forehead to his ear. And his shoulder got smashed up so bad it's now full of bits of metal holding it together. Nick's parents stayed at the apartment on the fold-out sofa and I didn't see Danny for two days because he was at the hospital with Nick. Nick was OK, though.

He was on the pavement. I think about that sometimes. The things that can happen when you're just standing on the pavement, how vulnerable a person's body is. All the different places it can break.

11

It is weird, I guess, that Danny is so much older than me.

There's this one photo that I found in the storage locker last year, that now I've got stuck above my desk. In it our mum has big eighties hair and she's wearing sunglasses on top of her head, and Danny is a little boy standing next to her in a Scooby-Doo t-shirt and holding her hand.

They may as well be two people from another planet for all they have to do with my life.

When I was in elementary school, somebody told me that when siblings are born really far apart it means that one of them was an accident. When I asked Danny which one of us it was, he said it was both of us. He was the first accident, when she was nineteen, and I was the second, when she was thirty-nine. "But we don't say *accident*," he said dryly. "We say *surprise*." Then he changed the subject.

"That's two really big surprises," I said to Nick once while he was making dinner. It's best to target Nick with this kind of stuff, and even better if you do it while he's thinking about something else.

"Yeah," he said, looking up from chopping vegetables. "I think she could be a bit—disorganized."

By then I already knew that Danny's father was some guy

called Michael Sloane, who was nineteen as well, and when my mum was pregnant he pretended that he *wasn't* the father, and then moved away, and no, Danny isn't interested in trying to find him because he obviously didn't care and so why should Danny. And my mum wouldn't tell anybody, not even Danny, who it was when she got pregnant with me. Some random guy. He probably didn't care, either.

It's obvious that Nick really liked her. He says she was funny and she used to write letters to the newspaper. She worked in a university library and students used to send her thank-you cards at the end of the year. If it wasn't for Danny I think Nick would talk about her a lot.

"Did she ever come to the coffee shop?" I asked him.

"I didn't have the coffee shop then," he said. "She'd have liked it, though. I think she'd have liked it a lot."

What do I know, but I think she'd have liked it as well.

× × × × ×

The next morning Ollie is standing in front of my locker with his headphones around his neck and when he sees me he says, "Teagan sent me a playlist of all this classical music." He is very pale and he looks exhausted and half-wired, scuffing his canvas shoes back and forth against the hall floor, tapping his fingers against his leg.

Since yesterday somebody has put a bunch of police posters up and down the walls, all about what to do if you see something suspicious. Half of them have been defaced already. *JUST RUN FOR IT*, somebody has written on the poster nearest my locker, with a picture of a screaming face.

I have an armful of textbooks but Ollie's blocking my locker, so I just have to stand there clutching them all against my chest. "Yes," I say. "She does that."

"Oh."

"She likes classical music. That's her thing."

"Oh."

"Have you listened to it?"

"No. Not yet."

I gently shove him out of the way and fumble for my locker key, stack my books inside and then force it shut again with my shoulder, and as I'm doing this, Ollie says, "Hey, did you know there's a video of your mum on the internet?"

I think I've misheard him. "What?"

"There's a video of your mum. On the internet. Have you seen it?"

"What are you talking about?"

"I think it's her. I dunno. It's at that Greenham Common thing. I found it by accident. I mean, not by accident, but—"

"What are you talking about?"

"I didn't know if you knew about it," says Ollie. "I thought, you know, in case you didn't. If you're into family history or anything. It's a video of a bunch of women at Greenham Common and one of them's this lady with a baby and she says her name is Heather Kennedy."

The postcard from Greenham Common is black and white and for some reason even though I know the eighties weren't really all that long ago, in my head it's still some long-lost historical time where they wouldn't have had video cameras— and so what Ollie's saying seems weird and impossible and also, also, I've never seen a video of my mother. Ever. Don't know what her voice sounds like. So what he's saying is impossible.

"What are you talking about?" I say. "How did you find it?"

"On the internet. I looked up your mum's name but there wasn't anything, and then I was just—I mean, I'm not trying to be weird or anything. I just got interested and after you showed me that postcard—because I've been doing this project about Vietnam protests, so I was thinking about—I mean, I know it's not the same thing, but I was just interested—"

"You can't look her up on the internet. There's thousands of Heather Kennedys. There's like, Heather Kennedy the porn star, Heather Kennedy the murder victim, the lawyer, the hairdresser."

"Yeah. I found the porn star as well."

"So how did you find—"

"I looked up that other woman. Lynn Wallace. And I found loads about her—you have to use her full name; it's Lynn Keller Wallace—and there's a bunch of stuff, like recent stuff, but there's also this old video of her from the Greenham thing, and then after I watched that, you know, like it suggests other videos to watch and so I was watching them and then on one of them—"

"Ollie. That *is* weird."

He stops. "Yeah," he says. "It probably is. Sorry."

"Don't you have any weird family stuff of your own to look up?"

He shakes his head. "No. I keep trying to find my brother but I don't think he really—I've sent him all these emails but—anyway, though."

It's a weird tangent and it distracts me for a moment. The last I heard, Ollie's brother left home and nobody knows where he is. The school told the police after they busted him for dealing at school. He didn't go to jail but he never came back.

Everyone remembers him. This was all last summer, just before the end of school. He was really skinny and had a tattoo on his neck, and I never saw him speak to anyone, not even Ollie.

Nick's mum would say that he was a bad egg. I would agree. He was awful. It's weird how people can be so different from their siblings when they've supposedly grown up in the exact same environment.

This doesn't count for me and Danny. We did not.

Ollie takes his headphones from around his neck and starts to fiddle with them. They're the kind that look expensive from a distance but up close you can see they're really cheap. "I'm not trying to be weird," he says. "I just thought it was interesting. I thought you'd be interested. I just like looking stuff up. I like research. I'm not trying to be weird." Looking properly worried now, he says, "Sorry, Alena."

"What for?"

"You look pissed off."

"I'm not." I am, kind of, but I don't know why.

"So do you want to see the video?"

I don't answer.

"Here." He holds his hand out. "Give me your phone. I'll find it."

I pause, and then I dig my phone out of the front pocket of my bag and hand it to him. It's second-hand, Nick's brother's old work phone, and the screen is cracked, but other than that it's good. Ollie taps at the screen for a few seconds and then hands it back, with a video paused, ready to play. The title of the video is *USAF Greenham, Women's Peace Camp, ITN December 1982.*

"It's only short," he says.

I look at the screen. "Oh, this," I hear myself say. "I've seen this." It's a lie and I don't know why I say it but I see his shoulders drop a little bit. "I've seen this already," I say again. "I forgot."

"Oh." He nods and there's a short, awkward pause. "She seems cool," he says, and I nod, a weird lump in my throat, wanting to press PLAY but not wanting to do it with him there.

"I have to go, Ollie. I've got math." I put my phone in my pocket, but keep my hand wrapped around it.

"OK," he says. "Yeah. OK. See you at lunch, maybe? And Teagan?"

I nod, feeling bad for lying to him. "You should listen to her playlist," I tell him. "It'll make her happy."

He nods and looks like he's about to say something else, but then I turn abruptly and walk away.

I walk to the math room, but instead of going in, I go up to the second-floor bathrooms that no one ever uses, go into a stall, and lock the door. I dig my headphones out of my bag and plug them into my phone and put them in my ears and lean against the stall door with my phone in my hand, and press PLAY.

The video is old and there's a woman reporter with a plummy voice and an eighties haircut, standing in mud. There's a voiceover—*"The protest continues, and as Christmas approaches, some have left the camp to be with their families. Others remain, and morale, they say, is still high—"* and there are shots of women with pots and pans and cooking stoves, and flags and banners planted in muddy grass. There's blue skies and it looks freezing, bright and bitter.

Then there's a couple of interviews, where the reporter asks women their names and why they're still there, and they all say good and smart and angry-sounding things, and then there's a woman—frizzy hair and younger than the others, not that much older than me. And she's holding a little kid: just a baby, really, a little boy who's all wrapped up in knitwear. She's wearing a green jacket and she's saying, in a proper south London accent that I never knew she had, *"My name's Heather, my name's Heather Kennedy,"* and she's smiling, radiant.

Plummy reporter says, *"And what do you say to people who say it's irresponsible to bring a child into an environment like this?"*

And my mother says, *"I think they're right, aren't they, but I'm not the one populating this earth with weapons, so you tell me who's irresponsible, you tell me who's putting children in danger."*

And then for just a second she glances right at the camera, the way you're not supposed to when you're being interviewed, right down the lens and through all the years and right at me—

And then it cuts to another woman, who says, *"We'll be staying here as long as it takes,"* and then it's the end of the video.

x x x x x

Outside in the corridor I can hear the bell ringing for the start of first period.

Feeling weird and spacey and kind of like I've just seen a ghost, I tuck my phone and my headphones into my bag and make my way out and down the stairs and into the math room, where I get a seat right at the back and stare blankly at the whiteboard where the numbers don't make any sense.

And I'm so busy thinking, *my mum, my mum, my mum,* that it's a while before I even think about the actual *child* that she was carrying, and then of course I remember it and I realize that it was 1982 and the child is Danny.

12

That night after dinner I'm supposed to be learning about weight and mass and gravity for a physics test. Danny and Nick have been drinking wine and they're both in a good mood; I can hear them laughing while they do the dishes. It's the first time they've stopped sniping at each other in days. Danny's supposed to start his job tomorrow, and Nick has obviously gotten sick of arguing about it and given up.

I'm flipping through *A Guide to Disobedience*. It's even more battered now that I've been carrying it around for days with highlighters and notebooks and everything else I keep in my bag, the pages all soft and dusty, a few of them loose. *Always question authority, and never stand for hypocrisy*, it says at the top of one page. *Taking action against injustice is our responsibility to future generations.* Somebody has underlined this with a green pencil and drawn a little exclamation mark in the margin.

There's a couple of old receipts tucked inside the book—one for cigarettes and one for milk and coffee. There's a cinema ticket stub, but you can't see what the movie was. I've left these where I found them, pressed flat between the pages where they've been for years ever since someone—ever since *she*—took the ticket stub back from the cinema attendant, tucked it absentmindedly into the book she was carrying around, went and watched the movie.

Maybe I was with her. Maybe it was one of those showings where you can take babies in with you and nobody's allowed to complain if they cry. Just the two of us, one afternoon. She never mentioned it to anybody. That might have happened. I will never know.

× × × × ×

In the kitchen, I can hear Nick talking.

"—just wanted a cup of steamed milk, basically," he's saying, "but she's still happy to pay, like, three quid for it, so I said, *Fine, you know, if that's what you want, no problem.*"

Danny says, "I know, she's crazy."

"And she keeps calling me *Nico*," Nick says. "Like she thinks I'm her personal Italian barista. *Ciao, Nico, I'll just have my usual this morning*—I just want to say to her, *Look, I'm from Essex, you know?*"

Danny is laughing. They are both laughing.

This makes me feel brave.

Danny flicks a wet tea towel in my direction when he sees me. "What's up, kid?" he says. "How's physics?"

Nick is drying glasses and Danny is just standing around doing nothing. I hesitate for a minute, on the other side of the kitchen counter, looking at them. I'm still wearing my school uniform, but with an old charity shop cardigan over the top, which I wrap around myself like I'm cold.

"What's up?" Danny says again. "You OK?"

"Danny," I say.

"I know a physics joke. You want to hear it?"

"You know when you were a baby."

"This is it. Why can you never trust an atom?"

"Danny."

He folds his arms. "Do I know when I was a baby? I don't understand the question."

"You never told me that our mum took you to Greenham Common. To the protest camp. You were there. When you were, like, a little tiny kid."

Nick turns the tap off and shakes water off his hands, starts to dry them slowly on a dish towel.

"What?" says Danny.

Nick hangs the dish towel on the hook. He turns to face me. He looks like he's about to say something, but then thinks better of it. Danny is staring at me. There's a long silence. I say, "When you were little. She took you to Greenham Common."

He says, in a weird, stiff voice, "What do you know about Greenham Common, Alena?"

"Nothing, basically," I say. "But I'd like to. Because I found this video. It's really amazing, Danny, it's actually a video on the internet with her in it, and you're there too, it must be you—"

"What video? What are you talking about?"

"I'll show you," I say. "Hang on." And then I go to my room to get my phone and when I come back out Danny is looking at Nick with an expression I can't read. Nick is giving him a *don't ask me* look.

"Here," I say, handing him the phone, and he holds it in his hand for a minute like I've given him a lit firework and he doesn't know what to do with it.

"You have to press PLAY," I say, but he doesn't, so Nick leans over and presses it for him.

And then all the women's voices fill the kitchen, saying all their smart, brave things again, and then there's *her* voice, and Danny watches with absolutely no expression on his face whatsoever, even though Nick totally grins when my mum comes on and says, "Danny, god, that's *you*. Have you ever seen this?"

He shakes his head, just slightly.

When it's over, he looks up at me and says, "How did you find this?"

"Someone at school found it by accident," I say.

"Who? Teagan?"

"No. Someone else."

"Who?"

"Ollie."

"Who's Ollie?"

"Ollie's the goth kid?" says Nick.

"Yeah. No. He's not goth, really. He's just like that. He likes art."

"He likes art," Danny repeats, like this is a sentence that doesn't mean anything. "Ollie who likes art. How did he find something like this by accident?"

"He's doing a project on the history of political protest," I say, which is sort of true. "He was doing research. And he recognized her name from my Greenham Common postcard."

Danny's shoulders hunch up a little bit and he glances at Nick again, like, *Is this your fault?* "What's your Greenham Common postcard?"

"It's this postcard I found in the storage locker. With her on it. Actually it's her and Lynn Wallace, that other person I was asking you about. So I suppose they were both—"

"Fine," says Danny. "Sounds like you know it all. Good for you." He hands the phone back to me.

I take it, glancing at Nick uncertainly, and say, "Do you want me to send you a link to it?"

"No," says Danny.

"Send me a link to it, Lena," says Nick.

Danny narrows his eyes at him. The whole atmosphere in the kitchen has changed. I think, *Broken glass, fire alarm.* I carry on anyway.

"You must have been really young," I say. "If it's 1982 you must have been—"

"I was one and a half," Danny says flatly. "Really responsible parenting. Story of my life. Being dragged all over the country with a bunch of women who think they're changing the world." His face has gone blank. "Why have I never heard of this Ollie person? You've got some goth friend now that only Nick knows about?"

"He's not a goth. Do you even know what a goth is? He's not anything, he's just weird. He's arty."

"Whatever. Are we done here?"

"I think it's kind of cool," I say. "I mean, she's so young. I never knew that she—"

"It's *not* cool," Danny says.

"Or not cool, more like—just, impressive, I guess. She looks like—"

"It's not cool, it's not impressive. None of it was. Ever."

"Danny," says Nick. "She's only saying—"

"I don't want to talk about it."

"Talk about what?" I say.

"Any of it."

There's a silence, and then Nick says, "I don't see why she can't—"

"It doesn't set a very good example, does it?" says Danny. "For starters."

"What doesn't?"

"It's a bad example. Her behavior. I know what you're like, Lena. You read about things or you hear about things or I'll tell you about something—"

"You don't tell me about anything."

"—and you'll get the wrong idea about it."

"So what's the right idea about it?" I say, at the same time as I'm thinking, *That's* not *what I'm like. I don't know what that even means.*

"It was irresponsible. It was dangerous. She shouldn't have been there with a baby. You have no idea how much looking after babies need."

"Neither do you," I say, and then, "Anyway, obviously nothing bad happened. You're fine, aren't you? She didn't drop you down a well, did she?"

Nick snorts a laugh and Danny glares at him.

I say, "Lynn Wallace isn't in that video but there's some other Greenham Common ones that she's in—"

"Oh, that's right, Lynn was everywhere," Danny snaps. "Any fucking place there was trouble."

"*Danny,*" Nick says.

My brother is not looking at either of us now. He's looking up at the ceiling like some divine being might come and save him from us both. "I can't talk about this right now. I can't talk about this right now. I've got work to do."

"No, you don't," I say. "You're just—"

"Yes. I do. I'm starting a new job tomorrow. I have stuff to do. Talk to Nick about it if you care that much about it. Do what you like." He looks at Nick. "Are we done here?" he says again.

It's not really clear if he's talking about the dishes or what.

"I suppose so," says Nick, and Danny says, "Good," and he leaves the room and goes down the corridor into their bedroom and slams the door.

"He doesn't have anything to do," I say, when he's gone. "He just doesn't want to talk to me. I can't even ask one single question about something that happened years ago."

I think Nick might scold me for sounding like a brat but he just stares after Danny for a few seconds, and then looks at me. "I know," he says. We've both lowered our voices. "You've just got to—you know, it's just hard for him to talk about certain—"

"I don't care," I say. "I don't want to talk about him. I want to talk about *her*."

Nick tilts his head to the side, looks at me very seriously. "You want to talk about her."

"Yes."

"Where is this suddenly coming from?"

"Oh god, you're just like him."

"Hey," he says. "I'm not. No, I'm not. I'd like to talk about her too but it's not that—"

"I think it's crazy that I've never even heard of Greenham Common when it's apparently *famous* and my own mother was there."

"Well, I think it's crazy too, but maybe your school should be—"

"It's not my school's fault. It's his."

"Alena."

"What about Lynn? Do you know who Lynn was?"

Because I'm looking closely, I can see him actually flinch, slightly. "She was your mum's friend. Her best friend, probably."

"Why have I never met her?"

"Do you want to meet her?"

"Yes."

"Danny and her—they fell out. Right after the funeral. They had a terrible fight. This was when your aunt was still trying to take you to Australia. He was under a lot of stress—"

"And they just never spoke again?"

"Not as far as I know."

"Do you know where she is now?"

"No."

"Does Danny know?"

"I doubt it."

She is somewhere, I think. *People don't just disappear. Not even people who die.*

"If you really want to know I can try and ask Danny about her," says Nick. "But not right now. When there's a better time. OK?"

My throat feels tight and I nod because I don't feel like talking anymore. We are quiet for a while.

"Do you want some ice cream?" Nick says. "There's about three scoops left."

I wipe my nose with my sleeve. "All right," I say.

"Do you want me to slice some banana or something on it?"

"All right."

"Listen." His voice goes gentle. "You just need to be a bit careful when you want to talk to him about—"

"I don't want to talk about anything," I say. "It doesn't matter. I have a physics test tomorrow. I have to study."

He pauses, and then turns to get the ice cream out of the freezer. He puts it down on the counter. "What's it about?"

"It's about gravity."

"Do you want me to help?"

"Not unless you know anything about gravity."

"What I don't know about gravity isn't worth knowing," he says. I sort of believe him.

13

"Listen," Nick said to me when I was twelve and he had just finished sweeping up the glass that I smashed on the kitchen floor. He was sitting on the end of my bed and I was wiping my eyes, still on the verge of tears. "You know your mum died very suddenly. Really out-of-nowhere suddenly. And I know you can't remember it, I know to you it's a hundred years ago, but to him it may as well have been yesterday. We just both have to try and remember that. Grief is very complicated. It can take a long time."

I nodded. I was trying to pretend to Nick that I was mature and that I understood. I didn't. I was thinking, *What about me, what about me, what about me?*

x x x x x

I am fifteen. This is the truth: I don't miss her. There is nothing to miss. There is nothing gone from my life that I can ever remember being there. Just sometimes there'll be this trace of her, somewhere unexpected—like Danny will say something accidentally, or I'll find an old shopping list—and it will feel for a moment like somebody trying to talk to me from very far away. And if I am very quiet—

My brother obviously misses her so much that if he tried

to talk about it he would just break into pieces like glass.

He says the same things, over and over: *It was a long time ago, I can't remember, I don't have time to talk about this right now, I can't remember.*

Since he's not ninety-seven years old and doesn't have amnesia, I can't see any reason why he can't remember. If anyone had an excuse to forget things it would be Nick since he's the one who got hit by a car and cracked his head open.

So sometimes I wonder if Danny just doesn't want to remember how things used to be. Like how he had a life where he didn't have to look after somebody all the time. Or sometimes I think he just wants to keep her memory all to himself and he doesn't want anybody else to touch it, not even me. Maybe especially not me.

If I actually had any memories of her, maybe I'd want to keep them to myself as well.

Or is it this?—he's scared that if he talks about her he'll say he wishes she was still here, which is the same thing as saying he wishes he didn't have me.

He's not just sad. I guess I've known this for a while, at least since the fire alarm incident, maybe since before; maybe I've always known, but I see it suddenly again while he's standing there, snapping at me, talking about responsible parenting. He's angry. He's angry with *her. Still.* And OK, maybe it is a little bit crazy to bring a one-year-old baby to a freezing, muddy campsite, but nobody who's not totally unhinged would still be angry about it more than thirty years later when the person is *dead.* He is angry about something else, I think. Really consumingly angry in some low-level way basically all the time.

And maybe it's that she died and left him stuck with me.

He must think that sometimes. Especially when I annoy him, when I make him angry. He must think, *This shouldn't be my problem.*

If she was still here, me and him would be like strangers, probably: he'd turn up at Christmas and buy me one of those gifts people get you when they don't know anything about you other than that you're a girl, like candles or pink stationery, and he'd say *How's school*, then he'd be gone again. Me and my mum would laugh at him for being uptight. I'd be more like her, I think. We'd go camping together and plan revolutions.

And Nick would be some faraway grown-up person who wouldn't even notice me: I'd be his boyfriend's little sister— half-sister, in fact—which is like nothing. It'd be like how I feel about Nick's brother's wife who I've only met a couple of times and who even though she's kind of in my family, she's like nobody to me: she's just a person who knows a person who knows a person I know. Nick would look at me politely and say, *Hello, Alena, nice to meet you*, and it would be like that. He wouldn't buy me a Christmas present. If Danny wishes she was still here—and he does, of course he does—then he wishes all of that was true, as well.

Maybe Nick and Danny wouldn't even be together, because, honestly, they met in some grungy London bar somewhere, and neither of them was really that old, and they weren't probably expecting to suddenly end up in a relationship that lasted forever. Except that when they'd been together for hardly any time at all my mum dies and Danny's like, *Oh, I have to take guardianship of my three-year-old sister now*, and Nick's like, *Oh, OK, well, I'll stick around*, because he's basically pathologically responsible—that's what I heard Zahra call him once—but if that hadn't happened, if she hadn't died and I hadn't arrived, wouldn't they probably have broken up over some little thing years ago? Wouldn't Nick have gone traveling around the world and wouldn't Danny have met some guy who loved Bob Dylan as much as he did and wouldn't they both have totally different lives?

I just think you have to ask yourself these things sometimes.

PART TWO

14

I am not making progress with the guitar.

Through my bedroom door I hear the front door open and close, Danny coming home late again, and I wonder how long before the fight starts up again. It's like my record player—another storage locker discovery—when you pick up the needle and drop it down again somewhere else, and the music just starts right up in the middle. Ever since Danny started his job, that's what this fight is like.

My fingers against the fretboard of the guitar are slack, and my hand won't form the right shapes; the skin on my fingertips is red and raw, little indentations from the steel strings. I can play a C chord, and if you wait ten minutes, I can change to a G. This is the beginning of "Let It Be." I work out that even if those were the only chords in it, it would take me about half a day to play the whole song.

All Danny has been able to offer in terms of guitar lessons is a battered old copy of *The Beatles Songbook* from his own failed attempts to be a musician, four hundred years ago. He also suggested I read volume one of Bob Dylan's autobiography. "For research," he said. "Inspiration. Meditation. Philosophy. Wisdom. You need to discover yourself as an artist."

Mostly I think he's trying to be funny but sometimes I think he's not.

In the kitchen, Nick is making dinner, and already their voices are getting louder. I lay the guitar carefully at the end of my bed and go into the kitchen, trying to think of some story from school or something that I can tell them to change the subject. They don't even notice me at first.

"And you know he has a teenage son," Danny is saying. "His wife died. He's a single parent. He's had to bring up his son—"

"Oh!" says Nick, slamming the cutlery drawer. "I see! So you have a *connection*. You have so much in common that you—"

"We *do* have things in common. I'm just saying that he—"

"*You*," says Nick, "are *not* a single parent."

"I know that," Danny says, his jaw set like a steel trap. He's wearing a tie but it's not done up properly. He is holding his laptop against his chest, and his bag is still hanging from his shoulder. "My point was, you don't know anything about him and in your mind you've created this cartoon villain when in reality—"

"Guess what," I say. I have no idea what I'm going to say after this, but they both turn and look at me.

"What?" says Danny.

I think wildly for a moment. "The library was closed today because the radiator was leaking."

There's a short pause. "Well," says Danny. "Thanks for the update." He puts down his laptop and bag and starts kicking off his shoes.

"Were any books damaged?" Nick says, as if I've just told a serious story in which he has to take an actual interest.

"And I'll tell you something else—" says Danny.

"Don't," says Nick. "Don't tell me anything else."

"All right." Danny turns to me. "I'll tell *you* something else, and I'll do it in a loud voice so Nick can hear."

"Don't drag her into it," Nick says.

"Don't drag me into it," I say, pulling up a stool at the kitchen counter. "I'm not going to pretend to like him."

Danny blinks. "Who?"

"Jacob Carlisle."

I can see Nick smirk although he tries to hide it.

"What, now you've decided you don't like him either?" says Danny. "You've never met him."

"Neither has Nick and he doesn't like him."

"So? Don't copy Nick!"

"What if I don't like what he believes in?"

"He doesn't believe in anything," says Nick.

"If he doesn't believe in anything, then I don't like him."

"Actually, scratch that," says Nick. "He believes in having all of us living in a police state, spending our lives spying on our neighbors, trying desperately never to do anything that might be construed as *suspicious*—"

"Nick, shut up," says Danny. "Seriously."

"Are you talking about the Safe Communities Initiative?" I say, and both of them turn their heads around to look at me. "What?" I say. "I read. I know about it."

The Safe Communities Initiative is all over Jacob Carlisle's website all of a sudden, like he's finally thought of an idea. It's about having more police, and giving people money for reporting suspicious behavior to the police. It's one of those things that sounds sensible when you read it but then you think about it later and it's sort of creepy.

"The two of you don't know what you're talking about,"

Danny is saying. "Maybe we should start talking about what *you* believe in."

"Well," says Nick. "For starters, I believe in an ethical commitment to—"

"Not you. I'm asking Lena."

I try to think of something, but my mind is blank.

"Leave her alone," says Nick, and Danny glares at him, and I think, *Nick, I believe in Nick, I believe him when he tells me stuff because he always tells me the truth.*

I can't say this. "I don't know. But I'm not running for mayor, am I?"

Nick grins. "That's a good answer. Danny, admit that's a good answer."

"That's a fairly good answer," says Danny. "It's an acceptable answer for now."

"Are you going to tell us what *you* believe in?" I say.

He leans over the counter and takes a piece of red pepper off the chopping board. Nick swats his hand away. Danny ignores the question and changes the subject. "So, hey, Lena. How's the guitar?"

"My fingers hurt," I say. He opens his mouth to reply. "Please don't say anything about Bob Dylan. Bob Dylan isn't the answer to everything."

"Wrong. That's just the kind of naïve thing only a child would say." He leans against the counter and folds his arms. "I'm going for a run. When are we eating?"

Going for a run is one of those things Danny always says he's going to do but in reality has done about once in his life.

"Ten minutes," says Nick. "Go after dinner."

"Fine," says Danny, and then, in his best *let's not argue anymore* voice, says, "Let me chop something."

I go back into my room before I get asked to chop anything, and check my email. I have two new messages since I last looked, fifteen minutes ago: a reminder about library fines and an email from Nick's mum with a picture of their cat that just says, *Hello Alena from Snowflake!* Snowflake is the cat. In real life Nick's mum is super serious and always has very thoughtful, intelligent conversations with people, but on email she is all cat pictures.

There's nothing else. It's been two hours since I sent an email to Lynn Wallace care of the Save Ocean Court campaign.

Dear Ms. Wallace,

I don't know if this is the right email address for you but if not maybe somebody will forward this on to your own email. I have signed the Save Ocean Court petition.

I found your name by accident on this website—

Lies. I trawled through hundreds of Lynn Wallaces to find it and it took ages, but I wasn't going to let Oliver Cohen be the only one with research skills, especially when the research was my family. Eventually, a few weeks ago, I found a site which had only just been created, and on the info page it said that the Save Ocean Court campaign was coordinated by Ocean Court resident Nisha Sawhney and housing law campaigner Lynn Keller Wallace. Even then it might not have been her but there was a picture of them both standing in front of Ocean Court looking pissed off and I held my Greenham Common postcard up next to it and you could believe she was the same person, just thirty-three years older.

It said: *For more information please contact info@saveoceancourt.org.*
I bookmarked the page and then I kept starting to write emails
and then changing my mind, not knowing what to say. Finally,
this evening, I just decided to do it.

—and I wondered if you were the same Lynn Wallace
who used to know my mum, Heather Kennedy, a long
time ago? She lived in Stoke Newington, I think, and
there is a postcard from Greenham Common with
both of you in it. If you are the same person, I guess
you know that she died very suddenly when I was little
and unfortunately I don't really remember her. I also
don't know anybody that she used to be friends with
but I would like to know more about her and what she
was like. So if you are the same person I would really
like to meet you. But if you don't want to, that's OK.
And if you're not the same person, then sorry. Please
could you send me a message either way? Thank you
so much.
Best wishes,
Alena Kennedy

P.S. I am fifteen now, but you might have even
known me when I was little as I think you were at
my mum's funeral, or you might remember my older
brother Daniel Kennedy who is my guardian.

When I read this back again I think that I sound like an idiot,
like a five-year-old, and that there's no way the serious lady in
the picture would take time out from saving Ocean Court to
talk to me, but whatever. It's done now.

"Marie sent me a picture of Snowflake," I say when I go back into the kitchen.

"Who do you think your mother loves more, Nick?" says Danny. He's setting the table. "Out of you, your brothers, and Snowflake?"

"She loves us all equally," says Nick. Danny says, "Are you *sure*?"

"I need a lift to Teagan's house after dinner," I say. "We have to work on our history project."

"Fine," Danny says. "I'll take you. Hey, do David and Rachel want me to come in so they can celebrate my diversity?"

Nick cracks up, as he did the last seven hundred times Danny made this joke.

The reason, I think, that they will never break up is that they find each other really, really funny, and practically nobody else does.

I'm almost sure this is enough.

15

I check my email twice more at Teagan's house but there's nothing new. Teagan is stressed because she's trying to learn some super-difficult piece of music for an audition and she can't get it right. I lie on her bed while she practices, trying to look supportive. I tell her it sounds fine and she says, Fine isn't good enough, and looks very determined. Sometimes I'm jealous of her ambition.

Over her desk I notice she's stuck a bunch of drawings that Ollie's done—either stuff he's given her or stuff he's left lying around that she's just taken. They look good, all together, like an art gallery or something. You can tell that it's the same person who's drawn them, the same way I can tell if it's Teagan playing the violin over anybody else at school. They have a way of doing the thing that they do that's totally unique to them.

Teagan's dad drives me home when it gets late. Trying to be polite, I ask if he wants to come in, but he says he has to get back, which is just as well because when I let myself into the apartment I know straight away that something's wrong. That feeling you get like if you walk into the middle of an argument. Nick is standing in the kitchen and Danny is standing in front of the TV and the moment I walk in, they both look at me but don't say anything. Danny is holding a nearly empty glass of wine. He finishes it and puts the glass down on the coffee table and says, "You're home."

Usually I would say something sarcastic to this, but instead I just say, "Yep," and look between them. "What's going on?"

"How's your history project?" says Nick.

"Good. It's good. We've nearly finished."

"Good."

"Yeah." I close the door behind me and lean against it for a moment, still holding my keys in my hand. "I invited David in for coffee but he said he had to go home."

Nick nods and looks like he's about to say something else but then Danny says, "We'd like to have a quick chat with you about something." I see Nick's eyes narrow a little bit at the word *we*.

"What is it?"

"Sit down."

"Do I need a lawyer?"

Danny gives me a brief, tense smile to acknowledge this joke. "No. You're fine."

I go and sit down on the sofa in front of him, still wearing my coat. I start to toe off my Converses and kick them under the coffee table. "What is it?"

"Does anyone want tea?" Nick says.

Danny says, in a voice strung tight like wire, "So apparently you got in touch with Lynn Wallace."

"I'm having tea," Nick says.

I say, "What?"

"You sent her an email."

"What?"

"There's no point looking at me like that, Alena. You sent her an email. Right?"

"How do you—" I panic a little bit, thinking he has been in my room, he has been on my computer. I'm trying to work out if denial or outrage or what is the best strategy. "How do you *know?*"

"Because." Danny picks up his wine glass, sees that it's empty, and puts it down again. "She just phoned me."

"*What?*"

"She just called me up. Fifteen minutes ago. *Hello, Danny, this is Lynn. It's been a long time. Et cetera.*" He picks up the glass again and for a second it almost looks like his hand is shaking. He circles around the sofa to the kitchen so I have to twist around to see him. He gets the bottle out of the fridge and pours himself another glass. Nick is watching him carefully. The kettle is boiling.

"I don't understand," I say.

"It's not really very complicated."

"How did she know your number?"

"God knows. Does that really matter? She probably keeps secret files on everybody who's ever disagreed with her about anything."

"Danny." Nick puts a hand on his arm. "You've had the same number for years. You had the same number before your mum died. She just still happens to have—"

"That doesn't give her the right to just—anyway." Danny looks at me and clears his throat. "Look. Look. You're not in trouble." He says this in a voice that says that I would be in trouble if he had anything to do with it but that Nick has talked him out of it.

"Of course you're not in trouble," says Nick.

"Why *would* I be in trouble?"

"You're not," says Nick.

"But I really wish if you were that desperate to talk to her that you would've spoken to me—"

"I did speak to you."

"—instead of going snooping around on the internet trying to uncover—"

"It's not snooping around; it's the internet. It's just there. I didn't even know if it was the same person." I am shaking my head, trying to understand. "Why did she phone *you*? She didn't even reply to my message."

"God knows," says Danny again. "God knows why she ever does anything."

"She called because she wanted Danny to know that you'd contacted her," says Nick. "And to ask his permission to get in touch with you. Which I have to say—"

"She does not have my permission."

"—I think is an amazingly responsible, respectful thing to do. That is really beyond what you would expect from most people and considering—"

"She doesn't need your permission," I say. "Why does she need your permission? It's nothing to do with you."

"Nothing to *do* with me?"

"You're obviously not interested in being in touch with her. Fine. But I am. I'd just like to hear some stories about Mum, and if you don't want to—"

"What stories? Since when? There are no stories. Whatever idea you've got in your head about this woman—"

"Don't call her *this woman*," says Nick.

"—is wrong. And she *does* need my permission, and she doesn't have it, and neither do you. I'll call her whatever I like."

Nick is now looking at Danny like he's a little bit crazy, so I do the same. "*Why?*" I say.

"She's a bad influence. She'll get you into trouble. You're at the kind of age where you'll—you know, it'll all seem exciting and glamorous to you—"

"What will?"

"*What* will, Danny?" Nick has taken a step back from him and his arms are folded, his head tilted to one side. He has given up on making tea.

"Her lifestyle."

"You know there are people who used to say that our *lifestyle* was dangerous for Alena, so that's exactly the kind of language—"

"Oh, please," says Danny. "Nick, support me or stay out of this, all right?"

There's a moment of dead silence. Then Nick speaks in a very quiet voice. "You're turning her into something she's not. She was your mum's *best friend*. If Lena wants to talk to her, then maybe—"

"Did you hear what I just said?"

"—maybe it's time that she—"

"Nick, shut up."

"You can't talk to him like that." I stand up again. "Don't talk to Nick like that."

"It's all right," says Nick flatly.

"She shouldn't be sending—Lena, *you* shouldn't be sending secret emails to people you don't know, all right? It might not even have *been* Lynn Wallace. It could have been—you know, it could have been Joe the Pedophile and he's reading this email from some fifteen-year-old girl; he asks you to meet him at a bus stop somewhere—"

"What?"

"Look," says Danny. "Look." He puts his wine down and

holds both hands up. "I don't want to fight. We don't need to fight about this. She asked for my permission to talk to you. I didn't give it to her. Alena, I'm sorry, I know it's hard for you to understand but when you're older—you know, when you're a bit older—if you want to talk to people, then I guess that's fine, but right now I'm telling you—I'm asking you *not* to go looking into things like there's some big conspiracy—I mean, I just—"

He stops, picks up his glass again. "I don't think it's really appropriate." He glances at Nick. "Right? Lynn's a grown woman, she's a busy woman, I doubt she really even has time—"

It's like he's hoping Nick will go, *Oh, actually, yeah, that's a great point* but he doesn't, so Danny trails off. Then he clears his throat and says, "Look. Please. I don't want her in my life again. Not right now. Just, please."

The obvious thing to say would be that it's not his life we're talking about, it's mine, but there's something about his voice and the glassy look in his eyes that makes both me and Nick go quiet. You can tell Nick is totally pissed off, but he just shakes his head and starts tidying up the kitchen and putting the dishes in the sink.

"What did you say to her on the phone?" I say quietly. "Did she ask anything about me?"

"I told her that I'd rather she didn't communicate with you at the moment. That I thought it would distract you from schoolwork. And you know she lives all the way down in—"

"So she's not going to reply to my email."

"—Kennington, anyway. No. She's not."

"That's just—it's *rude*. It's *impolite*."

"Well, she was never all that worried about good manners as far as I can remember."

"Not her. You."

His eyes narrow. "Alena, what's *impolite* is you going behind my back—"

"What's to stop me emailing her again and telling her to ignore you?"

"The fact that I'm asking you not to and that I trust you." He says this in such a strangled voice that it's hard to tell if he means it or if he's just casting around for anything to say.

I've never had much reason to think about whether Danny trusts me or not. I can't think of anything to say in response, because I'm trying to sound mature and I'm trying to work out if I even trust Danny, or what that even means—and suddenly all the lights in the apartment seem too bright and I feel like a headache is starting somewhere right in the center of my brain.

× × × × ×

I go to bed without saying goodnight to either of them. In the dark, under the covers, I check my email on my phone just in case maybe she wrote to me even after she spoke to Danny, said something like, *Who cares about him, let's get together anyway, I've got so many stories and I would love to meet you.* But there's nothing.

The first story she could tell me is what they fought about after the funeral. We can work back from there. Then I'll tell her about me. I will think of something to tell her about me.

I wonder if *right after the funeral* means, like, a couple of days after, or actually right outside the church while they're all still dressed in black. It's hard to imagine that people would argue at a funeral. You'd think everyone would be sad and respectful and think solemnly about the dead person that they have in common. You'd think everyone would probably have been really nice to Danny and concerned about his grief. Put their hands on his shoulder and ask him how he was. Whoever *everyone* is: I've no idea who was there. Maybe hardly anybody, maybe just Nick and Danny and my aunt and uncle and Lynn Keller Wallace.

Not that I'd know how people behave because I've never actually been to a funeral. I've never been to a wedding, either. Sometimes I wonder if Nick and Danny will bother getting married one day. I asked them a while ago, after it was legal, when they'd do it but they were in the middle of arguing about who should clean the fridge and Danny said, *Don't hold your breath*.

And then I'm lying in bed and I'm thinking maybe I *have* been to a funeral. Maybe I was at hers and I don't even know it. And suddenly I want to know this so badly that I almost can't stand it, that I almost get up and go and knock on their door just to ask—and then I can't sleep at all for thinking about it and when I hear one of them get up and go into the kitchen I have to get up as well—

But there's no one in the kitchen, so I don't know what I heard. It's all dark apart from the clock on the oven, glowing red. I go back down the corridor and I can see the light under their door, hear the murmur of their voices, rising and falling; then Nick's, getting louder, "—*sake*, Danny, do you have to *always*—"

I stand outside for a moment, then I slip back into my bedroom, let the door click shut softly.

16

"Are you still asleep?"

There's the creak of my bedroom door opening and Danny's voice, almost a whisper. My curtains are closed and my room is gloomy and warm and comfortable. I know it's nearly eleven o'clock and the murmur of the television in the living room woke me up a while ago, but it's Saturday and I've got no plans to get up and talk to anybody. I am thinking of maybe staying here all day. I burrow down under the covers, let him wait for a while before I answer. "Yes. Go away."

"I got you a chai latte."

I think about this for a moment, stick my head over the covers, and squint at him. "Really?"

"Yeah. Well, no. But I got Nick to bring one back for you. Here."

He comes into the room and puts one of the takeaway cups from the coffee shop down on my bedside table and then stands there for a moment. I sit up, tangled in the bedsheets, and rub my eyes. "Nick went all the way to work and then came back to bring me a chai latte?"

"We didn't have any of the stuff at home."

"I know, but—"

"He wanted to go in and check that Zahra was OK. The shop and everything."

"What do you mean?"

Danny sits down at my desk. He has to move a stack of magazines out of the way first. He doesn't come in my room that often and when he does he never says anything about all the old photos and postcards I've collected and stuck everywhere—all around my mirror—even though it's probably weird for him because there are photos of him when he was a little boy, even photos of our grandparents, who I never met but he did. One of our mum and Niamh when they were teenagers. I've always had them—just stuck there along with pictures of me and Teagan and collages I've made from magazines. I've got a picture of a young Ernest Hemingway with a dead animal, and a color photocopy of the front cover of an old eighties edition of *Pride and Prejudice*, which honestly I've never even read, I just like the guy on the front, even though he's a drawing. I try to pretend that my dead grandfather means as much to me as the *Pride and Prejudice* guy but honestly, if I had to save one of those two pictures from a fire—

Anyway, Danny sits down. He doesn't look at my pictures. I think he's going to start talking about Lynn Wallace again but instead he says, "There's been another bomb. Someone's been killed."

I pick up my chai latte from the bedside table but I can tell it's still too hot to drink, so I just hold it in my hands. Danny is watching me and I look away, look at the little recycling logo on the lid of the cup.

"Alena," Danny says. "Did you hear what I said?"

"What do you mean?" I say, my brain trying to grind into life. "How do you know?"

"It's on TV. It was early this morning. Near Liverpool Street."

"Who's been killed?"

"Don't know yet. It was another supermarket."

"So it's the same—"

"Looks like it."

I can't see Danny's face properly in the dark, but I realize, suddenly, that he's wearing work clothes. A white shirt and not-jeans. I reach and turn my bedside lamp on to make sure, and we both flinch in the light. He looks tired.

"Look, don't get up," he says. "Sleep as late as you like. Sleep all day. Don't watch the news. I just wanted to bring you a latte and say that I've got to go into work for a few hours."

"Why?"

"Nick's got to go to the shop later but he's home now. I think he's going to do frozen pizza or something for lunch. We have to—there's going to be a lot of media coverage; we've got to put together some kind of response."

For a second I think he means him and Nick, but then I realize he's talking about his job.

"But it's Saturday," I say.

"I know." He picks up a pencil from my desk, looks at it. "Listen. Alena."

There's a long pause. Then Danny's phone starts ringing. He takes it out of his pocket and looks at it, then turns it off. "Never mind," he says. "Later. Have a good day, OK? Don't watch the news. It's all bad."

"It's always bad," I say, but he's already out the door, and a few minutes later I hear the front door open and close and I know he's gone.

I don't bother to have a shower or get dressed or comb my hair or do anything respectable. I put a hoodie on over my pink-elephant pajamas and shuffle into the living room with my chai latte, where Nick has twenty-four-hour news on the TV, and they've stuck the *BREAKING NEWS* banner on the screen over the top of rolling footage of nothing: a police cordon and some ambulances with their lights off. *At least one fatality confirmed in London blast*, it says in smaller letters underneath. It looks cold, out there in Liverpool Street. The little people on the screen—police and random gawking strangers—standing around with camera phones; they're all bundled up in layers and you can see wind whipping the women's hair around. The sky is steel gray, no light at all, and even here Nick has all the lights on even though it's the middle of the day. I can see a few stray drops of rain on our windows, and then I see a drop of rain on the camera lens on the TV, as well, because it's all really not very far away from us.

The apartment is warm and smells like cinnamon and coffee, and Nick is standing in the kitchen slicing the film from a frozen pizza, with the oven already on. "You should turn that off," he says. "They're just filling up airtime. They don't know anything."

I keep watching. A terror expert comes on. *John McHane, Terror Expert.* He looks rumpled, like maybe he was still in bed too when he found out, when they called him up.

It's March now, more than a month since the last bomb, the one they found in Mile End. They'd only just stopped talking about it all on the news, like they'd run out of things to say. Now they're showing a timeline of all the failed ones from before, with a little map of all the different locations.

Nick crosses over in front of me and turns it off.

"Just remember," he says. "You're more likely to be hit by a car than caught in a terrorist attack."

Which is fine but, of course, that used to be true of the person who is now dead. So.

And anyway Nick *was* hit by a car, which I point out to him, and he pauses and says, "Well, and it's not likely to happen again, is it?"

I can't follow this logic. I turn the TV back on and the guy on-screen is saying, "*—of course, there's no evidence that that's even what we're dealing with here. We just don't know and that's what makes it so difficult and, now, tragic.*"

Nick sighs and goes back to the kitchen.

"*There's a growing sense of alarm in the city,*" the guy on TV continues. "*The police response is facing increasing scrutiny.*"

"Do you think Danny should have gone to work?" I hear myself say. "Is it safe to be on the subway?"

"Yes." Nick's voice is very calm. "It's safe. It's as safe as any other day. We shouldn't let this kind of thing frighten us."

I remember Nick's mum telling me at the time that his getting hit by a car was such bad luck that it had used up all the bad luck for our family in one go and now we'd have good luck forever. This seemed to make sense, back then.

I finish my drink and take the lid off the cup so I can scoop out the remnants of cinnamon foam with a spoon. I watch the news and worry.

"How was it?" says Nick, collecting my empty cup from the coffee table. "Danny made me promise to bring one back for you."

"It was good. Thank you." I realize that I never bothered to say thank you to my brother and I feel briefly sad about this. That way you just feel sometimes.

Nick sits down next to me, eyes on the TV in spite of himself, still holding the cup.

"Nick."

"Hm?"

"Was I at my mum's funeral? Did someone take me? Can you remember?"

He watches the screen for a few more seconds and then turns to me. "You weren't at the service. You were at the reception afterwards for a little while."

"Oh."

"You wouldn't talk to anyone. You held on to Danny the whole time and screamed whenever anyone else tried to talk to you."

"Oh," I say. "Like when I met Niamh for the first time and I screamed at her."

He frowns. "I don't know," he says. "I suppose. I don't remember that."

"Seems like I just used to scream a lot at people."

"Yeah," he says. "Well. I knew how you felt."

17

Later, we both go to the coffee shop.

The shop is bright and warm and totally empty apart from Zahra sitting behind the counter looking at her phone. The bell jingles as the door closes behind us, and she looks up. "Oh. I was excited for a minute there," she says. "I thought you might be a paying customer."

"Has it been like this all morning?" says Nick, looking at the empty tables.

"Uh huh. John called again. His driver's still sick. He says can you go and collect the order yourself and he'll give you another five percent, maybe ten if you're super nice about it and don't give him any hassle. Hi, Lena."

I hop onto one of the stools in front of the counter. "Hi."

"I'm not driving all the way out there today," says Nick. "Come on. Can't John do deliveries himself?"

"He told you, he's not allowed, he's got a bad heart or something."

"Well, I can't load all those boxes in the car either. My shoulder can't take it. I can't exactly—"

"Fine, but we're out of everything and they're closed tomorrow. I'm sure he's got someone who can help you load the car. And basically the only tea we have left is that vanilla stuff that everybody hates, so unless we're only going to serve—"

"All right, fine. Fine, fine, fine, fine. I'll have to go back for the car."

Zahra smiles and snaps her bubble gum. "Fine. And Lena can stay and keep me company."

"Fine." Nick gives me an apologetic look and says, "An hour, two hours max. Have whatever you like."

"She can't have whatever she likes since all we've got is disgusting vanilla infusion that everybody hates," says Zahra, and Nick says, "Good point," and ruffles my hair before he leaves, like I'm five.

Zahra is twenty-seven, and she's been working for Nick for almost as long as I can remember. She used to babysit me sometimes, and let me stay up late watching R-rated films on TV. She has a tattoo of a bird on the inside of her wrist and she knows a lot about Iranian punk music. Teagan finds her so intimidatingly cool she can hardly speak to her. She's not intimidating, though. She's sweet. She has a very complicated love life and she always tells me about it. And she's always reading serious things like Marxist history but then she also watches a lot of trashy TV. Last year she started a part-time law degree and Nick keeps joking that even when she's a hot-shot lawyer she'll still have to come and work at the shop in the evenings, since he can't cope without her. It's not all that much of a joke: I never want her to leave.

Danny wanted to study law once, he told me, after he finished university, but he never got around to it. I catch him looking at Zahra's textbooks sometimes, when she leaves them lying around the shop.

She takes her gum out of her mouth when I sit down and wraps it up in a piece of newspaper. "Scary day, huh?" She says it lightly but when I look at her up close she looks serious. "I am so sick of this world sometimes. Really."

"I just started thinking on the way here," I say. "Maybe he didn't really want anyone to get killed. Now they have, he'll feel so bad he'll turn himself in."

She doesn't look convinced. "Well," she says. "Yeah. Hopefully. Do you want a Coke or something?"

I nod.

"So," she says, turning to get a glass. "I didn't want to say this in front of Nick but they had Jacob Carlisle on TV about five minutes before you guys walked in here."

Every time I hear Jacob Carlisle's name I feel this pulse of anxiety, like it's cursed or something. I don't know when this started but I wish it would stop. Or that I could never hear his name.

"How do you know?" I say.

"Watching it on my phone." She scoops ice into the glass and turns back to me. "They had him talking about security and policing and all that kind of crap. Like he's an expert. It was a long conversation."

"I've never seen him on television before."

"I know. Quite a coup for the Carlisle campaign." She makes a face. "Honestly, I thought it was a little distasteful. Let them take the bodies away before you start reciting your manifesto, you know what I mean? No offense to your brother. Who you know that I adore."

"He's there today. At work. He went in this morning."

"Well, there you go. He probably scripted all those sound bites for him. If this turns into Jacob Carlisle's moment to shine, I am literally leaving this city forever, Lena. Tell your brother that from me, please."

I pick out one of the candies they keep in a bowl on the counter and start unwrapping it.

"I'd never have thought he'd exactly be Danny's cup of tea, you know?" she continues. "Jacob Carlisle. Nick's furious about it." She glances at me, gives me a sympathetic smile. "As you probably already know."

I stir my Coke with the straw, clink the ice against the side of the glass.

Zahra's dad died of a heart attack when she was twenty-one. He was at the airport on the way to visit his cousins in Tehran. She wears a necklace with a gold "D" for Dariush, which was his name. And maybe for Dad, I guess. I wonder if I should have something like this. A necklace or a bracelet or something, with an "H" for Heather, or an "M" for Mum.

It would seem fake. Like what I lost was the same as what Zahra lost, which it wasn't, because Zahra knew her dad for twenty-one years and I knew my mum for three.

Maybe I should get a necklace with a gold "3." The three years she loved me for.

Zahra is looking at her phone again. "I keep waiting for them to say who it is that's been killed. It's sick, isn't it? Like you can't help thinking, what if it's a *child* or something, or someone's grandma."

"You should turn it off. They're just filling up airtime."

"Yes. Yes. That is good advice." She turns it off, tucks her phone into the pocket of her jeans. "You are wise, Lena."

"Thank you."

"I'm thinking about going on a long vacation until this is all over. Somebody left their bag at one of the tables earlier and I was five seconds away from calling the bomb squad before they came back in and got it."

We both inadvertently glance around the shop in case there are any more unattended bags.

"Anyway, don't tell Nick that. There's probably some procedure I'm supposed to know. I'm supposed to be getting familiar with all the supervisory stuff in case he goes on this Colombian adventure," she says.

"In case he does what?"

"Well, not *adventure*. I know it's a business trip, meeting the growers and all that, but it still sounds kind of like—" She breaks off, looking at my face. "Or, he's probably not going, though. I mean, I don't really know anything about it."

The bell above the door rings as an old lady comes in and starts shaking out her umbrella. "If you're here to get out of the rain you still better *buy* something," Zahra mutters, and glares at her for a few seconds when she sits down at the table by the window without ordering anything. "Nice," says Zahra. "That's not rude at all." Then she gets up and starts dismantling the cappuccino machine to clean it.

18

Ten minutes later, there's a line of people and Zahra is busy explaining that they'll all have to drink vanilla infusion or black coffee. I go and slouch in the corner booth where me and Teagan sit, send her a message. *At coffee shop without parents. Want to join? Xx*

She replies instantly. *Have to keep practicing. Also scared to leave house in case blown up. Come over? XXX*

I don't feel like going to Teagan's house. I think for a minute about texting Ollie, calling him even, but I don't know what he does on the weekends, don't know if we have anything to talk about without Teagan there.

In my bag there is homework and the book I'm reading but my mind is all white noise and I know I won't be able to concentrate. I think maybe I'll go home again and watch the news, wait for Danny to come home, wait for them to say if the person who's been killed is a child or someone's grandma or what. Or maybe I'll get on the subway and go to the shops, except I have no money and I know there'll be police with machine guns everywhere and they make me nervous.

At the register, someone is complaining about being given the wrong change and Zahra is arguing with him, her cheeks flushing red. *People are awful,* I think. *London is a horrible city.*

Nick is going away somewhere and didn't tell us.

When the change-complainer stomps off, I lean over the counter and tell Zahra that I'm going home. She's trying to serve somebody else, so she waves distractedly and I slip out. It's dark now, although it's only four o'clock, and it's raining harder, car headlights glittering as they pass by, spraying water onto the pavement. I pull the hood of my coat up and dig my gloves out of the pockets. The supermarket across the road has closed early, pulled its security gates down. A dejected-looking man is standing in front of it, smoking. He glances across the road and meets my eye, stares at me for a minute. I turn abruptly and start walking up the road.

The first place I get to that's open is the library. I go in. It's empty. I have the idea that maybe there might be a book about Greenham Common. I read a lot about it on the internet but it would be nice to have a book.

I don't know where something like that would be shelved: history or politics or what? I wander the aisles for a while and eventually I ask a librarian. She's not that much older than me and she's never heard of it, but she types something into her computer and says, "Oh, here you go. It's in the women's history section."

I didn't know there was a women's history section and I tell her this, and she says, "Neither did I, to be perfectly honest with you." She helps me find it, but it's just one shelf at the end of the regular history section, and the Greenham Common book isn't there. She says it's probably been stolen.

Then my phone is ringing and I answer it in a quiet library-voice and it's Danny.

"Where are you?" he says. "No one's answering at home. Are you with Nick?"

"No. We were at the coffee shop but he had to go and pick up an order."

"Did he."

"John's got a bad heart and can't drive."

"Who's John?"

"I don't know."

"So where are you?"

"I'm in the library. I'm on my way home."

"On your own?"

"Yeah. Well, there's a librarian."

"I mean you're walking home on your own?"

"I will be in a minute."

"I'd like it if you went home, all right? You shouldn't be wandering aimlessly around the streets on your own when there's this kind of—"

"I'm not wandering aimlessly around the streets; I'm in the library."

"Well, I'd like it if you went home."

"I am. I will be. As soon as I get off the phone."

"Fine." Danny pauses, and says, "I didn't know I'd be here all day. I meant to be home by now."

Now I'm standing in the lobby of the library. A little kid is going around and around in the revolving doors while his mother stands inside waiting for him.

"What were you doing?"

"Drafting a statement. Press stuff. Jake wanted to get out there a little bit, talk about safety."

"Zahra said he was on the news."

The little kid tries to escape from the revolving doors at the last minute but he messes it up and falls over and starts crying like kids do. His mother goes and picks him up.

"Yeah," says Danny. "He was."

"Is that good?"

"It's good for him. I don't know. It is what it is."

"It is what it is."

"Yeah. Listen, when you see Nick, tell him I'm going to be really late. I'll have dinner here."

"Why don't you phone him and tell him yourself?"

"Because I'm asking you to tell him."

"Do you know anything about the bombing? Does anyone know who was killed?"

Danny sighs. "Yeah. They haven't released it yet but it sounds like it was a tourist. Some guy. They think he might be Italian."

This is terrible, I think. *Not any better than if it was a kid. Someone who thought that London would be a nice place to visit and look what happened.* He was probably buying snacks before he went to the museums or something. He probably had a guidebook in his pocket where he'd circled the stuff he wanted to see.

"Lena?" Danny sounds far away. I can hear people talking in the background, and a man laughing. "You still there?"

"Yes," I say. "I'm going home."

19

I say to Nick, "Apparently you're going to Colombia for a month." He stops in the doorway and stares at me for a few moments, and then comes inside and carefully closes the door behind him. He takes a few steps toward the kitchen, where I'm sitting at the counter with my laptop. He puts his keys down on the counter.

"I'd like to talk about your tone of voice," he says.

"I'd like to talk about you going to Colombia for a month."

"Drop the attitude," he says, "and we can."

It was nearly six o'clock when I got home and there was nobody here. I ate half a packet of cookies and two pieces of toast and rearranged the postcards around my mirror and read the first page of one of Danny's Bob Dylan books. I got out the Beatles songbook and tried to play "We Can Work It Out" but I couldn't even get my hand to form the shape of the first chord. I watched the news, and they replayed the Jacob Carlisle interview. He said that he was feeling devastated. I turned it off again. I looked up the Save Ocean Court campaign and looked at all the comments people had written on the website. When Nick finally gets home I'm tired of myself.

"I've never even heard of Colombia," I say, knowing this will wind him up.

He puts the lid back on the tub of butter that I've left out and puts it in the fridge, and takes the sticky knife from where I've left it on the counter and places it in the sink. "How many hours of your life have you spent in the coffee shop?" he says. "There's a huge map of the world on the wall and all the places we source from are labeled in huge letters."

Now that he says this, it sounds familiar, but without actually looking at it I couldn't tell him where Colombia was, which, anyway, is not the point. "Is it true?"

He takes his coat off and hangs it by the door, takes his shoes off and lines them up by the doormat, goes into the bathroom probably to fix his hair. When he comes out he has a face on like something he's practiced in the mirror. "Did you hear this from Zahra?" he says.

I don't really see why *that* matters either. "She seemed to think it was something I would already know."

"Well, she's wrong about it. I need to talk to her."

"So you're not going?"

"There's a possibility—" he holds up a hand "—a *small* possibility, an opportunity, a *chance* that I might go on a work-related trip to meet some of the growers we source from and look into building new possible—"

"For a month," I say. "A whole month."

"Yes," he says. "How would you feel about that?"

"I don't care," I say.

He looks at me steadily. "OK, then."

"How does Danny feel about it?"

"I only just found out about it."

"How could you only just—"

"I said I couldn't go, initially, but somebody just dropped out of the trip, so the space has opened up again, which means—"

"When is it?"

"Obviously I'm going to talk about it with Danny."

"When is it?"

"The end of April."

It's March. The end of April is not very far away.

I pinch the top of my thumb as hard as I can and look at it as the skin turns white. It leaves an indentation when I stop.

"Someone was killed today," I say.

He sits down at the counter and looks at me. "I know. How do you feel about that?"

I wonder if this *how do you feel about that* routine is something he's gotten from a book. One of the books they've got in the bedroom, hidden on top of the wardrobe where normal people probably keep porn, with titles like *Progressive Parenting* and *Understanding Your Child*, most of which I think Nick's parents gave them when I was little. After my thirteenth birthday they got some new ones. *Understanding Teenagers. Teenage Girls and What (Not) to Say to Them.* Some of them have Post-it notes inside. Like I'm a homework project or something, and one day, Nick is going to write a really good essay about his parenting experience. Danny, I know for a fact, has never read any of them, since he only reads detective fiction and Bob Dylan biographies.

How do I feel about it? I feel weird. On the news now they've said that he was a tourist in London with his family, and that he had a new baby daughter. He could have left his hotel five minutes later or stopped to tie his shoelace. He would have loved her for years and years. She will have one less person that loves her than she was supposed to have. And still no one even knows what the point of the bombs is supposed to be.

The last time the windows of the coffee shop got smashed

in—it's happened three times in the last two years—I remember standing on the street opposite and thinking that the front of the shop looked like a broken face, and thinking, *But why though, but why, but why?* Like if there was a good reason for it that would be better. *It's just kids*, Nick says, every time, but Danny says he's being targeted because of all the posters and stickers he lets people put up in the windows. Maybe it doesn't make a difference.

"They interviewed Jacob Carlisle on the news," I say.

A hard look comes into Nick's eyes and he rubs his hand over his face. "I know. I heard it just now in the car."

"What did you think?"

"I didn't think a lot of it, if you really want to know. I thought it was cynical and exploitative. If you really want to know."

I try to remember these words because they sound right; they sound like words that I could use myself sometime. *Cynical and exploitative.*

"So did I," I say, and he smiles half-heartedly.

"Are you going to Colombia because you're angry with Danny?"

"Who says I'm angry with Danny?"

"You are. I can tell."

"I'm probably not even going, Alena. Try not to worry about it, all right?"

"You think he's wrong about Lynn Wallace, don't you? You think I should be allowed to meet her."

"I never said that."

"But you—"

"I think he's got his reasons and they're complicated."

"So complicated that nobody will tell me what they are."

He doesn't answer.

"Why did you say no to going on the trip the first time?"

"What?" he says. We are sitting directly opposite each other, the counter between us, and it's very quiet, so you can hear the kitchen clock ticking.

Lately I get the feeling that Nick and my brother find me exhausting. That now that I'm a teenager and not a cute little kid, they don't really like me that much anymore. But there's nothing I can do about it. I can't switch back. I have to keep going.

"You said the first time you heard about the trip to Colombia you said no."

A long, long pause. "We didn't—it didn't seem like a good idea at the time."

"Like Danny didn't think it was a good idea?"

"Danny thought a month was a long time to be away and I agreed."

"And now you don't agree."

Nick gets up then, and I twist around on the stool to look at him as he goes to the fridge and opens it, stares into it for a while.

"Sometimes people have to do things for themselves. Like Danny and his job, for instance. Sometimes people have to make decisions on their own."

"OK," I say. "What decision do I get to make? What do I get to decide?"

"You get to decide what we have for dinner," he says, but it turns out all we have are baked potatoes and broccoli, so it's not true; I don't even get to decide that.

× × × × ×

I don't hear Danny come home but I wake up thirsty in the middle of the night, and when I go to get a glass of water he's sitting in the dark on the sofa, still in his work clothes, staring blankly at the news channel which is on mute. There's an empty bottle of wine on the coffee table in front of him and a plastic tumbler in his hand. The living room is freezing because all the windows are open.

Very slowly, he drags his eyes from the television to my face, and looks at me like he's not sure who I am.

"Why are the windows open?" I say, trying to keep my voice down, and then I see a red lighter and a pack of Marlboros on the table and work it out myself. "Were you smoking in the *apartment?*"

"No."

I grab a blanket that's hanging over the arm of the sofa and wrap it around myself. Danny squints at me. "Why aren't you in bed?"

"Why aren't you?"

He glances back at the TV. "I will be in a minute," he says. He rubs his eyes. "Do you need something?"

"No. I was just thirsty."

I drink a glass of water in the kitchen and then I go back and sit down on the arm of the sofa. I twist a loose thread from the edge of the blanket around the tip of my finger. "Nobody told me that Nick might be going to Colombia."

Danny blinks, stares at the television. Light flares over his face, red, blue, white, like police cars. "He's not going."

"What?"

"He's not going."

"How do you know?"

"I just had a conversation with him about it."

"You mean a fight."

"Yes."

I yank the loose thread and it snaps. "Oh."

"So don't worry about it."

"Did you tell him not to go?"

"I didn't tell him anything. Nick's free to do what he likes."

There's a silence. I don't know what to say. "I don't even know where Colombia is," I say eventually.

"Me neither," says Danny. And then, like he's talking to himself, he says, "My mum used to say I should be embarrassed how bad my geography was. Like hers was any better."

I freeze. I could swear this is the first thing in years he's told me about her without having to be asked, and I hold my breath for a moment in case there's more. But he just sits there for a minute longer and then he puts the plastic tumbler down on the floor and gets up to close the windows.

It's like conjuring her into the room, I think, *and just when I'm about to see her, she's gone again.*

20

Ollie's house is a ground-floor apartment and it smells like a hot day when nobody's taken the rubbish out. It's not overpowering or anything. It's just unfresh, like you'd think somebody would want to open all the windows. His dog leaps up and goes mental when we walk in on Monday after school, barks and barks and throws itself at our legs, super happy to see us.

"Is anyone home?" says Teagan.

"No," says Ollie automatically. But then he pauses, jingles his keys in his hand for a moment, looks around like somebody might appear and offer to make us all sandwiches.

Definitely no one is home. It's silent, apart from the dog.

In the living room, someone has left the TV on. There's an empty birdcage in the corner, jammed between the sofa and a big suitcase that's obviously too big to store anywhere else but the main room.

"What's that for?" Teagan says, looking at it. "Are you getting a bird?"

"Huh?"

"The birdcage."

"Oh. No. I dunno. We just never got rid of it. My dad wanted a bird. He got this bird once but it died right away. So."

It must have been standing there for years because as far as

I know, Ollie's dad left before he even started secondary school.

"Anyway, sit down or whatever. If you want. Hang on a second." Ollie disappears down the corridor to what must be the bathroom.

Me and Teagan look at each other and sit down on the edge of the sofa. There's one sofa and two wicker chairs that look awful and uncomfortable.

I get my phone out and take a photo of Ollie's dog while it rolls around on the floor trying to get its belly scratched, waggling its little dog legs in the air.

"Ollie, your dog wants love," says Teagan, when Ollie comes back into the room. He has washed his face, and his hair is damp at the edges, pushed out of his eyes for once.

"She's not mine." Ollie looks at the dog and she leaps up, starts running rings around his ankles, yapping. He nudges her away but she tries to scrabble up his leg, so he bends and picks her up, holds her like you'd hold a baby, and she goes still and happy. "She's Aaron's. My brother's. Only somehow now I've got to take her out all the time and feed her and everything like that." He looks at Teagan. "Do you want her? Her name's Brandy."

"No, not at all," says Teagan.

"Alena?"

Brandy's head is dangling back over the crook of Ollie's arm so she's looking at me upside down and it looks like she's smiling.

"I'd be scared your brother would come back and then hunt me down for stealing his dog or something," I say.

Ollie nods, and looks at Brandy for a moment. Then he puts her down, very gently. She tries to scrabble up again. "He's not coming back," Ollie says.

I've always thought *Aaron* was a nice name. It didn't suit Ollie's brother at all. I don't like to make judgments about people I don't know, but I'm pretty sure Aaron was—*is*, because I don't suppose he's dead—a really bad person. Just like a fundamentally not-nice person that nobody liked and everybody was frightened of, including teachers. After he got busted and he disappeared it was like when Christmas returns to Narnia the way everyone talked about it at school. And what should Ollie even care because Aaron never even spoke to him.

Ollie obviously does care. I have no idea what to say about it.

"She loves you," says Teagan. "Look at her. You can't give her away. Look at her little face."

I hold up the photo I took to show him, just in case he doesn't know what she looks like. "Look. She's cute. Girls will like her."

"You're girls and you don't seem that interested."

"Well, my dad's allergic," says Teagan.

Ollie takes Brandy out to walk her around the block and leaves us sitting in his living room, Teagan picking dog hair off the sofa carefully. I go into the kitchen wanting a glass of water. There are glasses and plates piled in the sink but there's nothing clean, and when I look in the fridge it's empty apart from half a bottle of tonic water and some out-of-date milk. I go back into the living room and sit down again.

"This place is a bit—you know."

"I know," says Teagan.

Then I feel bad. "I mean, where I live is a mess, too, most of the time," I say, but Teagan shakes her head.

"No. This is like no one really even lives here."

"Do you know what his mum does?" I say. I lower my voice a bit even though I know there's no one here.

"He told me she drinks a lot," says Teagan, which isn't really what I was asking, but then we hear the key in the lock and the dog barking, Ollie coming back.

We stand up, ready to leave.

"You can bring her to the coffee shop if you want," I tell Ollie, as he puts out a bowl of water for Brandy.

"Nah. She'll bark and everything. She doesn't like lots of people."

We all watch the dog for a moment as she laps at her water. You'd think Aaron would have had some big ugly dog called Spike or something. Maybe she was a rescue dog if she doesn't like people. One of those dogs with lots of psychological trauma.

"Let's go," says Ollie. "She's fine."

x x x x x

There turns out to be a long, looping walk you can take from Ollie's house to the coffee shop that goes by the canal. It's pretty, in a grungy, littered sort of way, and the dog would like it, I think. I feel sad that we didn't bring her. We stop and sit for a while, scuffing little stones from the gravel pavement over the edge into the green water.

"This is probably murder central around here," says Teagan. She looks suspiciously at two men in suits walking past us on their way home. "I'm not sure if I'm allowed to go walking by canals. I think I'm not. I think my parents have some kind of rule about it."

"Mine too," I say.

"Yours *definitely* do," says Teagan. "Danny would, anyway. Remember when we were little and he wouldn't let us go to the corner shop because we had to cross a road?"

"Yep."

"What was wrong with crossing a road?" says Ollie.

"Nothing," I say. "Just, my brother thought we'd be hit by a car."

"Me and Aaron used to skateboard by this canal all the time when we were younger," Ollie says. "Like ten and thirteen. Except one time these other kids came and pushed me off and stole my skateboard and then threw it in the water."

"What did Aaron do?" says Teagan.

"Nothing. He went home."

"That was nice of him."

"There wasn't anything he could have done."

"Did you get your skateboard back?"

"No. It sank. It's probably still down there."

"OK," says Teagan. "Thanks for that depressing story."

"You're welcome."

"I don't have a brother or anything, but aren't they supposed to defend you if you get your skateboard stolen?"

Ollie is silent for a minute. "I don't know," he says. "I guess."

"They are."

"Teagan." I give her a look. Neither of us knows anything about having brothers: she's got no siblings and I've only got Danny who doesn't count because he's so much older. I can tell that she wants to say to Ollie that his brother is a creep, but honestly, who understands how anybody's family works?

There's a low cloud hanging over us and it's cold even though I'm wearing my coat and my scarf and my green gloves with stars on. Looking at the murky water then, I have this heavy, anxious feeling, like everything is dangerous and the cold water is inside me, rising. It gets worse when I open my mouth to start to try and explain it to Teagan and Ollie and realize I can't because I don't know what it is. Instead I just say, "I'm cold. Can we go?"

21

On the chalkboard it says, *Monday's Special: Kindness!*

There's a rack for flyers that stands in front of the till, and Ollie has taken one of each of them, so he has a stack of about twenty to read and doesn't have to talk to anybody. There's a post-work rush on and all the tables are taken, so when my brother walks in at about six o'clock there's nowhere for him to sit and he has to come and join us. He's carrying a newspaper and when he drops it on the table there's a picture on the front of the guy who was killed on Saturday. Danny sees me looking at it and flips it over.

"What are you doing here?" I say.

"I need to use the Wi-Fi. Ours keeps cutting out." He gets his laptop out and starts opening it. "I'll be twenty minutes, Alena. Don't look at me like that. Do you want to introduce me to your friend?"

"Danny, this is Oliver. From school. We're doing a science project."

Danny looks at our empty Coke glasses and Ollie's stack of subversive leaflets and my notebook lying open with a drawing of a zebra wearing a top hat. I like drawing animals in formal clothing. "Uh huh," he says.

Ollie is staring at Danny with an unreadable expression on

his face, and when I see Nick come out of the back office, notice Danny, and head toward us, I think, *Please don't kiss*—and then I'm immediately ashamed of myself but it doesn't matter because they don't; Nick just touches Danny's shoulder very briefly and says, "Hey, guys, how are we all doing out here?"— all charming like he's our waiter in a nice restaurant. Teagan immediately starts blushing and Nick smiles at her as he slides into the booth next to Danny. "You guys mind if I join you?"

"I don't mind," Teagan says, and I roll my eyes at her.

There's something a little bit wild in Ollie's eyes once there's five of us around the table, and he starts folding up his leaflets and tucking them into his pocket. Danny tries to engage him in conversation but he goes monosyllabic and nervy and finally Teagan has to get up to let him out and he leaves, mumbling something about the dog. Honestly, I don't blame him. Other people's families can be stressful. Having dinner with both of Teagan's parents always makes me exhausted. They are way too nice.

"That kid needs a coat," Danny says absently, watching Ollie leave. Then he turns to his laptop. Nick frowns at him. "Are you here to work?"

"Yes. Wi-Fi's dead at home. Sorry."

"Why don't you give it a rest for the night? I'm nearly finished here. We could all go out for food or something. Or get takeout. Teagan, you want to join us for takeout?"

"I told my mum I'd be home by seven," Teagan says, massively disappointed. "Sorry."

"That's fine," says Danny. "Because I have to work."

"I'll have takeout," I say. "Me. I don't have to work."

"Danny, take a break. Whatever you're doing can't be that important—"

"Right," says Danny. "It's not important at all. Not like selling coffee, is it?"

Both me and Teagan go very still. There's a short, cold silence and then Nick says, "So what's his policy for keeping us safe this week? Martial law? Capital punishment?"

Teagan, who has probably never seen Nick in sarcastic mode, shifts uncomfortably and says softly, "I should really go home, then."

"You don't have to," I tell her.

"No, I should."

Nick and Danny both say, "How are you getting home?" at the same time and then glare at each other, and Teagan says, "I can walk. It's still light. I think I'll walk." And you can't blame her either, really.

"I might go home as well," I say when she's gone, but neither of them are paying attention to me and I don't honestly want to go home, so I gather up my stuff and go and sit at the counter and talk to Zahra who, in between serving customers, tells me about how she has been sleeping with a revolutionary communist she met on the internet.

× × × × ×

Later, as me and my brother are getting ready to leave, somebody bellows "Danny!" across the shop, and we look up and it's Mike, Danny's old boss, coming in for his evening espresso on the way home from work. Danny always says he doesn't know how anyone can drink that much caffeine at night, and Nick says *Who cares, it's good for business*, which I doubt is true since half the time he doesn't let Mike pay.

Danny flinches at the sound, but then he gets up, goes over, and him and Mike do a complicated back-slapping man hug, and Mike says, "How's life on the other side?"

"Do not start," says Danny.

Mike is tall and has gray-black hair and nice, kind eyes, and he once told me that he was the first Irish-Lebanese man to go to Oxford University, which for all I know is true. He's been editor of the *Hackney Standard* for years. He gave Danny his first job, supposedly, so he's known him forever, and he likes sitting around and talking politics with Nick and Zahra.

I like him a lot. He buys me overpriced Christmas presents and takes us all out to dinner with his wife, who loves me. If Nick and Danny are ever killed in a plane crash I hope that the Feghalis will adopt me.

"Alena," says Mike. "Lovely Alena." Nobody calls me lovely apart from Mike. He says, "Will you tell your brother to stop working for that crook and come back to me?"

"Stop working for that crook and go back to Mike."

"Tell Mike to triple my pay and I'll think about it," says Danny. I don't know if this is a joke or not.

"Lena, how would you like a job?" says Mike. "I'll take either of the Kennedy siblings."

"Yes, please," I say.

"Right, glad that's solved," says Danny. "We're going home. Nick's in the back office; go and bother him."

"You don't call, you don't write," says Mike. "You know Trevor's wife just had a baby?"

"Congratulations to Trevor," says Danny. "We've got to go." Like he realizes he's being rude then, he says, "How's circulation?"

"Down, down, down," says Mike. "You know how it is. East End Bomber's been good for us, though."

"Uh huh," says Danny. "Well, send him a gift basket."

Nick comes out of the back office then, shrugging into his coat, and he sees Mike and says, "Hey!" and comes over for some more manly half-hugging.

"Don't you have to close up?" Danny says.

Nick glances at him. "Zahra's doing it. Thought I'd walk home with you guys."

"Right."

They look at each other in silence until Mike gets uncomfortable and says, "Well, Zahra makes better coffee anyway." I'm suddenly sick of them both behaving like this in front of people who are our friends.

× × × ×

"Right," says Danny. "He's not Muslim, so the only other option is that he's a Nazi."

"I didn't say *Nazi*."

"Yes, you did. You just said *Nazi*."

We are walking home past all the locked-up shops, and on to the quiet residential street on the way to our apartment. They both look tired and orange under the streetlights and their voices are loud and echo against the empty road.

"My point was that all the bombs have been in ethnically diverse areas of London and it might be that this is some sort of white supremacist kind of—"

"Every area of London is ethnically diverse."

"Yeah, but these areas are *particularly*—"

"How do we know he's not one of your lot? One of your eco-activist friends from the coffee shop?"

Nick stops for a moment so that I almost walk into him because I'm trailing behind. He gives Danny a very hard look. "Since when is my lot not your lot too?"

"You've had hundreds of *stop the evil supermarkets* posters up in the shop. How do we know the bomber isn't back there right now drinking an organic black soy Americano and planning his next target?"

"There's no such thing as a black soy Americano," says Nick. He starts walking again.

"If he is a white supremacist," I say, trying to keep up with them, "it's not actually a very good *tactic*, is it? Like there's no white people in Tesco's in Shoreditch?"

Nick shakes his head. "Some people just want to burn things down," he says. "That's all they really want. Whatever they believe in. Some people want to build things and some people want to burn things down."

"That's really profound, Nick, thank you," says Danny, and I say, "Can we stop talking about it?" and both of them say, "Yes," at the same time.

22

Danny was twenty when they met, and Nick was twenty-three. Or Danny was nineteen and Nick was twenty-two. Or, Nick told me once, Danny was twenty-two and Nick was twenty-five.

"Nick," said Danny, sitting next to him that time. "No. You're getting senile. I was still at university. I was nineteen. Or twenty."

"Right," said Nick, looking totally confused. "OK. Yeah. That's right."

"Twenty-two and twenty-five are the ages you were when you got me," I said, and Nick said, "Right. Yeah. Of course," and still looked confused.

I swear they have told me different ages every time I ask. They are both getting senile.

"My parents are the same," Teagan says. "It's because they can't deal with being nearly sixty."

Teagan's parents are twenty years older than mine. Teagan's mum had her when she was nearly forty. She sometimes tilts her head to one side and says, sort of wistfully, how young Nick and Danny are. I have, on very rare occasions, heard her refer to them as *the boys*. They'd probably love this.

My parents and Teagan's parents are super nice to each other these days, ever since the *celebrating diversity* incident.

Extravagantly polite, always sending each other Christmas cards and invitations to dinner, and then skilfully avoiding the actual dinners since they have nothing to say to each other except to talk about us.

Teagan's parents were both married before, to other people, and in fact her mum was still married when she met Teagan's dad, although the details around this are all very sketchy and not to be talked about. But now we're teenagers, sometimes Rachel will have a few glasses of wine and start telling stories. I always listen. I love stories like this. I am starving for them.

I think it's romantic, actually. Like you're already married but then you meet the person you're *really* meant to be with: you'd have to really be in love to go through all the hassle of breaking up with the other person. I think of her parents' relationship as a very deliberate thing. They didn't just stumble into a relationship and stay that way forever. They had to choose. Which I think is romantic although Teagan thinks basically the opposite.

Nick and Danny met in a bar where Nick was working, and that's all they can remember about it. I've tried for years to get them to tell me about this in some way that makes it a story. I'd like for it to be romantic and funny and brilliant. Or just important and deliberate in a way that makes it seem like everything that came after was important and deliberate and not just a series of accidents they couldn't find their way out of. Instead, it goes like this: Danny walked into a bar one evening—he can't remember why he was there—and Nick started speaking to him—he can't remember what about—and they exchanged phone numbers—they can't remember why—and then the next week they met up in another bar—they can't remember which one.

"That's great," I said to Nick once, rolling my eyes. "That's really romantic."

"It doesn't need to be romantic," Nick said. "We're here, aren't we?"

"But you must have fallen in love," I said. "At some point you must remember falling in love."

"What do you want to hear, exactly? Candles and flowers and caught in a rainstorm?"

"Yes!" I said.

"Our relationship's not like that," he said, and I said, "No kidding," and he said, "Yeah," and I said, "But you do love each other," and he said, "Yeah, but—"

I said, "Don't say *but*! There's not supposed to be a *but*!" and that made him laugh. Then he said, "I was just going to say that love isn't necessarily romantic in the way you're asking." He said, "Sometimes it's more like—" and then he paused for a while, frowning like he was thinking really hard, and eventually said, "I can't think of the right word."

"*Nick*," I whined, and he said, "It's just that it's not really a romantic story. How I met Danny. It's more difficult than that. It's more complicated. It's better. It's more like—"

He paused again. He was thinking really hard. One thing I will say about Nick is that he tries to take these questions seriously. Even when I was little, asking really stupid stuff. He tries to give serious answers.

"It just changes you," he said. "Sometimes you meet someone and it changes everything. In a good way. And there was all this awful stuff that happened, your mum dying and everything, and we went through all of that together, and you just end up being changed by it all. Like you've broken a bone or something, and then it heals differently. The other person becomes part of who you are."

"So being in a relationship with my brother is like breaking a leg?"

He grinned. "Yes," he said, "exactly. Except it's not like the breaking. It's like the healing."

I said, "That makes no sense," and he said, "You'll understand one day," which is absolutely the number one most infuriating thing an adult can say.

When I told Teagan he'd said that to me she went starry-eyed and said it was the most romantic thing she'd ever heard and gave herself a pen tattoo on her arm that said, *It's not like the breaking. It's like the healing.*

I gave myself one that said, *Teagan Esler is fucking ridiculous* and Teagan said, "You'll get in trouble for having the word *fucking* written on your arm," and she was right, I did.

Whatever.

23

So now anyway, lately, I am thinking that's not even the important story. The important story, the place where I start, is not Nick and Danny. It's her.

I've got my Greenham Common postcard propped up by my bed and I keep looking at her face and trying to find the place in my mind that recognizes her, the place where all my memories are hiding. And I'll watch the video sometimes before bed, or on my phone at lunchtime, her saying, *I think they're right, aren't they?* and her glance flicking to the camera at the end. She is really young. Not that much older than the girls in sixth form. She could almost still be at school but instead she's in a green raincoat on an Air Force base. *But I'm not the one populating this earth with weapons, am I?*

She has a baby. I keep thinking, *There's my brother,* and then I think, *This woman is nothing like my brother,* and then I think how I ended up with Danny when for a little while I had *her.*

× × × × ×

Things we might have done together before she died:

She might have taken me to a political protest, like you see babies at the Pride parade sometimes, flags and banners unfurling from their strollers. There might have been a walk through the wild, overgrown cemetery near where she used to live, me picking up dried leaves and interesting stones and showing them to her. Our faces both flushed from the cold. My first birthday, a badly iced cake that she made herself and was proud of. Her making up songs and putting my name in them. Sunday afternoons, just the two of us, at home. Toys. Coloring books. Maybe she accidentally left me in the car one afternoon when she went shopping. Maybe she accidentally dropped me down the stairs and I cried for a few minutes and then I was fine and she never told anybody because she felt so guilty. A visit to the London Aquarium on a Monday morning when it's quiet. She held me up to the tanks so I could press my hand against the glass.

Maybe she killed a rabbit and drew symbols on my face with its blood in a pagan ritual for long life and well-being.

All of these things might have happened. Since no one can ever tell me otherwise—since Danny won't tell me anything—I'm starting to believe that all of them did. Starting to imagine these stories and collect them, and carry them around like stones in my pocket. There was an *us* once.

24

It's Saturday again and I spend the morning on a charity shop pilgrimage. It's the start of April and they still haven't found the East End Bomber, so I have promised Danny that I will avoid supermarkets. Instead I go to Cancer Research and the British Heart Foundation and Oxfam and the Salvation Army and the Arthritis Society, and I come home with two bags of t-shirts and skirts and beaten-up paperback books that smell like somebody's attic. I'm in a good mood when I get back and there's a note on the fridge saying, *Gone food shopping, N+D x*, which I interpret as meaning that they're trying to be nice to each other.

When they come back I'm in my room, trying on a sweater and looking in the mirror, wearing my mum's old glasses from the storage locker to complete the vintage thing. I hear the front door open and thwack against the wall the way it does if you kick it open.

"—and don't even get me started on the *strategy for safety* or whatever the hell it is, because it's the most—"

"I know that isn't what you really want to talk about, so why don't you just say whatever it is that you—"

"I actually *do* want to talk about it because I think you've lost your mind if you can justify to yourself—"

"Just drop it, Nick, just shut up about it. I'm sick of hearing—"

"—and I'm sick of being told to shut up every time I say something that you find difficult to hear. *Jesus*, Danny, I mean, you seriously—"

The door slams shut again and I hear Danny's voice. "Don't. Don't. Don't even start."

"You can't just shut down every time something you don't want to talk about—"

"Don't do your ridiculous psychoanalysis whatever-the-hell-it-is you're going to—"

"—and after everything I've done and all the times I *have* kept my mouth shut when what I really wanted to do—"

"What you really wanted to do was go and hang out with coffee growers in Colombia while I'm left here with Alena trying to track down Lynn fucking Wallace and somebody going around trying to blow us all up, and you know what, if that's *still* what you want to do—"

"Oh my god."

"—then *fine*, you know, fine, why don't you just—"

"To try and make it sound like I don't even—"

"And I'm doing my best, OK. I'm doing my best and there's no need—I mean nobody ever forced you to stay with us; you're the one who can leave any time you want, and you know what, go ahead, if it's such a big problem for you. Nobody's forcing you to be here; you don't have any *duty*—"

"*Please* don't start this again, *god*. I can't have this conversation again. Do you have any idea how I feel when you—like I haven't earned the right by now to tell you when I think you're making *bad* decisions, when I think you're making seriously *bad* parenting decisions, if you honestly—"

"Don't you *dare*—"

There's an awful crack in Danny's voice then, and a sound like somebody slamming their hands on the kitchen counter. Then there's silence for a long time, and then Nick says something quiet that I can't hear. There's a weird, gasping noise like somebody crying and trying not to, like Danny crying, but I know it can't be, because in my life I have never seen Danny cry and I never want to and if he ever did, I think I would hate him.

I'm absolutely still and I'm quiet, so quiet, so if they haven't realized that I'm home, then they won't. I very carefully put my charity shop things into a neat pile and then put it all on the floor under my bed. And then, even though it's the middle of the day, I get under the blanket and pull it up to my chin, stare at my door, and wait for something.

After a while, I hear them go into their bedroom, and then I can't hear anything else. It's all quiet for a long time, and eventually I'm hungry, and I make myself get out of bed and go into the kitchen and make a lot of noise pouring myself a glass of juice and making toast and a cup of tea, and I even make a pot in case anyone is going to come out of the bedroom, but they don't. There are shopping bags on the kitchen counter that haven't been unpacked. From their bedroom I can hear very, very low voices, and the sound of someone moving around. I could knock on their door, say *What's for lunch?* but I don't. I wait.

And then so later, I'm in my bedroom getting crumbs all over my desk and butter on the keys of my laptop, and I'm playing this old Joni Mitchell album really quiet, and then there's this gentle, polite knock on my door, and I say "Come in," and it's Nick.

His face is very serious, one of those faces where you can't even fake a smile because the muscles around your mouth just won't work right. He closes the door behind himself and looks at me for a long while. "I'm sorry if you heard some of that," he says. "We didn't know you were home."

"What's for lunch?" I say.

"I need to talk to you for a minute."

"OK."

Then he just stands there, eyes roaming around my room, and I see him looking at my wardrobe which is hanging open with clothes falling out, and my mirror with all the postcards, and my schoolbooks under the bed. Then he comes into the room and sits down on my bed, which for a change I actually made after I got out of it.

I have a purple blanket with green and pink and orange flowers on it. It was a birthday present.

"C'mere," he says, so I go and sit down next to him, on the side of the bed facing the window.

"I know what you're going to think when I say this," says Nick. "So I'm going to tell you right away that you're wrong."

"When you say what?"

"I think you know that Danny and I have been fighting a lot recently, and to give us both some time to clear our heads, I'm going to go and stay with my brother for a few nights."

He stops, and wipes the palms of his hands on his jeans.

"You're breaking up," I say.

"No," says Nick. "We're not. We're not. That's not what this is."

"Is this because of Jacob Carlisle?"

"No, Lena. Of course it's not."

"Because he's like—he's not even a real person. He's like a person on the television. You can't move out because of him. Over something that isn't even a real thing."

"It *is* a real thing," Nick says then, short and blunt and like he didn't really mean to say it. "Jesus Christ. What's wrong with you two? It is a real thing. Jacob Carlisle tried to close down the coffee shop. Do you understand that? He tried to close down my business."

"Danny says he didn't."

"Danny's lying."

I think I might have misheard him for a second. He doesn't say Danny's wrong. He says Danny's lying. Actually lying.

I have the odd sensation of everything tilting, slightly; skewing sideways.

"So it *is* about him."

He puts his elbows on his knees and his face in his hands and for one awful moment I think he's going to cry too. I get up and go and lean with my back against the window, folding my arms tight. Nick takes this deep, dramatic breath and rubs his face very hard, so that when he looks up there are red marks on his face.

"Lena," he says. "Lena, Lena, Lena."

"Nicholas," I say, and he smiles a little bit.

You're my favorite, I think. *Don't leave. You're my favorite.*

"Are you going today?"

"Yes."

"Now?"

"I have to go to work this afternoon anyway. I'll go to Adam's afterwards."

"I'll come to work with you. I'll come to the shop."

"Maybe not, Lena. Maybe you should stay here this afternoon."

"Nick," I say. "Please. Please don't."

"It's just for a few nights. Maybe a week. That's all."

"How's that supposed to help? How's that going to solve anything?"

"Look," says Nick. "We've both been working really hard and we've got a lot on our minds, and I don't—we don't seem to be able to speak to each other right now without fighting. We're just taking a little bit of space to clear our heads. And then when we've calmed down we're going to talk and start working it out. You know that I wouldn't just leave, OK? So, make sure you know that."

"And I'm staying here."

"Lena."

"That's just been decided for me."

"This is where you live."

"This is where *you* live."

I think about Nick and Danny meeting in that bar, Nick being all charming and straightforward the way he knows how to be, getting them both a drink, no idea of the Kennedy family drama he was about to give his life over to.

"I bet you wish you'd never met Danny," I say. "Never got stuck with any of this. Then you'd be in Colombia and you'd be free and you'd be doing whatever you wanted."

Nick stares over my shoulder out my window. "You know what," he says, in a different tone of voice. "It's actually insulting when the two of you say stuff like that."

"Like what?"

He looks at me. "Nothing. I'm sorry. None of this is your fault. Everything's going to be OK."

It's somebody's fault, though.

PART THREE

25

On Monday at lunchtime there's a hazy, washed-out kind of early April sunshine, just about warm enough to sit out on the benches in the center of the quad, in our coats. Teagan is wearing fingerless gloves and she has painted her fingernails green. The color is really beautiful. I keep staring at it.

"I don't understand," she's saying. "Just for a few nights?"

"That's what he said."

"Are you OK?"

"No," I say. "I don't know. Not really."

"When he said a couple of nights did it seem like he meant it or was he just saying it?"

"I don't know."

She thinks about this. "Sometimes my dad sleeps in the guest room when my parents are mad at each other."

"Well, we don't have a guest room, so."

"So maybe that's all this is."

"He's never done it before." My voice comes out shaky in a way that I don't mean it to, and Teagan's eyes go wide and she grabs my hand and squeezes it for a second.

"I think that's what it is. This is just like sleeping in the guest room except that you don't have a guest room."

Behind her, I see Ollie come out of the dining hall and

stop, looking around the quad and trying to seem like he has something to do.

He sees us, waves, and then shoves his hand back in his pocket and walks toward us.

"Ladies," says Ollie when he gets to our table. Then he stands there like he's waiting to take our dinner order.

"Hi, Ollie," says Teagan. And then, after a pause, "Sit down if you want."

"What's up, Alena?" he says as he sits down.

"Nothing. My parents are breaking up."

He blinks a few times, looks like he regrets sitting down. "Oh," he says. "Shit."

"Yeah."

"You mean your brother and his—"

"Yes," Teagan interrupts. "Her parents. And I don't think they are."

"I don't want to talk about it," I say.

Teagan gets a Kit-Kat out of her bag and starts unwrapping it.

"Which one of them do you live with if they break up?" Ollie says.

"She says she doesn't want to talk about it, Ollie."

"Danny, I suppose." I pick at a splinter of wood on the bench until it breaks free. "He's my guardian."

"So he can't just leave?"

"What?"

"Your brother. Is it like—is he, looking after you, like, the law? Or does he just do it? I mean, what's to stop him from just leaving?"

"Oh my god." Teagan scowls at him.

"What do you mean, stop him from leaving? Leaving to go where?"

"I don't know, just—"

"Yes," I say. "It's the law. He can't leave. He's my legal guardian."

"And that means he can't just, like, give you to somebody else?"

"No. He can't just give me to somebody else. There isn't anybody else."

"Ollie, her brother *loves* her," says Teagan. "He's her *parent*. He's *amazing*. He's like the nicest person, and him and Nick are like these *heroic*—"

"Teagan," I say. "Don't." Because it suddenly sounds a bit like she's telling him that my brother is nothing like his—that Danny is nothing like Aaron—and I don't want to think about it like that. It makes me feel awful—sad for Ollie, and pissed off that Danny gets credit for looking after me, like he ever even really had a choice.

Looking good in comparison to Aaron is not exactly difficult.

"Just, don't say bad things about Lena's family," Teagan says firmly.

She has this way of curling her lip sometimes, like a snarl. Like when we were in primary school. Her hair in bunches, snarling at people who ever said weird or bad things about who my parents were. She never even thinks about it. It's frightening. Ollie looks frightened, a little bit, until Teagan snaps her Kit-Kat into two pieces and offers us both half.

"I feel sick," I say. "I need to go home."

× × × × ×

The thing about my school is, it's huge. They have this big thing about how they have small class sizes, but there's still hundreds and hundreds and hundreds of kids. It's supposed to be a good school. I don't know. Nick's parents tried to get me put on the waiting list for the school in west London that Nick went to, but a) it was miles away, and b) Danny accused them of wanting to send me to an all-white school. This is one of their favorite long-running arguments.

"You know that's not what they said," Nick will say. "They never said *all-white school*! They never said *all-white school*!"

Danny: "They said Mayfield was too diverse. Too diverse!"

"They said diverse," says Nick. "They did not say *too* diverse. They said diverse. They said diverse!"

Et cetera, et cetera.

The point is, my school is huge, and there's only one nurse, and if you go and see her and tell her you feel sick and have to go home, she will tell you to sit in the reception office for half an hour and see if you feel better, and then she'll forget that you're there. Except first she'll give you a stamped card that says you've been seen by the nurse and that's why you're not in class. At which point if you go home, or go to the cinema, or go out and get hit by a car or abducted, then the next day you can just hold up your nurse's card and you won't get into trouble.

So that's what I do, but instead of getting hit by a car or abducted, I get the bus to the coffee shop. I think that if Nick isn't sleeping in our house, then he doesn't really have the right to tell me off, and anyway, I have a nurse's card.

"Slacker!" Zahra says when I walk in. "Slacker! You're a slacker. You are so guilty. I can see it in your face." She's wearing a yellow and pink tie-dyed t-shirt.

"I felt sick," I say. "I have a nurse's card."

"Liar," says Zahra. She grins at me. "Nick's not even here, so you might get away with it."

"Where is he?" I lean over the counter and take a red hard candy from the bowl, sit down on one of the high stools, and carefully unwrap it.

Her face suddenly goes serious. "Actually," she says, "there's been a bit of a thing. Nick's parents turned up here as part of some surprise visit on their way to the theatre or something. And they wanted to have dinner with all you guys, and Nick was like, *That's probably not going to happen.*"

This isn't surprising to me at all. Nick's parents love to get involved in drama and I'm pretty sure they can just sense it, somehow, from all the way in Essex.

"And then what happened?"

"Nick tried to distract everybody with free coffee but it didn't work. As I'm sure you can imagine."

"And?"

"And then they all left. I think they went back to your place. I think his parents might have called your brother and asked to speak to him."

Like me, Zahra is good at listening in on other people's conversations.

"That's really bad," I say.

"I agree," she says. "If I was you, Lena, I would not turn up home with your nurse's note right now. Stay here for a bit. I'll make you a chai latte."

× × × × ×

I have two chai lattes and a slice of cake, so by the time I go home at four o'clock, I feel sick and sugary and like my heart is beating too fast. Nick is there. So are his parents. Nick's dad, Gerry, is sitting on the sofa pretending to read a book, like he's not involved in the conversation. Everyone else is standing around in the kitchen while the kettle boils. Nick and Danny both have their arms folded and look identically exasperated. Nick's mum, Marie, is surreptitiously tidying the kitchen counter and saying, "—after all the effort you've both put in, and don't think we don't recognize that—"

"What's going on?" I say, the door closing behind me.

"Hi, love," says Gerry from the sofa. Gerry has always liked me. Nick, he's not so sure about. And he always seems confused by Danny, as if he likes him but he can't quite work out why their lives are connected.

"Gerry and Marie are here," says Danny, pointlessly.

"Hi!" I say, trying to act surprised.

"You're just in time for a cup of tea," says Marie. "Have you had a good day at your school?"

"Are you here for dinner?" I say.

"No," says Marie. "We're going to the theatre. And since we had to come into London we thought we'd call in on you. See how you're getting on." She looks at Nick. "Not very well, by the sound of things."

"Yes, we're a bit of a disappointment," says Danny. Nick just looks like he wants to die.

"I'm going to get changed," I say, edging around the wall toward my room. "No sugar in my tea, please."

From my room, I hear Marie speak in what she probably thinks is a low voice. "This is about Alena, after all. Hasn't she had enough instability in her life?"

I don't know what this is supposed to mean and clearly Danny doesn't either. "Excuse me," he says. "She's had almost no instability in her life whatsoever."

"Well, she lost her mother."

"Well, so did I."

"And if you don't mind me saying, Daniel, I think it probably affected you rather more seriously than you've allowed yourself to admit."

"Mum, for god's sake," says Nick.

"I do mind you saying," says Danny.

I turn my radio on, loud, while I change into my jeans and an old gray t-shirt that says *NYC Superstars 1988* on it that I got for a pound at a car trunk sale. Sometimes Marie buys me clothes for Christmas. She always gets it wrong, but I don't mind. It's nice anyway.

"—if it was about money, then you should have just—" she is saying when I come back out. They all fall silent and look at me. The elevator rumbles in the center of the building, going up or down I can't tell.

Gerry clears his throat. "How about all this East End Bomber business, then, eh?" he says, which is obviously his idea of a good subject change.

"Dad," says Nick. "Please."

"Isn't it terrible?" says Marie. "Just terrible."

"Whole world gone mad," says Gerry.

"Do they think he's a white supremacist, then, or something else?" Marie looks at Danny like he might be an authority on the matter.

"I think they haven't ruled anything out," Danny says, but in the voice he uses when he's really, really pissed off about something.

"Such a tragedy," says Marie.

"I'll be glad when all this is over," says Gerry. It's not really obvious what he means, but I totally agree.

26

I think maybe Nick will stay when his parents finally leave to go to the theatre, but he doesn't. He says that he has to go back to work, and Danny just nods. "I'll call you later," Nick says to him, which is good, I guess, except that it means he's obviously not coming back here tonight. "And I'm sorry about that. I didn't even know they were coming into the city. So. I'm sorry."

"Don't worry about it," says Danny. "It's always a pleasure."

I'm sitting on the arm of the sofa, and Nick leans over to hug me before he leaves. He kisses the top of my head and says, "I'll see you very soon." I feel like crying.

× × × × ×

Even though it's only April, for some reason I start fixating on Christmas—like what if Nick is gone by then, so we don't visit Gerry and Marie either, so it's just me and Danny alone in the apartment opening presents from each other. Plus the present I always get from Niamh and Drew, which is always uncomfortable since Danny never gets anything, not even a card.

I spend the next evening at the coffee shop, and the one after that, and Nick keeps telling me to go home but actually I think he's pleased that I'm there. And I turn my phone off so

Danny has to phone him to ask where I am. "She's doing her homework," Nick says. "She's fine. I'll walk her home." And I think, *Now it's been two days, now it's been three days.* On Saturday, Nick said to me, *A couple of days.*

"It's Wednesday," I say to him, when he comes to sit opposite me near closing time, turns my physics homework around to look at it.

"Yes," says Nick. "It's Wednesday. What's this supposed to be?"

"It's a bat," I say. "I'm drawing the way a bat knows where things are. From listening to echoes. Because it's blind. It's a drawing of a bat."

"It's very good."

"Are you going to stay at Adam's again tonight?"

He looks at the picture for a few more moments, and then turns it back to me. "Yes."

So this means he will walk me home but not come inside and I will go inside on my own, and Danny will be doing work at the kitchen counter and he'll try and be really nice but it will be totally fake and I'll snap at him and then he'll snap at me and then he'll look guilty and then I'll go to my room and go to bed and the light will be on in the kitchen until really late.

"Do you have enough socks, and everything?" I say. Because as far as I know he didn't pack a suitcase when he left and Nick is *not* somebody who would ever wear the same socks two days in a row.

He looks at me for a while. "I'll be home in a few days," he says.

Nick doesn't lie to me. I make myself think this, deliberately: *Nick does not lie. Nick does not lie.* Apart from the thing about Colombia, which was more of an *omission*.

I keep accidentally reading about the person who was killed. His name was Eduardo Capello, which is a really beautiful name to say out loud. All the papers print the same picture of him, holding his new baby daughter and looking like the happiest person you've ever seen. He's lovely in the picture, all soft brown eyes and huge smile. And he kept exotic fish, it said in an article I read; he was an exotic-fish enthusiast and he had an aquarium in his living room.

I wish that I didn't know this.

I hope that somebody will look after his fish now that he's dead.

Nobody looks after the things my mother loved. I've been thinking about that recently. They are all locked up in storage, in the dark, all the things she ever cared about or bought for herself as a treat or presents that she saved, and nobody touches them or looks at them. All those things that are pieces of her. There are probably toys from when I was little, stuff we played with together. Pieces of us.

Wednesday is feminist book-club night at the coffee shop. They have pushed two tables together in the corner, and they're sitting around them with copies of the book. They're reading *The Bell Jar*, which I read a couple of years ago even though my English teacher at the time said that I was too young, and actually wrote a letter to Nick and Danny telling them that I was too young. And they were both really cross about it and massively overreacted and spent ages writing this letter back about how you can't protect children from everything and reading was a powerful and liberating act and they wanted me to read whatever I wanted, and then they were really pleased with themselves for ages, and bought me a whole bunch of Sylvia Plath poetry for my thirteenth birthday, which I read sometimes although it's really intense and honestly I think my English teacher might have had a point, but still.

I think this is a good story. This is one of the stories I would tell you if you asked me to tell a story about my family.

27

Then, the next night, Thursday evening, Danny comes to get me. He comes straight from work but even so, it's nearly nine o'clock. I don't see him come in. I am sitting at a table opposite Mike, who came in for his evening espresso and sat down to talk to me, and Danny suddenly looms up next to us, his laptop bag over his shoulder and his tie halfway undone and looking ill, like he has the worst case of the flu or something. He says, "Hey," and makes both of us jump so that Mike spills his coffee and swears softly.

"What are you doing here?" I say. Nick is behind the counter and the shop is busy. When I twist around to look for him I see him giving someone their change and staring in our direction.

"Since when do I need a reason?" says Danny. "I'm just coming home. I thought you'd be here. Thought I'd come and pick you up. Save Nick walking you back."

"I'm not going home yet," I say. "I'm doing homework." My copy of *Hamlet* is on the table, face down and open in the middle. "I'm doing *Hamlet*."

"Danny, sit down," says Mike. "Long time no see. Get a coffee. I keep meaning to call you." He nods in my direction. "This one's doing homework. She's got some interesting things to say about *Hamlet*."

Danny looks at Mike briefly, then back at me. He is very deliberately not looking at Nick, who has a line of five people but is still watching us.

"I'm not staying," says Danny. "Just stopped to get my sister. This is late to be out, Lena."

"This is late to be coming home from work," I say.

Mike clears his throat. "Come on, Danny, sit down for ten minutes. Have a chamomile tea, for god's sake."

"I'm here to get my sister," he says again.

"And what's the rush? She's right here."

I tuck myself back into the corner of the booth and make my bag into a barrier between me and him. I pick up *Hamlet*, look at the front cover. At the end of the school year we're supposed to go and see a production of it.

"Really, Danny," Mike is saying. "Daniel. Sit down. Let her finish her milkshake. Sit down. Relax a bit."

It's weird, people telling Danny what to do but Mike is about a hundred years older than him, so I guess he's allowed to. Danny's shoulders sag. He puts his bag down and then, as he does, he leans over to pick up my coat which was next to me but has fallen on the floor. Straightening up, he brushes it down with his hand and folds it, puts it back on the seat.

"All right," he says. "Ten minutes." But before he sits down, Nick comes toward us. Zahra has taken over at the till.

"Hi," says Nick, walking over, sticking his hands in his pockets, fake casual. "How are we all doing over here?"

Danny turns to him, folds his arms. "We're fine. How are you?"

"Good. That new Ethiopian coffee is going great."

"Yeah. Seems like you're busy."

"Uh huh."

"I'm doing *Hamlet*," I say faintly.

"Are you here to pick up Lena or do you want a coffee or something?" says Nick.

"I'm here to pick up Lena."

"I was going to walk her home in half an hour."

"Well, I've saved you the trouble."

"It's no trouble."

"No," says Danny. "But it's not your responsibility, is it?"

Nick's face goes very, very hard. "Is it your responsibility? Because if it is and you're not finishing work until nine o'clock, then it doesn't seem like you've exactly—"

"Exactly what?"

"—exactly got your *priorities*—"

"Unless I'm wrong, you're *still* at work, Nick. Whereas I am done and I'm taking Lena home."

"She's fine where she is."

"Except of course you're allowed to work seventy hours a week because your job is good and fun and morally superior and more important than anyone else's."

"Fellas," says Mike. "Comrades. Get a room. Neither of us wants to be involved in your intra-marital problems. I've got enough of my own."

Danny and Nick glare at each other for a few more moments. They are actually a lot alike when they're pissed off about something. The rest of the time they're different, but when they're angry with each other, they both get exactly the same. All snippy and sarcastic and defensive.

Maybe I get the same way too. Maybe we are all the same.

"Alena, what do you want to do?" says Danny, in a clipped voice.

"I want—" My voice comes out croaky, so I stop and clear

my throat. "I want to stay here. I'll walk home with Nick."

Nick is a nice person, so he doesn't look smug.

But Danny looks totally betrayed and I think, for a moment, *He came here specially*, but then I shut that thought down. I look down at my book, flick the edge of it with my thumb.

"OK." Danny picks up his bag again. "OK, whatever. Yeah. Fine."

"Half an hour," says Nick.

"Fine."

"I'll come up for a coffee, maybe," says Nick. "We can—"

"Yeah, maybe," says Danny, which means no. I don't know why he gets to decide since it's Nick's apartment as much as his, but Nick just says, "Yeah, or maybe not tonight."

× × × × ×

"Is everything OK at home?" says Mike after Danny leaves and Nick goes back to the counter. "What's going on?"

"Nick's not at home," I say. "He's staying with his brother for a while."

Mike looks at me, all serious and kind. "Oh."

"It's like sleeping in the guest room but we don't have a guest room."

He nods, looks at me for a while longer. "Lena," he says. "You ever want to stop by the office, come and say hi, you know you're welcome. Come and have a Sprite one afternoon. I'm there all hours. Just ask my wife."

I try to smile but my mouth is stiff and stuck in a straight line. "OK. Thank you."

"And your friend, too, with the violin. You're always welcome. Any time you want to see inside the glamorous world of local news."

The *Hackney Standard* office is above an electrical shop on Grove Road. You wouldn't know it was there except for a tiny sign above the buzzer. It's cramped and it's a mess, which is why Danny always used to work from home or the coffee shop. Why Mike sometimes works from the coffee shop, too.

I nod my head, mute.

"Look, now," he says, lowering his voice. "I can't say I understand these things, but I'm sure it'll all work out fine. They're grown-ups. They'll work it all out. Those two can't be away from each other for five minutes."

Obviously not true, I think, but I nod again. I finish my milkshake as slowly as possible.

x x x x x

Nick walks me home but we are mostly silent. When we get back to the apartment I see him reach for his keys and then stop himself, so I have to get mine out instead.

He waits for the elevator with me. "Listen, Lena. Maybe you should just go home after school tomorrow," he says. "You've been at the shop every night. Danny's missing you."

"How would you know?" I say. It comes out meaner than I intend it to but Nick is unfazed.

"Because I know," he says.

The elevator door pings and opens. I ignore it. "You've been away for a week now," I say. "Almost a whole week."

The door realizes nobody's getting in and closes.

"I know." Nick presses the button so that it opens again. He squeezes my shoulder. "I'll see you soon, OK?"

I step inside the elevator.

No, I think. *Not OK.*

28

Mike has written the article that's on the front page of the *Hackney Standard* website on Friday morning. I'm supposed to be finishing an essay for history but instead I'm reading the news while I eat a bowl of cornflakes, my laptop balanced on a stack of newspapers on the kitchen counter. Danny has had three cups of coffee already and can't find any clean shirts because he's only just realized that it's Nick who always does the laundry.

I used to be excited when Danny's articles were on the front page of the *Standard*. I used to tell my teachers like it was something really impressive, like it was something I'd done myself. I'd secretly tear out the articles and bring them to school. Half his articles used to be about stabbings and murders and fires and I'd get sent home with letters, *We do not think "Gang warfare claims another victim" was an appropriate piece for show-and-tell,* and Danny would have to call the school and apologize. I never even thought about what the articles said. I just liked seeing his name printed out, *Daniel Kennedy,* since I was Kennedy as well.

Maybe all those stabbings and murders and fires were part of why he stopped working for Mike.

But there's no murder on the front page today.

Residents of Hackney are responding to Jacob Carlisle's "strong leadership," a *Hackney Standard* poll has suggested. Asked about the top five candidates in the race for the mayoral election—including Mr. Carlisle, who has stormed ahead from seventh place into third in an unprecedented popularity surge— and their responses to the actions of the "East End Bomber," 62% of respondents stated that current mayor Christopher Buckley's response had been "hesitant" and "indecisive." A majority of respondents—68%— said that they were "very convinced" that Jacob Carlisle's proposed policing reforms and his "strategy for safety" would reduce the threat of violent crime and terrorism in the city. See full poll results below.

In a television interview yesterday morning, Mr. Carlisle announced that he had spoken to the widow of Eduardo Capello, the Italian tourist who was fatally injured in the explosion in March. He appeared emotional as he spoke of Lucia Capello's grief, and, for the first time in public, recalled the sudden loss of his own wife in a car accident seven years ago. "The shock is devastating," he said. "You feel numb. You feel disconnected from the world around you. You feel as though you are trapped in a nightmare." He continued: "If there is anything we can do, anything at all, to protect other people from these kinds of tragedies, we must do it. I am as devastated by this as we all are."

"If Jacob Carlisle wins," I say when Danny comes into the room, buttoning a creased shirt, "does that mean you'll keep on working for him?"

"It's too early to think about that."

"Not really. The election's in a few weeks, right?"

"Right."

"So?"

"So, yeah, maybe. We'll see."

"But if he loses, that's it? You'll have to do something else?"

"Probably. Depends what he does next."

"What do you think he'll do next?"

"I don't know, Lena. I think he's writing a book. Who knows? Maybe he'll open a delicatessen. I have no idea." He picks up his bag and slings it over his shoulder. "Listen. It's nearly the weekend. I was thinking. Do you want to go out tomorrow night? Go and get a pizza or something? We could go to that place you like. Or wherever you want."

"I can't. I'm staying over at Teagan's."

"Since when?"

"Since I arranged to stay over at Teagan's."

"Arranged with who?"

"With her parents. And Nick said it was fine."

"Oh." Danny shifts the weight of his bag on his shoulder. "Sounds like your evening's been arranged, then."

"Sounds like it."

He pauses. "Alena, can you not—can you not talk to me in that tone of voice all the time?"

"What tone of voice?"

"You know what I mean."

"I don't."

"Lena—"

"This is how I talk."

"It's not. You don't even sound like you anymore. This is how you talk when you don't want to talk."

"You're a good one to talk about not wanting to talk," I say, which is a totally confusing sentence and he's right, anyway, because when I say it my voice doesn't sound like me at all. I can feel blood rushing toward my brain.

We look at each other for a few moments. Then Danny says, "This isn't all my fault, you know. Nick not being here."

"I never said it was."

"I'm doing my best."

I don't even know what this means. I don't even want to know.

I say, "So am I."

"It would help me a lot right now if you would just—"

"If I would just do nothing and say everything's OK and let's all just carry on, la, la, la."

His face has gone very dark. I know that I'm being a brat. I know I am. He would probably even be right if he yelled at me.

"Yes," he says. "Yes. It would help me if you would just do nothing and say everything's OK. All right? Yes, it would."

"Everything's not OK."

"And I am trying to fix that but it's not—"

"It's my life too. You make all these decisions like they don't affect me. Nick belongs to *me* as well, but I don't get to have any say over anything that happens in my own—"

"God, do you think that I have any say over anything that happens? My whole life is basically one long—I am doing my *best* while everybody else is just—" He stops, breaks off, holds his hands up in a *stop* gesture, although who or what he's trying to stop I don't know. "Never mind. Never mind. Look. Never mind. I have to go to work. I need you to just—"

"You need me to just what?"

"I need you to just stay out of trouble and not—"

"I'm not *in* trouble. I've never been in trouble *ever*. There are people in my class who smoke and drink and bring knives to school and I don't even—"

"There are people in your class who bring knives to school?" he says, turning pale.

"Well, there might be."

"Are there?"

"I don't know. That's not the point. The point is—"

"Lena, if there are people in your class bringing knives to school, then you need to tell your teachers or the police or—"

"Or maybe I can tell Jacob Carlisle and he can tell us about the *strategy for safety* since he cares so much about people getting hurt." My heart is going too fast and I have to press my hands against the kitchen counter so they don't shake. Sometimes I think I might have a heart condition. I know about heart conditions. I look these things up.

"What's that supposed to mean?"

"Just that apparently he cares a lot about people getting hurt." I make myself look at my brother very steadily. "Apparently since he knows how it feels to lose somebody."

"He does know how it feels to lose somebody."

"I know. He said so in an interview. Unless that's just something you wrote for him to say." I slam my laptop shut and gather it up against my chest, slide off my chair. "I have to get ready for school," I say, pushing past him on the way to my bedroom.

He follows me. "His wife died in a car accident, he's got a fifteen-year-old son at home—you know, I'm not saying he's perfect, but there's no need for this constant—"

"It doesn't matter," I say. I dump my laptop on the bed and then go around to the side and kneel down, reaching under it for my geography textbook. "I don't care."

He comes into my room, stands by my desk. "I'd like to talk about this with you properly but you're not making it very—"

He stops, trails off.

"What?" I say.

"What's that?" he says.

"What?" I stand up again.

"Stuck to your mirror."

There are about a hundred things stuck to my mirror. Tucked in the corner of the frame is the black-and-white Greenham Common postcard, my mum and Lynn Wallace with their fists raised.

"This," he says. It's only stuck with tape and he pulls it off easily, stands and looks at it for a moment. "Where did you get this?"

"I found it in the storage locker. I told you. I told you ages ago."

"Why is it stuck to your mirror?"

"Why shouldn't it be?"

He's distracted then, and I see him start looking at all the *other* pictures I've got stuck around my mirror: pictures of my mum, pictures of my mum and Niamh, him when he's a little boy holding her hand, most of which have been there for years, but it's like he's seeing them for the first time.

"Why have you got any of these pictures? You don't even know these people, Lena. Why have you got all these pictures?"

"When you say *these people* are you talking about my own mother?"

He looks at me, blinks a few times, looks back at the postcard in his hand. "You know, people act like Greenham Common is this great moment in history, this heroic thing, and it's exactly like every other protest, every other thing she did; it never changed anything in the world. It was just stupid, dangerous things, one after another, nuclear weapons, the arms trade—"

"I know something about the arms trade," I say.

"Excuse me?"

"I was reading about the arms trade. They have these dinners, here in London; all these guys in suits get together and work out how to make money out of selling weapons, and it's all completely—"

"I really don't need a lecture on the arms trade, OK, Lena? I heard this stuff every day of my life when I was growing up."

"Well, I didn't. I never heard a single thing about it."

He doesn't answer. He rubs one of his eyes the way he does when his contact lenses hurt. He is still looking at the postcard.

"Do you know what else I found out?" I say.

"What?" he says. His voice has gone quiet.

"They have protests outside of these things all the time, and this year someone from the BBC was going to give a talk at one of the dinners, but everyone protested, so he didn't."

"And?"

"And a couple of years ago Jacob Carlisle gave a speech at one of the dinners. To a bunch of arms dealers."

There's a long silence. I can tell that Danny didn't know this. Truthfully, I only found it by accident and it was a tiny mention in an article about something else entirely.

"Where did you find that out?" he says.

"I just found it on the internet. It's not a secret. Anyone can find it. He was talking about what the rest of the world can learn from London police. Like probably how to beat people up and never get—"

"Alena," he says, in a choked voice. "Stop, all right? Look, the world is a lot more complicated than just—"

"Give it to me," I say. I hold out my hand for the postcard.

"No," he says. "You shouldn't have this kind of stuff. You're romanticizing something that's not—I mean, it's morbid, Alena."

I see what he's going to do just before he does it.

I scramble over the bed and try to grab it out of his hands, but it takes him no time at all to tear it in half and then in half again.

What does it matter because it's just one stupid picture when I have dozens more, when I have a video, even, but it's still mine, something that belongs to me that he has decided I can't have, and I am *furious* then, blood behind my eyes, and I say, "I can't believe you—" and my voice almost breaks and I grab the pieces of the postcard from his hand and then I punch him on the arm, twice, as hard as I can, which is not very hard. He says, "Hey, *ouch*," taking two steps back. "Wow, not OK, Alena. Not OK at all. What's wrong with you?"

"What's wrong with *you*?" I am almost screaming at him. "What's *wrong* with you? There is something really, really wrong with you and it's like you don't even know it. You think it's everybody else and it's *not*. It's *you*. There's something *seriously wrong with you*."

He is still taking steps backwards as if I'm a bomb that's about to detonate, which maybe is what I feel like. His jaw is set and his eyes are very bright. "All right, that's enough. That's enough. We're done. That's enough."

"I hate you," I say, and I guess that is the detonation because his face changes into this expression I've never seen before, and there's a long, long, awful silence, and the fact that he doesn't even answer makes me want to say it again.

"I have to go to work," he says, finally, in a hollowed-out voice. "I'm going to work now."

"I'm not stopping you," I say and he turns and walks out of my room and out of the apartment and the door slams and makes the walls shake. It is not even nine a.m.

29

My heart is still beating too fast when I'm sitting outside the math room with Teagan at first break and telling her that I've looked up the Save Ocean Court campaign website again. They've gotten thousands of signatures for their petition and Lynn Keller Wallace is giving a seminar called "Housing Justice and Standing Up to Power" at three o'clock this afternoon. I'm going to go, I tell her. I've just decided.

"At three o'clock."

"Yes."

"We have hockey."

"I'm not going."

Teagan bites her lip, looks worried about this. "All right," she says.

"Will you cover for me?"

"Yes. Will you be all right?"

"Yes."

"What are you going to say to her?"

"I'm going to ask her why I've never met her before."

"You probably have met her," Teagan says. "You just don't remember."

"Maybe."

"It's weird," Teagan says. "I think it's strange. How you

don't remember anything. I remember a lot of stuff from before I was three. Like getting stung by a bee. And when I got lost at the Natural History Museum."

"You just remember that stuff because people have told you about it," I say, which is true, I think, and when I say it I feel this anger in my chest, under my ribs, thinking that I *would* have remembered her if we'd ever talked about her: that memories feed off stories and that if I'd ever been told any, maybe all of mine wouldn't have burned out and disappeared so quickly. I would close my eyes right now and be able to see her.

"No," Teagan says. "Nobody talks about the National History Museum thing. It just starts a fight about whose fault it was. I was lost for like two hours in the reptile area. I just remember it because it was so terrible. And then when my parents found me my dad cried. I have a whole bunch of memories like that."

"Lucky you, then, I guess," I say, not very nicely, and then the bell goes for next period.

× × × × ×

The problem with the video—and the postcard, and the photos I've collected—is that these things fix her, so she is stuck at nineteen, or twenty-four, or thirty, or however old she is when somebody films her or takes her picture. And so every time I watch the video she gets more stuck. It gets harder to imagine her any other way. So, I think maybe Lynn Wallace can tell me new things that will unstick her. I'll find her in some way that's shifting, changing: still here. Everything Danny doesn't want.

Nobody looks twice at me on the Northern line at two in the afternoon in my school uniform, even though don't people know that it's the middle of a school day and why would I be on the tube on my own? Nobody cares. I guess why would they.

I get out at Clapham North and look at the directions I've written on the back of my hand. I'm early and when I find the building I'm too nervous to go in, so I search through my bag to check if I have any money and I go into a coffee shop and buy a hot chocolate. The lady behind the counter does look a bit suspicious but she doesn't say anything, just makes my drink, which costs 30 pence more than it would at Nick's. I go and drink it at a table by the window, where I can look across the road straight at the Clapham Community Study Center, which has a sign outside saying, *All-day housing teach-in, join us!*

Ocean Court is apparently being torn down and replaced with luxury apartments. I wonder if Lynn Wallace is still worried about nuclear weapons or if she's moved on, if she's all about housing now. Maybe she can tell me the main things I should be angry about.

Her talk goes from three to three forty-five p.m. and even after I get up the nerve to cross the road and go into the building—it says, *Join us!*, after all—I can't find the right room and when I do, it's five minutes past and the door is shut and I'm too scared to go in, so I sit down on the floor outside and wait for it to finish.

It runs late. It's nearly four when people start coming out. I stand up and try to smooth out the creases in my school skirt. While I was waiting, somebody brought tea and coffee and snacks and arranged it all on the tables in the corridor, and all the people head straight for the tables, but inside the seminar room there's a black woman in a smart suit behind a desk, still talking to a girl with blue hair and a tie-dyed dress that makes me think of Zahra. They come out together, talking.

"Excuse me," I say, and the blue-haired girl looks at me.

"Hi," she says. "Can I help you?"

"I'm looking for Lynn Wallace."

She's right in front of me. I know this.

"Oh," says blue-haired girl. "Sure. This is Lynn."

Lynn regards me silently. She is super tall with short hair and is dressed all in navy with a chunky silver necklace, and she's holding a folder and a stack of papers. I am short and young and awkward and I'm sweating. I suddenly wish I'd worn something else, brought a change of clothes to school, combed my hair, worn make-up, made up a question about housing justice. Pretended I was a young, single mother about to be evicted. For two seconds I almost say this anyway, but then I think what's the point, I didn't come here to lie.

"Can I help you?" says Lynn, sounding kind of snippy. "Were you in the seminar?"

"No. I got here late. I'm sorry."

"Well. What can I help you with?"

"I'm Alena Kennedy," I say. "You knew my mother."

Blue-hair girl is smiling pleasantly—she is wearing a badge, I notice, that says *Becky Saville, Teach-in Coordinator*— but her smile falters as she looks at both of us. She says, "Lynn, are you OK?" because Lynn is standing perfectly still and her expression hasn't really changed but she has one hand over her mouth and her eyes have gone wet and bright.

It's hard not to feel self-conscious when someone is looking at you like you're some tragic, miraculous woodland creature that's just appeared. I wrap my hand around the strap of my bag and say, "I wanted to come to your seminar but I was late. I got lost. I'm sorry."

Becky Saville, taking in my uniform and looking completely uncertain now, says, "Are you at a school nearby? Is this—is school finished already?"

Happy to be offered this explanation, I say, "Yes. School's finished."

Lynn, recovering her composure, says, "It's OK, Becky. Thanks. This is the daughter of a friend of mine."

I never hear the word *daughter* in reference to myself, and I feel something wild and new and lovely flare in my heart for a second. *Daughter.*

Becky scurries off and Lynn looks and looks at me, starts to speak, stops herself, and then says, "Has school really finished?"

I glance at a clock on the wall. "It probably has by now."

A smile flickers across her face.

Around us people are gathering into groups with plastic cups of tea, talking about the meetings they've just been in. There's a blur of noise and the smell of cheap, bad coffee and warm fruit. It's hard to concentrate.

"Alena," says Lynn. There's the tiniest tremor in her voice. "Alena. Look at you. Look at you."

Then she clears her throat, refocuses, and says, "What are you doing all the way down here? Isn't this a long way from home?"

"I wanted to meet you. I wanted to know why—" Then I stop. I say, "Hang on," and then search in my bag for the four torn pieces of the Greenham Common postcard that I brought to school tucked into *Hamlet*. I take them out and give them to her. My hand is shaking a little bit. I don't know why. "I found this postcard, a little while ago. I didn't know about Greenham Common. I wanted to hear about it. But I had a fight with my brother and he tore it up."

She takes the pieces, looks at them for a long time.

"I can give you another copy of this," she says eventually, handing the pieces back to me. "There were hundreds of them printed. I've got copies at home. I can send you another. Although I don't suppose your brother will want that."

What I want to say next is that I would like to go somewhere and ask her questions, somewhere quiet where we can talk—but what is suddenly real to me is that I don't know anything about her or how to talk to her—and she is old, she is twenty years older than Nick or Danny, more like Nick's parents' age, and she has a stack of papers and things to do.

I say, "I was wondering if we could—" but she has started shaking her head.

"No. No. I'm sorry, no, I can't. I really can't. I'm meeting the head of Lewisham Council in twenty minutes and I'm worried you're going to make me cry."

"Or maybe we could—"

"I want to tell you that you look just like your mother. That's what people always say at times like this, isn't it?"

"I don't. I already know that I don't."

"No. In fact you look like the image of your brother when he was your age." Her hand hovers for a minute like she's going to touch my arm but then she doesn't.

"Did you know my brother when he was my age?"

"Did I—Alena. Yes. I knew him his whole life. Since he was a baby. Until he stopped speaking to me."

"It's just that I've never—"

"And I have to respect his wishes. I have to respect Danny's wishes. This shouldn't be happening. I have to respect him as a parent."

"You don't. You don't."

"Does he know that you're here?"

I don't answer.

"Alena—"

"You don't know him, though. You don't know what he's like. He doesn't even have to know. You don't have to respect him. Honestly. He's just weird, he's a weird person; you have to ignore him. It's because of—it's because of his grieving process or something—you don't have to respect him at all." *He doesn't respect you, I think. He pretty much hates your guts.*

But that look is coming into her eyes, that adult look where they think they understand something that you don't. "Alena—"

"Why have I never met you before? Nick told me that you and my mum were best friends. Didn't you want to—I don't know. Didn't you ever want to meet me or something?"

She looks a bit devastated. "Of course I did. Of course I did. I can't tell you how many times—"

"Then why—"

"But it's a complicated situation, with a lot of complicated feelings, and much as I would like so much to get to know you—"

"You can get to know me, you can—"

"—I decided a long time ago that I was going to respect your brother's wishes. I'm so sorry. I really am."

Somebody else is gently edging up on us, putting a tentative hand on Lynn's arm. "Lynn, if you're ready—"

She nods. Still looking stricken, she says, "Yes. Alena, I really have to go. We can call someone for you. How are you going to get home?"

I don't even answer. I don't trust myself to speak. I just turn and walk away and since there's no point going back to school I go to a seminar about what to do if you're facing eviction.

Everybody in the room looks pissed off and depressed, so I fit right in.

30

When I get home, Danny is waiting for me. Lynn has called him. Which I suppose was predictable.

I start to wonder if I might hate her, a little bit.

Danny says, "You don't cut school. You do *not* cut school. You do not go to Clapham on your *own. Clapham.*"

"It's on the Northern line," I say, pointlessly.

"I don't care if it's on the Trans-Siberian Railway. Do you understand how dangerous this city is right now? Have you watched the news lately? And you're riding around the subway in the middle of the afternoon on your own. Do you have *any idea*—"

"It's in Zone 2."

His eyes flash. "I know where Clapham is, Alena. My point is, you don't go there. You don't go there, you don't go anywhere else when you're supposed to be—"

"You're banning me from Clapham."

"I am. I am. I am banning you from Clapham, and I'm banning you from going anywhere or doing anything apart from school. This is it. I've had it up to here with this. Give me your phone."

"What?"

"I want your phone and your laptop. Give them to me."

"No."

"And you know what? No more hanging out at the coffee shop. You know what you're doing this weekend? You're coming to work with me."

"What?"

"I have to work this weekend and guess what? Now you do too."

"I want to talk to Nick."

"Tough."

He's walking circles around the coffee table while I stand in the kitchen. Everything is the wrong shape without Nick here. This is an apartment where three people live. This space is meant for three of us, and me and Danny don't know how to fill it on our own. We don't know where to stand or how to talk to each other. There's all this space that should be filled up with Nick saying something sensible.

"I'm so angry with you," Danny is saying. "I am so angry. I am *so* angry. I've had it up to here with this shit. I've had it up to here."

It carries on like this for a while. He's had it up to here. With me. He is angry. He is *so* angry.

I have no idea what I am.

31

Danny makes me get up at eight a.m. and stands by the front door impatiently while I eat a bowl of cornflakes. I make zero effort to look presentable: a messy ponytail and my oldest jeans. We get the Central line and change to the District. The trains are quiet because no normal people go to work on a Saturday morning. Danny looks at his phone the whole way and doesn't talk to me.

His office doesn't feel like an office: just somebody's— Jacob Carlisle's—posh apartment with the furniture replaced by desks and computers. There's a lobby with a photocopier, a closed door on one side with a printed bit of paper saying *Campaign Manager* stuck to it, and an open door on the other side. We go through the open door into what obviously used to be someone's living room. The only person there is a woman behind a desk eating crackers and writing notes on a long list of numbers. Danny puts his hands on my shoulders and says, "Leila, this is my little sister. Alena."

"Oh!" Leila looks genuinely happy to see me. "Alena! I've heard so much about you. It's so lovely to meet you, how exciting, we're all really—"

Danny interrupts. "Yesterday she cut school for the afternoon and went to Clapham on her own, so now she's grounded and has to come to work with me."

"Oh," says Leila. "Oh, well. OK. Welcome!"

"But I have a strategy meeting with Will and then we're meeting the bus drivers, so I have to leave her in here with you for a couple of hours. Is that OK?"

"Of course it is. Is that OK with you?" She is asking me, not Danny. "There's nothing very exciting going on. Melissa was supposed to come in and help me with these supporter calls but she's phoned in sick." She gestures to a sheet of paper on her desk. "There's thousands of them. How's your telephone manner, Alena?"

"Not great," I tell her.

"No, neither is mine."

"Nothing exciting is what we want," says Danny. "She's not supposed to be having fun. No fun." His hands are still on my shoulders and he turns me around to look at me. "No fun. Understand?"

"I'll try," I say.

He gives me a brief smile.

"Will's in his office already," says Leila. "He says he's feeling *invigorated*." She rolls her eyes slightly.

"Fantastic." Danny takes off his jacket and hangs it over the back of a chair, then points to a desk opposite where Leila is sitting. "So sit there and do homework or something, Lena. Please. I'll be back soon."

When he goes, I say, "Who's Will?"

"He's our campaign manager. He's very—*energetic*." Leila offers me a ginger snap. She has a lot of snacks: Kit-Kats and little Tupperware boxes of cashew nuts and grapes and cookies. "I'm trying out vegetarianism," she tells me, starting to carefully peel an orange. "And I'm starving. Literally starving, morning to night."

I feel like I should respond in some way, so I say, "Nick says brazil nuts are good if you're trying to give up meat. There's a lot of fat in them or something."

"Yes!" she says. "Brazil nuts are incredible. It's like eating butter. Who's Nick?"

"Danny's partner."

I sometimes think that this doesn't really do Nick justice, *Danny's partner*, but it's the simplest explanation, or at least it used to be. Leila looks a bit confused and for one tiny moment I think that I've just outed my brother in his workplace—maybe they are all massive homophobes and he's been living a lie—but then her face clears and she says, "Oh, *Nick*. Of course. Of coffee shop fame."

"Right."

"I always thought I'd quite like to run a coffee shop."

"Me too."

She smiles. "So it sounds like you're in trouble. What was in Clapham?"

"Oh. Nothing. There was nothing. I was just—we had hockey at school. I hate hockey."

"God, me too."

I haven't brought any homework with me. There's a Jacob Carlisle manifesto lying on the desk. When Leila's phone rings, I pick it up and flick through it. On the first page, it says, *My vision: a safer city for our children. Let's cut violent crime by half. Let's take back the streets.*

There's a picture of him with a teenage boy—his son, I guess—grinning and sweaty with marathon numbers on their chests, holding medals.

The boy looks a bit like this boy at my school who once, for no reason at all, wrote *dyke* in Tipp-Ex on Teagan's violin case. I remember because she didn't bother to remove it until her parents made her.

"Will he be here today?" I say, when Leila hangs up the phone.

"Who? Jake?"

"Yeah."

"Could be. Can't promise it. He's in and out. He's a bit of a hard man to pin down. He likes to run his own schedule." There's a tone in her voice when she says this, like she doesn't really like him very much. She nods at the manifesto I'm holding. "Your brother wrote almost all of that, you know. He had about three days to do it. The manifesto we were working with when he started was a mess. Seriously amateur. He rewrote the whole thing. Daniel's been our *savior*, I don't mind telling you. We're all crazy about him. Will especially."

"Will especially what?" says a voice behind me. I turn around. Danny is standing in the doorway with one of the best-looking non-famous people I have ever seen. He's holding a Starbucks coffee and leaning against the doorframe. He's got artfully tousled brown hair and twinkly eyes and an immaculate white shirt.

"I was just telling Alena that we all worship her brother around here."

"We do," says Will. "That's true."

Danny looks appropriately awkward and doesn't meet my eye. It's suddenly clear to me why he might like working here, where everybody thinks he's so fantastic and doesn't pick fights with him all the time, like his family. Some part of me feels weirdly angry about this, like, *Tough, you can't have him.*

"So you're Alena." Will gives me a very direct smile. "We've heard a lot about you." He's got one of those impeccable, neutral BBC accents.

"Yeah," I say, not particularly politely. "I'm Lena."

"We just need those budget numbers," says Danny. "Sorry, Leila. Can you send them again? Then we'll get out of your way."

"So." Will is still looking at me. "Are you interested in politics, Alena?"

"Yes." I don't follow this up with anything and he looks a bit disconcerted.

"And what do you want to do when you're older?"

It has been my experience that adults, when introduced to a young person, cannot go more than seven minutes without asking this question. As if this is all just killing time before my real life starts, as if my life isn't actually happening to me right now.

"I don't know," I say. "I haven't decided."

"You can't blame her," Danny says. "I'm thirty-one and I still don't know what I want to do when I grow up." Ha ha. They both laugh.

"You're thirty-four," I say, and get a dirty look.

"Well, keep up the good work," says Will, and they leave. I see Leila roll her eyes again as she picks up the phone. Danny's jacket is still hanging over a chair and when they're gone I lean over and search through his pocket to find his phone since he's confiscated mine. I flick it on.

The picture saved on his home-screen is of me and Nick on vacation last year.

I feel like calling him—Nick—telling him where I am. Maybe he will come and save me. But then that seems rude, in front of Leila who is being so nice, so I look to see what games Danny has instead.

"You look bored out of your mind, Alena." Leila has the phone tucked between her ear and her shoulder and is slicing the foil on a Kit-Kat with her fingernail. "Do you want something to do? Say no if you want."

× × × × ×

I say yes. The job she gives me is photocopying. So when I first hear about it I am standing in the lobby of the campaign office, leaning against the photocopier, tugging at a thread that's come loose in the sleeve of my sweater. The photocopier is churning out some sort of fundraising leaflet.

In the office next door, I hear Leila say, "Oh no. Oh no."

Danny and Will are both behind the closed door of Will's office and I am alone in the lobby. There's suddenly a bunch of voices next door and I realize that Leila has switched on the television that's mounted in the corner of the room: "*—information from a number of sources—no casualties have been officially confirmed but we're showing live pictures now from—yes, you can see here, these are live pictures, and we should have our correspondent—we're just waiting for our correspondent—*"

Leila barrels through the open door and marches across to Will's office without looking at me. She bangs on his door a couple of times and then opens it without waiting for an answer. I see Will come into view, slouched in a leather chair with his feet on the desk. He says, "Leila, we're in a meeting."

She says, "You need to come next door and see the TV."

"Why?"

"There's been an explosion in Bethnal Green."

I can't see Danny, but I hear him say, "What kind of explosion?"

Will gets to his feet and Danny appears from the corner of the room.

"They're not saying yet," says Leila.

"Just now or when did this happen?" says Will.

"Just now. Just this morning. About an hour ago."

"Is anyone hurt?" says Danny.

"They're not saying," says Leila.

They all come out of the office and walk back across the lobby and nobody asks me anything about my photocopying, so I just follow them back into the main office. We all gather around and look up at the TV in silence.

On the screen, it's just like last time. There's a police cordon at the end of a street, and about seven hundred feet behind it there are ambulances and police cars almost blocking the view of a Tesco Metro. In front of the camera is a reporter with a raincoat over his shirt and tie, holding one hand against his ear the way they do when they're trying to hear the person back in the studio.

"That's Chris Mahoney," says Will to no one in particular. "He was in my year at Cambridge."

Chris Mahoney says, *"It does seem as though—it's too early to say with any certainty, but obviously everybody is going to be assuming this morning—obviously, Sophie, everybody is going to be asking if this is the action of the so-called East End Bomber, who has targeted a series of big-name supermarkets in the past four months and who tragically, last month, claimed his first victim."*

Sophie says, *"Chris, can we confirm that there have been casualties this time?"*

Chris says, *"Sophie, the police as yet have not given any details, but I can tell you that I have seen—I have myself seen evidence that this was an explosion of considerable size—that there have almost certainly been some injuries, though it's far too soon to say any more than that."*

"Chris, thank you," says Sophie. *"Chris, we'll be coming back to you very shortly."*

I wonder if Chris and Sophie are friends in real life.

Sophie says, *"That was Chris Mahoney in Bethnal Green. Confirming there what we have heard so far, which is that police are not confirming anything at this stage but are reportedly advising the public, who are understandably alarmed right now—"*

"Fucking right," says Leila, then puts a hand over her mouth. "Sorry," she says. She looks at me and then at Danny. "Excuse my language. Sorry."

"She's heard worse," says Danny.

"It's Bethnal Green," says Leila. "Jake needs to say something. That's his old constituency. Does he need to say something?"

Will is standing with his arms crossed, looking rapt at the television. "Of course he needs to say something."

"I mean, before anybody else? If he has a connection to the area?"

"Yes," says Will. "He does."

"He needs to say something soon, then," she says. "Before everyone piles in, am I right? Get ahead of it? Before the one o'clock news maybe. Do you think they'll have him on?"

"On the news?" says Danny. "I doubt it."

"Not even local?"

"Maybe local."

"Or should he wait until they know if anyone's been killed, or what?"

"We should wait," says Danny. "We should be careful."

"No," says Will. "He needs to be quick."

"God, I feel cynical," says Leila. "I hate myself right now. Don't listen to this, Alena. This is a very cynical conversation." She looks at Will. "Where *is* Jake? Is he still at the carbon strategy thing? He probably doesn't even *know*."

I am still trying to watch the television, where now they are showing a different angle of the street, and Chris Mahoney is listening to his earpiece again.

I'm wondering if I have ever been in that Tesco's. I am imagining smashed vegetables and tins of soup and bodies on the floor. Wondering if there was a bomb just lying in the middle of aisle five or if it was behind the cereal boxes or what. Wondering if this will go on forever and we will all be always just waiting for the next one.

Chris Mahoney says, "*Obviously, Sophie, we can't get any closer than this but I can tell you that I have seen a number of superficial injuries and—but obviously at this stage we are just waiting for more information—*"

Danny has stopped watching. He gets his phone from his jacket pocket and goes back into the hall with it. I follow him.

"Are you calling Nick?" I say. He nods, phone pressed to his ear.

"Nick would never shop in Tesco's," I tell him, and then someone obviously answers and Danny says with relief, "Hey, it's me—I was just making sure—Have you seen the—yeah. I know. OK."

"Can I talk to him?" I say, holding out my hand. Danny shakes his head.

"Yeah. That's Lena. She's here, she's—no, she wouldn't answer; I've still got her phone."

"Please," I say.

"Yeah," he says to Nick. "I know. OK. All right."

"Danny."

"No, that's all."

"Danny, please—"

"Fine. Here." He hands me the phone and goes back to the office.

"Alena," says Nick, sounding far away. "Before you say anything, I know all about your little Clapham adventure and I'm just as angry as Danny, so don't even try—"

He doesn't sound angry. He just sounds tired. "Are you watching the news?" I say.

"I've just switched it off. You shouldn't watch it either."

"Danny made me come to work with him."

"I know."

"Can you come and get me?"

He goes silent, so I say, "Are you at the shop?"

"No, I'm at home."

"At home?"

"I mean at Adam's. Sorry. Not at home."

I bite my lip. There's a red light blinking on the photocopier to say that there's a paper jam. "Nick, this isn't fair."

More silence, and I hear him sigh. "Do you want me to come and get you?"

"Yes."

"Let me speak to Danny again."

"He's not here. He's gone back to work."

"Well, I need to talk to him before I—"

"Fine," I say. "You know what, never mind. I'll stay here."

"Lena."

I hang up the phone and immediately feel like a brat, want to call him back and say sorry and tell him not to go to any supermarkets today, but I don't.

Like that time I smashed a glass on the kitchen floor, I feel strange and absent, vaguely out of control.

32

The meeting with the bus drivers is canceled. Everybody makes a lot of phone calls. I stand in front of the office window and press my forehead against the glass. The street outside is quiet—no cars or dogs or anything—and the row of beautiful white houses opposite all look like they're empty. Dark, curtainless windows and no movement.

Here's what I am thinking about. I am thinking about my mum at nineteen. Only four years older than me and she had a baby. Imagine that. I think of her with her curly hair and a baby in a sling, imagine her in dungarees and a bandanna, her and her friends with a rainbow banner saying *Women Against the Bomb*, shouting at the police. I've made this picture up. What else can I do? I have a twenty-second video and a torn-up postcard. But I can imagine: wet grass and mud, sleeping in a tent and sharing their food. The baby crying. She is *brave*. Wild and very strong. Determined. She doesn't watch television helplessly, turning it off when things are too bad. The world is a thing that she thinks she can change. She sleeps with men and forgets their names. She loves her friends most of all. She has a best friend, like I do. They are inseparable. She is nineteen. She has a baby. She is never lonely. She is not interested in being safe. She is part of something. She's alive: wet grass between her toes, heart beating and neurons firing, breath clouding the morning air, baby crying for her. She is needed. She is doing something. That's what I'm thinking.

× × × × ×

I'm spacing out. Danny is talking to me. "Lena. Alena. Are you listening to me?"

"What?" I turn around. He's standing with his arms folded, tie loosened.

"I don't want you to go anywhere. All right? You're staying here." He looks at Leila. "I don't want her to go out."

"Lockdown," says Leila. "Got it."

"We'll be an hour. Two hours, maybe. That's it."

"What?" I say. "Where are you going?"

"Do you listen to anything I say?" says Danny.

"Apparently not."

"We're going to go and meet with Jake. He's on the other side of town. There's a taxi on its way."

"Can't he come here?"

"He needs to stay where the cameras are," says Will. He appears behind Danny wearing a black wool coat that looks expensive.

The whole office is overheated and my eyes feel dry and tired, my skin prickly. There is black ink from the photocopier smeared on my jeans and Will in his super-smart office clothes makes me feel uncomfortable. I ignore him and look at Danny.

"Is it, like . . ." I start and then I stop. "Is anybody worried there'll be another one?" I say.

"Yes," says Danny.

"No, they'll catch him," says Leila. She's at her desk.

She looks up at me and smiles. "Don't worry, they'll catch him now."

"Right," says Danny. "No, that's right. They probably will catch him now."

"I need my phone back. In case there's an emergency."

Danny considers this and then says, "Yeah, all right."

He has never been very good at punishment. He always loses the heart for it too quickly. He takes it out of his bag and hands it over. I have six messages, all from Teagan, and a missed call from Nick, earlier this morning.

"Would you like something to do?" Will glances at his watch, and turns to Danny. "Would she like something to do?"

Neither of us answers but Will doesn't seem to be paying attention. He crosses the room and logs in to one of the computers, swivels the screen around to face me.

"We had a volunteer doing our press clippings for us but he hasn't shown up all week. We like to keep track of all the mentions Jake's getting in the press. Good, bad, indifferent, whatever."

I stay where I am for a few moments and then I realize I'm supposed to be shown something, so I have to drag another chair over to the computer.

"We've got news alerts set up for his name," Will says, "and for a few other things we think are relevant. A news alert is—"

"I know what a news alert is."

"Oh. Well. Good."

His smile is a bit stiff then. The job he gives me is finding and printing out every mention of Jacob Carlisle in the London media for the last week, and filing them in date order. This sounds like a colossal waste of time and paper to me, and it takes me a huge effort to say, "OK. All right. Thanks."

"I wouldn't bother, if I were you," says Leila when they're gone. "No one reads our press clippings. Will shouldn't be giving you work, anyway. It's a little exploitative."

"I don't really have anything else to do."

"Here." Leila takes a copy of *Cosmopolitan* out of her desk drawer and throws it to me. "Read something trivial. Don't think about bombs."

× × × × ×

I print out two Jacob Carlisle articles just so it looks like I've made some kind of effort. Then I check the news. It says there are four people confirmed injured.

I read an article in *Cosmopolitan* about face contouring, which is apparently a thing.

A little later, I'm checking the news again and I realize I'm still working on Will's computer log-in when a little alert pops up in the corner of the screen: *You have a new message.* Without really meaning to, I click it, and his email opens up. I jump back a little bit, like the time me and Teagan accidentally found porn on a computer at school—but you can't not look at something when it's right in front of you, so after glancing over at Leila, who is on the phone again, I read the message. It's from Jacob Carlisle. It says: *Have to agree—thanks for your work today. JC.*

I guess Will and Danny must be on their way back to the office. I scroll idly down to see what the message is replying to. Will's original email is underneath.

Jake,

Confirming 8:30 meeting with Shannon Lees on Monday. Leila—cc'd—please put in diary.

After today we can expect another busy week ahead. The ee-bomber is clearly on our side—1st explosion was great timing, so is this one. Maybe you should thank him in your victory speech?!!

Will

I stare at this for a few minutes, feeling my headache starting to creep back. Leila is talking on the phone, peeling another orange. "He'd be very happy to talk to you," she's saying. "Can we do that early next week?"

I read it again. *Maybe you should thank him in your victory speech.*

In one of the articles I've just printed out, a columnist is saying how Jacob Carlisle is the only politician who seems to truly understand the mood of shock and fear. *A widower himself,* it says, *he speaks to a frightened electorate with compassion.* There was a picture of him. Blue eyes, serious face. I thought about that, while I was reading it. Whether he spoke to people with compassion. I thought, *Well, maybe he does.*

Underneath, there was the lovely smiling photo of Eduardo Capello and his baby daughter, which they still print all the time, any chance they can, like they know how upsetting it is.

His baby daughter, I think. *His pet fish.*

It feels like my blood is rising, thumping in my ears. I imagine Jacob Carlisle talking to people—right now, tomorrow, all week—saying how devastating it all is and if people vote for him he'll make them safe. Him and Will laughing together at the end of the day, looking at poll results in their expensive coats. It's not just that they don't care that somebody died: they're happy about it. Because it gets them attention. It gets them power. They're probably hoping that it happens again.

The next thing I do is click *Forward*. Then I enter Mike's email address.

Dear Mike, I write at the top. *I saw this accidentally.*

I look at the screen. *This could be faked*, I think. It wouldn't be hard to fake a forwarded email. But there's nothing I can do about that.

I stop for a long time, thinking what else I want to say, and in the end I just write: *You should put it in the paper. Don't tell Danny. Love, Alena.*

I click *Send*.

Then I go into the *Sent Mail* folder and delete it. Then I mark Jake's reply as *Unread*. Then I shut down his email and shut down the whole computer and wipe my hands on my jeans and nearly jump out of my skin when Leila touches my shoulder and says, "God, are you OK? You were miles away. You've gone white as a sheet. What's wrong?"

"I think I need some fresh air," I say faintly, and she pulls me out of the chair, saying, "Fresh air, got it. White as a *sheet*, Alena; you're not going to pass out, are you? What's your brother going to say to me? It's the heating, isn't it? For some reason it's permanently set to keep us all *roasting*—"

"I'm fine," I say. "I'm fine, I'm fine, I'm fine."

33

Outside, Leila says, "I used to pass out all the time when I was your age. I went to a girls' school and we used to drop like flies. I think it was contagious. Are you feeling better?"

We are on the steps outside the office and the air is cool and damp. I hug my knees against my chest and look at the ragged laces on my Converses. When I don't answer, Leila says, "Do you want me to call your brother? I'm sure he'll be back any minute."

It's hard to concentrate on what she's saying. I'm thinking, *If Mike is like everybody else in the world, then he checks his email every five minutes, and he will have already read it.*

"Alena?"

"No. Don't call him. I'm fine. I'm sorry. I'm totally fine."

She pauses. Then nods. "I'll make some tea in a minute. Or I could go on a coffee run. There's a Starbucks around the corner. You probably don't drink coffee. Do you drink coffee?"

"I like chai lattes," I say. My voice has disappeared and it comes out almost a whisper.

"Chai lattes. Got it. I'll go in a minute." She still looks concerned. "You know," she says, "he talks about you all the time. How bright you are and everything. It's really sweet."

There's a watery afternoon sun casting long shadows down the road and I turn and squint at her. "Danny does?"

"Of course he does. *Alena this, Alena that.* I'm sure you'd be embarrassed."

I don't know what to say to this.

She smiles at me. "*Alena*'s such a pretty name."

"Oh," I say. "Thanks. It's OK. People pronounce it wrong."

"I love it. It really suits you. Did it come from anywhere special?"

"I don't know. No one's ever told me."

"It's not a family name or something?"

"I don't know." I look down at my shoes again. "My mum's dead," I say. Which is a stupid thing to say. I don't know why I say it. It sounds stupid and overdramatic, like it just happened yesterday.

"I know," says Leila. "I'm sorry."

I nod. I try to say thanks, but my mouth is really dry and instead I just sit there nodding like an idiot, thinking about what it's supposed to mean when people say *I'm sorry*.

34

When Danny gets back he knows something's wrong with me right away. He thinks I'm upset about the bombing. Which I am, I guess, and he keeps telling me that it's OK and no one was really hurt this time, which is apparently true, and they'll definitely get the guy because they've got more CCTV footage, and it's clearly all taking him this huge effort because being optimistic and reassuring is really more Nick's style, and in fact I think Danny would just like for us all to go home and lock the doors and stay inside forever.

He stands outside the office on the steps for a while, talking on the phone. I watch him through the window and I can tell he's talking to Nick. I can just tell from his expression, from the way the phone is tucked between his ear and his shoulder.

They are no good at being apart. They are like Danny trying to give out punishment. No staying power.

When he comes back in, he says, "Do you still want to stay over at Teagan's this evening?"

"I thought I wasn't allowed," I say.

"You're allowed now," he says, and I look at him and think, *If you knew what I've just done.*

× × × × ×

When Danny drops me at her house it's evening, and getting dark, and Ollie is standing outside her door looking at his phone.

"What are you doing?" I say, walking up the drive toward him.

"Teagan invited me over."

"So why are you standing outside?"

"I was just texting her."

"Why don't you just knock on the door?"

"I dunno," he says. "In case her parents answer."

"Who cares if—"

"I don't know what they're like."

"They're fine," I say. "They're like normal people." Although actually I think they probably would make Ollie nervous if he was alone with them. They're always very *present* when people are at their house: asking a lot of questions and offering snacks like sliced carrots and mineral water.

"Have you been watching the news?" says Ollie. "Pretty fucked up, right? Can you believe they still haven't—"

Teagan flings open her front door then, and stands looking at us. She's wearing purple socks and cut-off jeans. "Why are you two just standing out here?" she says, frowning. "Are you coming in?" Almost immediately her dad appears in the hall behind her, holding a bowl of olives. "Ah," he says. "Welcome!"

There's supposed to be a meteor shower that one of our teachers has told us to watch, so after Ollie gets awkwardly introduced to Teagan's parents, we all go and sit out in the yard and look at the sky. As usual, you can't see a thing because of the city lights. Ollie has to borrow Teagan's dad's coat because it gets cold, and when her mum and dad go out somewhere

Teagan steals some whiskey from their drinks cabinet, pouring it into three plastic cups, and we drink it looking up at the bright burned-out sky.

I tell them what I did. When I look at them Ollie is staring at me with his eyes slightly wide, an expression that I choose to interpret as respect or possibly awe, and for a moment I feel good, proud of myself. But Teagan is looking alarmed.

"Not that this Will person doesn't sound like a creep," she says, "but aren't you worried you're going to get Danny into trouble?"

I stare at her. "Danny had nothing to do with it," I say.

"But won't people think that he—"

"If anybody gets in trouble it's going to be me. If Mike tells him—"

"Yeah, but Lena, that's where Danny *works*; won't people think—"

"Why do you care so much about Danny?" I say irritably. "I thought it was Nick you had a crush on."

Teagan looks confused for a second, then hurt, then gets up to go and get snacks from inside, saying, "All right, never mind then."

I feel bad. The whiskey is making me feel sick.

Ollie is staring into his plastic cup with his shoulders hunched up.

"Ollie," I say, "what's your first memory?"

"Huh?"

"What's the first thing you can remember? Can you remember being really little?"

"I dunno," says Ollie, and then, "My dad took me to the beach once and we got lost in the fog. I remember that."

"How old were you?"

"Like two or three. And my brother kicked a football in my face when I was three or something. I remember that."

"Anything else?"

"Don't know. Probably. Why? What's your first memory?"

"It's this thing with my aunt. Me screaming at her. It's nothing."

"Oh."

"I can't remember anything before living with Nick and Danny."

"Oh." Ollie looks uncomfortable. "That's probably normal, though."

"It's not normal. It was my mother. That's when my mother was alive. It's like I just wasn't paying attention."

"But. Yeah. I mean, that's not your fault."

"It is, though."

"Not really."

"It is. And you and Teagan remember all this stupid stuff that doesn't even matter. It's not fair."

Ollie goes quiet for a minute. His breath is misty in the cold air.

"If you get in a lot of trouble with this email thing," he says. "If it's really bad. I'm thinking about going to Swansea. You could come with me."

"What are you talking about?"

"I got this email from my brother. He didn't really say anything but—I think that's where he is. I dunno. I think I'm just gonna go. On the train. I'm saving for a ticket. So when I've got enough I'm going to go."

"For the weekend or something?"

"No. I'm going to stay there."

"Stay where?"

"I'll find somewhere."

"Ollie." I think this is the stupidest plan I've ever heard but I can't bring myself to say this to him. "Ollie. Don't do that. I don't think you should."

"My mum doesn't want me around," he says. "She'd be happy if I left."

I'm about to say, *That can't be true,* but then I think, *What do I know, maybe it is true.*

"You could come with me," he says again. "It'd be better with two of us."

"Ollie."

"Come on," he says. "You obviously don't like your brother that much or you wouldn't've just totally screwed over his job and everything."

"I haven't screwed over his job. It was nothing to do with him."

He falls silent, looks back at the cup he's holding.

"Anyway, what would I do in Swansea?" I say.

"I don't know. I'll find Aaron. Maybe we could stay with him. I'm going to get a job."

"Ollie. I really don't think you should do that."

He turns away from me. "All right, never mind," he says. "That's what I'm going to do but you can do whatever."

"Ollie—"

"Don't tell Teagan, though, all right? Just forget I told you."

In the house behind us, I can faintly hear Teagan singing in the kitchen while she bangs open cupboards and looks for snacks.

I make my voice go quiet. "You should talk to Teagan; she's actually good at things like—I mean, she has good ideas. She could probably help you look for Aaron if that's what you want to do."

"She wouldn't understand."

"She would."

He shakes his head, gestures vaguely back at her house and her yard like, *Look at all this*, like that explains something, and says, "No. Just forget it."

I wonder, then, what it is he thinks Teagan's got that I don't, what he thinks I understand that she wouldn't.

Maybe it is true that Ollie's mum doesn't want him around. Maybe I know the feeling. Those times when it seems like Nick and Danny forget I exist, and then remember.

Teagan comes out again, clattering the back door open and kicking it shut with her foot as she carries platefuls of potato chips and cookies. "Anybody see anything yet?" she says.

"There's nothing to see," says Ollie. He pulls the hood up on Teagan's dad's coat and goes silent, and the atmosphere between the three of us takes a weird, wrong turn. We stop talking and just watch the sky.

× × × × ×

"What were you two talking about?" Teagan says later, after Ollie leaves and her parents are back. She is standing in the doorway of her bedroom holding her toothbrush while I check my email on my phone. There's an email from Nick's mum offering to take me shopping next weekend and saying, *Isn't it dreadful about the bombing?* and that's it. Nothing from Mike.

I put my phone down on the bed. "What?"

"Before. Ollie was talking to you about something and then you both shut up and went weird when I came back."

"He was just—nothing. He was talking about his brother and stuff."

She has pinned her bangs back with a barrette and washed her face so her cheeks are flushed and red. She looks uncertain, like she thinks I'm lying but isn't sure. I'm not sure if I am either. Other people's secrets are difficult. It's hard to know where they're supposed to start and end.

"You both seemed like you were in the middle of something important. Ollie was all, like—"

She trails off, looks at her toothbrush in her hand, and twirls it through her fingers a few times.

"He told me not to tell you," I say, and then immediately regret it because what a stupid thing to say.

"Not to tell me what?" she says, clearly hurt.

I lie back on the bed, look up at the glow-stars Teagan's had stuck to her ceiling for years.

"What can he tell you that he doesn't want me to know? We've known him for the exact same amount of time; what's the difference between—"

"He thinks his brother's in Swansea and he wants to run away, or something. He wants to go to Swansea and live with him."

There's a silence, and I sit up and look at her. "Don't tell him I told you."

She's upset. I can tell.

"So why can he tell you that and not me?" she says.

"How do I know?"

"Lena."

"He just thought you wouldn't understand."

"Thanks a lot. Why wouldn't I understand?"

"How do I know?"

"Do you understand?"

I sit up again. "I don't know. I suppose so."

Teagan looks at me for a few seconds, blinking, and then she turns and goes back to the bathroom. She comes back without her toothbrush and sits down at her desk. Her pajamas are an old pair of tracksuit bottoms and a pink t-shirt with a music note printed on the front. She's had this t-shirt for years and years; I remember her wearing it on a school trip when we were eleven or twelve.

I lie back down. I feel exhausted and wide awake at the same time. I want to check my email again but it's late now. If anything's going to happen it's not going to happen tonight.

"I always thought he was jealous of you," Teagan says.

"What?" I say, still looking at the ceiling.

"Ollie. He thinks you're really interesting. He's always asking me all these questions about your family. I thought he was jealous of you because you've got Danny and he's got Aaron."

"That's ridiculous."

"I don't know."

"What's so great about Danny?"

"Lena. You don't even realize. He's like the nicest person and you don't even notice."

"Nobody thinks that apart from you, Teagan."

"That's not true."

"Danny hardly talks to me anymore, Nick moved out because of him, you've got no idea—Ollie only told me about going to Swansea because he thought I might go with him."

"Why? Because he thinks you've got something to run away from? The two of you have so much in common all of a sudden?"

"I don't know. Just." I close my eyes for a second. "Our families aren't like yours."

In the quiet I can hear her breathing, and then she says, "He thought you might want to go with him."

"Yes."

"But not me."

"Why would you run away from home?"

"Right. Because my life is perfect. Why would *you*?"

This is getting ridiculous. I sit up. "I'm not," I say. "Nobody's running away anywhere. Nobody's going to Swansea. This is stupid."

Downstairs I hear somebody switch on the TV, the news starting.

"Nick's going to come back," Teagan says, quietly. "I know you're upset but he'll come back."

"You don't know that. You don't know them. Just because you hang out at the coffee shop and they try and impress you by acting like these great parents—"

"They *are* great parents, though. It's like—your family is nothing like Ollie's. You're so lucky and you don't even—"

"Ollie has *actual* parents. And you. You and Ollie have actual mothers and fathers and I don't have any of that. My mum died and I don't even know—"

"Oh, all right, we know your mum died," Teagan says. "We get it."

She looks instantly guilty, but then she bites her lip and folds her arms, defiant.

"What's that supposed to mean?" I say.

"Nothing."

"Nothing. Right."

"Just that until recently you've mentioned your mum about twice in your life. And now suddenly you're really sad about it. And I can honestly understand why Danny wouldn't want to talk about her. I mean it must be different for him, it must be—"

"You don't know what you're talking about."

She presses her lips together and won't look at me for a minute.

We never fight. This already feels like the worst fight we've ever had. It's like there's something about me right now, like I'm radioactive, in a fight with everybody.

I get up and go into the bathroom and shut the door, sit on the toilet seat thinking that I'd like to cry but I don't know which one particular thing to cry about.

I don't cry. I just sit there for a while, listening to the sounds of the house, the TV downstairs and somebody loading the dishwasher.

And then I wash my face and brush my teeth with one of the spare toothbrushes still in the packet that Teagan's mum always keeps stocked in the bathroom, squinting at myself in the bright bathroom mirror and thinking of Lynn saying I look just like Danny when he was my age.

When I go back into Teagan's room she's turned the light off, pretending to be asleep.

35

Usually we'd both just sleep in Teagan's huge double bed, but instead I sleep on the sofa underneath her window with a blanket pulled over my head. We sleep late in the morning, with the curtains shut. When I wake up, I lie there half listening to the sounds of her house, her parents talking quietly, and morning news talking about the bombing. I keep imagining that the phone is ringing and that it's Will from Danny's office telling me that I'm going to be arrested for reading his email. And then the phone really is ringing, and I hear Teagan's mum answer it, and a few minutes later she comes into the room and sits on the end of the bed.

"Girls," she says, "it's time to get up." There is something strange about her voice and it wakes me up like cold water. I sit up straight and look at her, and I know instantly that she knows what I did.

"Alena," she says, gently, "I've just spoken to your brother. He'd like me to take you home."

"What's happened?" I say, just in case maybe hopefully somebody has been in a car accident.

"I'm going to take you home and your brother would like you to stay there until he gets home."

"Where is he?"

"He said he had to go in to work but he's going to be home very soon and he'd like you to be there."

"What's going on?" Teagan mumbles, sitting up and rubbing her eyes.

"I'm sure you already know, Teagan," she says. "It's time to get dressed, Alena. Do you need some breakfast?"

"I'm OK," I say. I can feel my stomach twisting itself into a knot. I couldn't eat. If I ate I would be sick. "Thank you."

"I'll meet you downstairs," she says, and leaves, closing the door behind her.

Me and Teagan look at each other for a few seconds, and then Teagan lies back down and pulls the blanket over her head and mumbles, from underneath, "Well, good luck, then."

x x x x x

In the car, my hands are sweating. Teagan's mum is talking about the weather, like trying to distract me, until she's interrupted by my phone ringing from the bottom of my bag. She gives me a sort of sympathetic glance as I fish it out and look at the name on the screen.

"Hi, Nick," I say, almost a whisper.

"Alena," he says. "Alena, Alena, Alena."

"Hi," I say again, and I wonder, wildly, how everybody knows already, and whether I could just deny it, say that Mike was making it up.

"I just spoke to Danny," Nick says. "And he says he had a phone call from Mike this morning. Who apparently had an interesting email from you yesterday afternoon."

"Oh," I say in a tiny voice.

"I'm not even going to ask how you—I don't even know where to start."

"This guy Will said that it was good timing that that guy was killed and he said—"

"I don't want to hear about it right now."

"But, Nick—"

"Really. Not right now."

"OK," I say, and he sighs and the phone crackles with static. Nick is worse than Danny when he's angry with me, because he just goes quiet and sad and disappointed and makes me feel awful.

"What's Danny going to do?" I say.

"Where are you?"

"Rachel's driving me home."

"OK. Here's what you're going to do. OK? You're going to go home and wait there and not answer the phone unless it's me or Danny. OK?"

"Why can't I answer the phone?"

"Because I say so. I'm serious. Just go home and wait for us."

"Are you coming home?"

He pauses. "Yes," he says. "I'm going to come over. I'm the only one in the shop but I'll be over as soon as Zahra gets here."

"Is Mike going to do something?" I whisper.

"I can confidently say, Alena, that you're going to find out all about it as soon as Danny gets home."

"Is he going to kill me?" I say.

I must sound genuinely scared, because Nick says, "No. He's not going to kill you. I'll be there as soon as I can, sweetheart, OK? And then we're all going to sit down and talk about it."

I think the last time Nick called me *sweetheart* was this time when I was ten years old and I was ill and I had such a high temperature they nearly took me to hospital. I remember sitting on the side of my bed and holding this stuffed penguin

I used to have while Nick looked at a thermometer. Everybody was being so nice to me.

× × × × ×

The apartment is deadly quiet. There's a half-drunk mug of cold coffee on the kitchen counter. I kick off my shoes and sit down on the sofa, try to ignore my skittering heartbeat and do what Danny always tells me to do, which is to pretend to be brave even when you don't feel like it.

All he can do is shout at me, I think. That's all he can do. That's all that will happen. Nobody else will even care about the stupid email.

I put twenty-four-hour news on for a few minutes in case I'm famous, but they're talking about the economy, and the sight of somebody in a suit talking about the markets calms me down a bit. But then there's a short, hard knock on the door, and I jump.

I stare at it for a moment, and then I switch off the television and get up. As I'm opening the door I'm thinking maybe it's Danny and he's forgotten his keys.

It isn't.

It turns out that Jacob Carlisle really *is* quite good-looking.

"Are you Daniel Kennedy's little sister?" he says.

"Yes," I say. "I'm Alena."

"You," he says, "are an extremely disruptive young lady."

36

I stand in the doorway and I can't work out if I'm supposed to let him in, so we just face each other, me with my hand braced on the side of the door and him with his arms folded and his spine perfectly straight. I can see a broken blood vessel in his eye, a tiny red explosion. His eyes really are very blue: I thought they touched them up in the photos but they don't.

There is a woman standing behind him in the hallway, typing into her phone. She looks up briefly and we make eye contact and then she looks back at the phone. There's a man, as well, further down the hallway, and he has his hands in his pockets but he's standing stiffly and just watching us. He has a thick neck, like a rugby player, and a squashed face and he doesn't look like a politician: he looks like a boxer.

Maybe he's a bodyguard. Not that long ago nobody even knew who Jake Carlisle was and now he has an *entourage*.

I wonder if the bodyguard thinks that I am dangerous, in my socks and jeans and with my uncombed hair.

"Is one of your guardians here?" says Jacob Carlisle, and I can see him looking over my shoulder at our apartment and I think about slamming the door shut so he can't see it, can't see our dishes in the sink or my shoes in the middle of the floor or

Danny's jacket on the back of the sofa: so he can't look at it and think that he knows anything about us.

"No. They're not here."

He turns and looks at the woman behind him and she shrugs.

"Maybe I should call them," I say.

"I think that would be a good idea."

And he is good-looking but he's *short*, though, not that much taller than me, and he could be anybody, could be somebody's dad picking them up at school.

"Is this—are you here because of the email?" I say.

He gives me an incredulous look and is about to answer when the woman with the phone looks up again and says, "Don't talk to her without one of her guardians, Jake. The last thing we need—"

"It's not my fault that I saw it," I say. "I just saw it. It was an accident. And I can tell whoever I like. It's not illegal."

The moment I say this I wonder if it *is* illegal to read someone else's email. I actually have no idea.

"I didn't come here to talk to you," he says. "So you can save your explanations. I'm here to talk to your brother."

"He didn't have anything to do with it."

He stares at me like I'm some strange creature he's never encountered before. "How old are you?" he says.

Before I can answer, the elevator door pings open, and we all turn to look as my brother steps out. He has his bag slung across his chest and he's texting somebody but as soon he sees us he stops dead for a second, and then comes quickly toward us.

"Whoa, hey, OK," he says. "Hey, what's going on?" He catches my eye for a second as he gets to the door, and then he steps around Jake so that he's standing directly in front of me with his arms held out at his sides, either like surrender or like he's making himself a bigger target. He doesn't look at me again. I have to step out from behind him just so I can still see. Jake looks at me for a few seconds, and then turns to Danny.

"Will has just called me and offered to resign," he says.

Danny is breathing too fast. "Will has just—OK. What? The thing's not even online yet."

"But it will be in a couple of hours, is that right?"

He pauses. "Yes."

"And what do you think I should do about it?"

"It might not get picked up," says Danny. "I think this is an overreaction. It might not be that big a thing. There's plenty of other stuff going on this weekend."

"It will get picked up. It'll get picked up right away. Our whole campaign has been about this, Daniel. How is this going to make us look?"

"I've asked him not to post it."

"Asked who?"

"Mike Feghali." He pauses. "Mike Feghali. That's who she sent it to."

"Is Mike Feghali the person who's been trying to contact me all morning?"

"Probably."

"Who is he?"

"From the *Hackney Standard*."

"And how did she know how to get in contact with the *Hackney Standard*?"

"We know him. He's a family friend."

"How touching," says Jake. "You've asked him not to post it?"

"Yes."

"And what did he say?"

"He said he was going to post it in a few hours."

"Oh," says Jacob. "Very well done, then."

"Yeah."

"You've seen him?"

"I've just come from his house. He says he's confirmed it. She didn't make it up or anything."

"How has he confirmed it?"

"He wouldn't tell me. I got the impression he spoke to someone else who'd seen it. Mike's very good at his job. He's very thorough."

"Who else would have seen it?"

"How would I know?" says Danny, starting to sound rattled. "*I* haven't seen it. The point I'm making is that she didn't make it up."

"Am I supposed to be impressed by that?"

I am standing right here, I think. But it's hard to make myself speak when they're both suddenly acting like I don't exist.

I do exist: this whole conversation is about me. I made this happen.

Danny lowers his arms slightly. He is still holding his phone in his hand. "So you can't—I mean, that's the actual text of the email?"

"How would I know?" says Jake. "I don't even remember the email. I doubt I even read it."

Danny says carefully, "It was only yesterday. You replied to it."

"I have no memory of replying to it. I probably didn't even read it."

"That might be difficult to argue," says Danny.

There's a shakiness in Jacob Carlisle's voice, I realize suddenly, like he's genuinely upset. "Do you know what this is going to do to us?" he says. "This campaign has a few weeks left. Do you understand how this is going to look?"

"Yes." Danny's voice has gone very flat, and Jacob's is getting louder.

"For god's sake, you're telling me a *girl*, a *teenager*, who thinks she's some kind of—did I even approve her coming into the office? What was she even doing there? Was she just left to run wild? Do we have any basic security procedures on this campaign?"

"She's my sister," Danny says. "She's not a terrorist. And she's not—this is out of character. She's never done anything like this."

"I just can't *conceive* how she managed to end up reading a private email exchange. Am I being told that she *deliberately*—"

"I haven't really had a chance to ask her—"

"Well, she's right here, so let's ask her now."

I open my mouth to speak and Danny says, "No. She's not talking to anybody right now. You can talk to me."

"Danny," I say, and he glances at me. "All I did was—"

"Not now."

Jake is shaking his head. "I'm just finding this hard to understand," he says. "From you, Daniel. You're the one who turned this around for us."

"He didn't have anything to do with it," I say. "He wasn't even—"

"Be quiet," says Danny, and something in his voice makes me do what he says.

"She saw this email and you didn't know anything about it?"

Danny doesn't answer. He folds his arms.

"You are responsible for her, is that right?" says Jake, with another quick glance at the apartment like maybe there's an actual grown-up around.

"Yes. I'm responsible for her."

This hangs in the air for a moment, and I wonder what that even means, that he's responsible for me. Like he's responsible for looking after me or like he's responsible for everything I do wrong, or both.

"I was advised not to come here," Jacob says, and then stops and rubs his eyes, pinches the bridge of his nose. "Everyone's always got a lot of advice. This is my *life*. This isn't a game, this isn't a children's—" He stops, glances at me. "Perhaps we shouldn't have any conversations in front of this young lady," he says. "I can only assume the transcripts will end up on the front page of *The Times*."

"Then we should go somewhere else," says Danny. "Because I'm actually not really comfortable with you coming to my home and talking to her when she's here on her own anyway."

"I'm not sure you're in any position to be the one who's angry here, Daniel. This whole incident raises some very serious questions."

"I know. I know that."

Then Jacob looks directly at me. "It seems very strange to me that you would want to do this," he says.

"It seems very strange to me that someone who works for you would say something like—"

"*Alena*," says Danny. "Shut up."

Jake looks back to Danny and there's a long silence. "I don't know what to do here," he says.

"I can come into the office and we can talk about it with Will. We can work out how you're going to respond, we can work out—"

"I don't think we'll need you to come into the office. I don't think that would be appropriate right now." He pauses. "In fact, I'm not sure that it's appropriate for you to continue coming into the office."

Without meaning to, I reach toward Danny, grab the sleeve of his shirt with my hand.

"You don't want me to finish the campaign," says Danny flatly.

"People are very upset about this."

"I understand that."

"It's not appropriate that you continue. It's just not appropriate. I'm sorry." Then: "People will find it hard to believe that a fourteen-year-old engineered this by herself."

"She's fifteen," says Danny, like that's any better. "And I think people will be more interested in the contents of the email than in who leaked it."

"Nevertheless," says Jake.

I let go of Danny's shirt and try to speak again. "This isn't fair; he didn't even—"

"Be quiet," says Danny, eyes fixed forward.

"If anyone should be in trouble it should be—"

"Shut up, Alena."

The woman in the hallway has stopped typing into her phone and she says, gently, "Jake. We need to meet with Des."

Jacob nods, still looking at Danny. "Is Mr. Feghali going to reveal his source?" he says.

"No."

"I suggest you sit down and have a very long conversation with this girl about why exactly she felt the need to get involved with something I assume she knows nothing about."

And then, I suppose because he's just lost his job, Danny says, "I don't need any advice, thanks."

They look at each other for a very long time. "This isn't constructive," Jacob says.

Danny doesn't answer.

"I came here to talk to you," Jacob says. "I didn't come here to intimidate her."

"I hope not," says Danny.

"Someone from the office will be in touch with you," says Jacob, and there's a short, uncomfortable silence, and then they turn and walk back down the hallway.

They take the stairs instead of the elevator, and you can hear the doors in the stairwell slam an echo on each level as they go down, like gunfire getting further and further away.

Danny closes the door but for a few seconds he doesn't turn around. I can hear him breathing like he's just finished a marathon. When he does turn around, he looks at me and his face is totally blank and when he folds his arms I can see that his hands are shaking.

"Danny," I say, my mouth dry. "I didn't know—"

"I got a phone call at nine o'clock this morning," says Danny. "I got a phone call from my friend Mike saying that last night he'd had an email from my little sister, and he thought I should know about it. He wanted to give me a couple of hours as a courtesy before he posted it online." He's shaking his head slowly as he speaks, like he doesn't really believe what he's saying. "And so before I do anything I have to phone up the people I work with and warn them that this is going to happen, and they all say, *But* how *did this happen?*, and I have to say, *I don't know exactly but it has something to do with my* little sister *who I brought into the office with me and who, for some reason despite her recent behavior, I thought was responsible enough to be left on her own for a few hours.*"

There's a long silence. Then Danny says, "You actually do hate me, don't you?"

I don't know if it would make it better or worse if I started crying. I can feel the tears building, pressure somewhere behind my eyes, but I can't make myself cry, can't make myself do anything. I have no idea how everything got this bad this quickly. The expression on his face is terrible.

I try to think of the right words to explain, wanting to say something smart and brave, like the women on the Greenham Common video, to explain what I did, but nothing comes together. The idea is all broken up in my mind. I know there's something I have to say but I don't know what it is.

When I don't answer, Danny says, "Forget it. I can't talk to you right now. I need you to go somewhere else."

"Where do you want me to—"

"Just go to your room," he says. But before I can even do this, he's gone into his own room and slammed the door so hard that the coffee cup on the counter shakes.

× × × × ×

I'm still wearing the clothes I was wearing yesterday, so when I go to my room I change into a gray hoodie and an old pair of cropped jeans. I sit on the bed and look at my toenails, which I painted purple a few weeks ago and now the polish is all chipped. I think about summer and wearing flip-flops and whether we'll go anywhere this year. My laptop is lying on the desk but I don't power it up, don't look at the *Hackney Standard* website or at anything else.

I get a message from Teagan. It says, *I might have been being a stupid idiot last night.* Then, a few seconds later, *What's happening at yours? xxx*

I text her back. *Me too. don't know yet. big trouble. xxx*

Nick gets home at exactly ten minutes past one. I hear him open and close the door and then stop because the living room's empty, and I wonder which room he'll try first.

He tries mine.

"Come in," I say when he knocks, and my voice still sounds normal, still doesn't sound like I'm going to cry. He opens the door and leans in. "What's going on?" he says.

"Danny's in your room," I say. "I think he lost his job."

Nick's expression doesn't change as he absorbs this information. "Don't go anywhere," he says, and closes my door again. Like there's anywhere I could go.

37

So then, nearly an hour later and after Nick and Danny have been talking in their room very quietly and not so quietly for ages, there is the most awful and excruciating family conference ever, which the only good thing you can say about is that it doesn't last very long.

It starts with Nick knocking on my door and saying, "OK, Alena, can you come into the living room and talk to us, please."

When I go into the living room, Danny is standing in front of the window, looking at his phone. "Mike's just posted it," he says. He scrolls down the screen. "He posted it—seven minutes ago. Front page." He looks up at me. "Pleased with yourself?"

"What does it say?" says Nick.

"*In an email leaked to the* Hackney Standard *yesterday afternoon*—et cetera et cetera—*Jacob Carlisle's campaign manager describes the East London bombing that claimed the life of an Italian tourist as 'great timing'*—"

Danny stops and shuts his eyes for a moment.

"Jesus," he says. "*Jacob Carlisle's campaign manager goes on to say*—blah, blah, blah—*Jacob Carlisle responds to this email with the words 'Have to agree.' Mr. Carlisle, whose response to the tragedy has been credited with his unprecedented rise*—" Danny stops.

"Well, great day for the *Hackney Standard*," he says. "You and Mike must be really pleased with yourselves."

I take a deep breath and I'm about to speak, but Nick interrupts.

"I think we should all sit down," he says. He gestures toward the table.

"Yes, *let's*," says Danny, and he pulls out a chair and sits down abruptly, his phone on the table in front of him. He crosses his arms and stares at the table like he wants to kill it, and I take a seat opposite and Nick sits between us at the head of the table. I try to start speaking again but Nick says, "I think we should start with why you were looking at somebody else's email in the first place."

This isn't where I wanted to start. "It was an accident," I say, and attempt to explain the computer log-in thing which, admittedly, doesn't sound that much like an accident when I say it out loud.

"So you saw it by accident," Nick says. "She saw it by accident, Danny."

"And then she *accidentally* fell on the keyboard and forwarded it to Mike?"

"No," I say. "I did that on purpose."

"No kidding." He is looking at me like he doesn't even recognize me.

"Have you seen what those emails actually say?" I ask. "Will Rofofsky goes, *Hey, brilliant, someone's dead, so you're going to win the election* and Jacob Carlisle goes, *I know, it's really brilliant, isn't it.* That's what they're saying."

Nick clears his throat. "And so that—what? That made you angry?"

"Doesn't that make *you* angry?"

His mouth twitches and you can tell it does make him angry. It's *exactly* the sort of thing that makes Nick angry.

"And so you decided you wanted people to know about it because—what? You wanted to get this guy fired?"

"His name is Will," says Danny.

"No, I just—it's not about him. I don't even care about him."

"Clearly," says Danny.

I can feel my resolve falling apart. "I didn't know that Mike would actually post it," I say.

"What did you expect him to do with it?" says Nick.

"I don't know."

"Is this about me and Danny?"

"No. *No.* It's what they're *saying*. It's about what's *morally*—you know, what's *morally wrong*. Don't you think that people should know about—"

"You know what?" says Danny. "You know what? I am *sick* to *death* of hearing about what's morally right and what's morally wrong. It's bad enough with him, and now you've started up as well. This is some line you've gotten from Nick, and you're doing it to get at me or punish me for something and that's fine, go ahead, but I've given up *half* my *life* for you, you know, so *don't* tell me about what's morally wrong—"

"Danny," says Nick, putting a hand on his arm.

"—because if that's what this was really about, then you should've spoken to one of us first instead of deliberately sabotaging me, and you know what, if you're that angry with me for doing nothing except doing my best for you like there's nothing else I ever wanted to do with my life—"

"Danny."

"—then maybe I should never have bothered, maybe I

should have said, *Fine, take her to Australia*, maybe we'd all have been happier—"

"*Danny.*"

He shuts up, finally, and puts his elbows on the table and his face in his hands.

Nick's hand is still on Danny's arm, gripped so tight that his knuckles are white, that it probably hurts. I see that Nick knew what Danny was going to say and that he tried to stop it. Too late.

Nick is shaking his head, obviously trying to come up with the right combination of words to erase what Danny's said, but I don't want him to. If that's what he thinks, then why shouldn't he say it.

"I didn't know you'd lose your job," I whisper, since that's true.

"Yes, you did," says Danny without taking his hands away.

"Danny, I don't think she could've known."

"She's not stupid." He takes his hands away and looks at me. "Those people are my friends," he says. "Will is my friend. They all think I had something to do with this, Alena."

"I'm sorry," I say, but my throat is closing up now and it comes out wrong.

"I didn't get this job for kicks. I got it so you could have clothes and vacations and guitar lessons and god knows what else. So when you're eighteen you can go to college and you can—" He stops, and swallows. "Never mind."

"I don't want to go to college."

"Yes, you do."

"I don't. Just because you had such a great time—"

"That's not what we're talking about right now," says Nick. "One fight at a time, please."

"I don't think Will should be your friend," I say. "I don't think he's that nice."

"You don't even know him," says Danny.

"That's true, Lena," says Nick.

"Whether I know him or not, I know what he said. I think people have a right to know—"

"Don't finish that sentence," Danny says. "Don't say anything else. I don't want to hear it. I've changed my mind. Nick, I can't do this right now. I need both of you to go away. I need both of you to go somewhere else."

I look at Nick, a little desperately, like he could get up and make a pot of tea and we'd all be friends again. For a minute he looks like he's going to argue, but Danny has gone back to staring at the table, and finally Nick says, quietly, "OK, Lena, let's go out for a little while."

"Thank you," says Danny. Not to me.

× × × × ×

We walk up the high street toward the coffee shop, glassy April sunlight in our eyes. I wipe my nose on my sleeve, rub away a few escaping tears, and look at my shoes, black canvas Vans that I got last summer. I replaced the black laces with green ones but now they're all frayed.

Nick tugs me loosely into his side and squeezes my shoulder.

"You shouldn't listen to everything Danny said just now," he says. "People say things they don't mean when they're upset."

"Which bits should I listen to then?"

"You know what I'm saying."

Like presumably I shouldn't listen to the bit where Danny said we'd all have been happier if I'd gone to Australia. Except it sounded true enough when he said it.

"If Mike's put it online that means it's important," I say. "That means people *should* know about it."

"Yeah," says Nick quietly. "Yeah. OK. But I can't be on your side about this."

"But you hate Jacob Carlisle. And you wouldn't like Will, either: you'd think he was pushy and fake and shallow." I sniff and wipe my nose again. "You're always talking about your ethical responsibility."

Nick sounds very tired suddenly. "I know," he says. "But that's not—" He stops, and then says, "I have a responsibility to Danny too."

"Then why did you move out?"

"I didn't move out. I haven't moved out. Is my stuff still at the apartment? Do I still have my keys?"

"It felt like you moved out. You haven't been there in a week after you said only a couple of nights." I pull my sleeves over my hands and cross my arms and squint up at him. Nick is like 6' 4" or something. He's really tall. "You left me alone with Danny and you know what he's like, you know he doesn't talk to me about anything. He's angry at me all the time."

"He's got a right to be angry at you when you're cutting school and running off to Clapham for secret meetings with your mother's friends."

"Which I would never have done if he would just let me meet my mother's friends like any normal person would."

Nick stops walking suddenly. "She didn't have anything to do with this, did she?"

"What?"

"Lynn Wallace. Did she put you up to this? Did you tell her who Danny was working for?"

"What? No. She didn't even want to talk to me."

"What do you mean?"

"She didn't want to talk to me. She told me to get lost."

"She told you to get lost?"

"Basically. She said she had to respect Danny's wishes."

"Oh." We start walking again. Then Nick says, "I'm sorry. That must have been disappointing."

I don't answer.

"It sounds like she was trying to do the right thing," he adds.

I don't answer that, either.

× × × × ×

When we get to the coffee shop, Zahra is behind the counter looking at her phone, and when she sees us she says, "You guys. You guys. Have you seen this Jacob Carlisle email thing that's happened? Have you seen it? This is *brilliant*. Do you guys know about this yet?"

"Yes," says Nick. "We know about it."

"Is Danny going mental?"

"You could say that," says Nick. "What site are you looking at?"

"It's all over the internet." She waves her phone at us. "And it was Mike from the *Standard* who got the emails. We know him! Isn't this brilliant?" Then she looks guilty. "I mean, I'm sorry for Danny. I know Jacob Carlisle's his man. So no offense to him or anything."

"Zahra, let me talk to you for a minute," says Nick. "You, sit there," he says to me, pointing at the booth nearest the counter.

"What am I supposed to do?" I say.

"Just sit there and try not to overthrow the government," he says, and goes into the back office with Zahra.

A few minutes later she comes back out and there's a customer waiting, but before she serves him, she grabs a napkin and writes something on it, and then she comes over to me and says, "This is really terrible, what you've done, Lena." She hands me the napkin and goes back to the counter. On the napkin she has written: *YOU ARE AWESOME xxxxx*.

I fold it up carefully and tuck it into the pocket of my jeans.

I feel like one of the kids at school who's gotten in trouble and has to wait in the corridor outside the principal's office while they decide what the punishment is going to be.

Usually they just have to say they're sorry, but sometimes that isn't enough.

38

We can't stay away forever and I haven't eaten anything all day apart from coffee shop flapjacks; I don't have any homework with me, or a book, or anything. I get a text from Ollie. It says: *holy shit what you did is on the news nice one. ollie.*

I text him back. *Ollie please don't go to Swansea. Even if Aaron is there.* I want to write, *Especially if Aaron is there* but I think better of it. Then, because it's true, I write, *I'd miss you.* Then I delete that and write, *me and t. would miss you.* Then I hit *Send.* He doesn't reply.

I sit in the corner and read an old magazine cover-to-cover while Zahra flits around cleaning things and humming to herself. Nick comes and joins me after a couple of hours. He says, "You're going to need dinner at some point, aren't you?"

"Yes."

"Your email thing is all over the news. You'd be a celebrity if Mike had used your name. This Will Rofofsky guy isn't going to be in a job much longer."

I think of Will Rofofsky in his expensive coat, leaning over to log in to the computer. What I was about to do to him, and he thought I was just some kid. It was only yesterday afternoon. It feels forever ago.

"I thought people might think I'd made it up."

Nick pauses. "You didn't think Mike would believe you?"

I shrug, and he sighs.

"Doesn't matter. Apparently he went and found someone to confirm it anyway. He's not an idiot."

This is what Danny said earlier. "Who?" I say.

"Don't ask me, Lena, you're the one who read the email. You know as much as anybody else right now."

I'm the one who read the email. I picture it, suddenly, in my mind, the whole thing.

The bit that said *Leila—cc'd*. She saw it as well.

I'm distracted by this thought for a second, but Nick is looking at me like there's something else I'm supposed to be saying.

"Maybe now he could work for the *Standard* again," I say. "Danny could."

"Angry as he is with you, Lena, he's even more pissed off with Mike right now. So I don't see that happening any time soon."

"Nick." I look down at my magazine, but I can't see the words properly. "I didn't know it would be this big of a deal."

"Drop the *I didn't know what I was doing* act, OK? I know you're not stupid. You're not helping yourself. And if you feel like you did the right thing, if you did this out of some kind of moral imperative, then take responsibility for it."

I look up and meet his eye.

"I think you knew exactly what you were doing," he says, and Nick has always known me probably better than anyone.

"I didn't know that Danny would lose his job," I tell him.

"You didn't even think it was a possibility?"

"I don't know."

"Alena."

"I was thinking about what you said a while ago. You said you thought my mum would've hated Jacob Carlisle."

"I don't remember saying that."

"Well, you did."

He sighs. "All right. If you say so."

"If she knew something that would stop people voting for him, she'd have used it. That's what I think. This is exactly what she would have done if she was here."

I am certain like a rock that Nick will tell me that I'm right; I have known this all day—that when Nick is alone he will privately tell me that I'm right and, god, that I'm just like her, do I know that? Sometimes we just have a human duty to take action against injustice—

—but he's shaking his head before I've even finished the thought. "No, no, no, no, no, Lena. Is that why you did this? You've got that one wrong, kid. Maybe if Jake was just some politician, but this is *Danny's* life you're messing with. She'd never have done anything like that to him."

I squeeze my hands into fists underneath the table. "She *would*. If she thought it was important."

He looks very, very sad for a moment. "She was his mum. She was like all mothers. She thought everything he did was wonderful. She'd never have done anything to deliberately hurt him, no matter what she thought about Jake Carlisle. Not in a million years. You've got that one wrong, Lena. Mothers don't do things like that."

It's like being punched in the stomach. "Well, I wouldn't know, would I?" I say, and for a moment I look across the table and it's like a tunnel and Nick looks like he's very far away from me.

When we get home, at the threshold of the door, while Nick is looking for his keys, I say, "So you're not going back to Adam's tonight?"

He hesitates. "No. Not tonight."

"Tomorrow night?"

"It's probably a good idea for me to be here right now."

"It was probably a good idea for you to be here last week, as well," I say, but before he can respond the door opens and nearly hits him in the face.

"Oh!" says Leila. "I'm so sorry. I was just—I'm sorry. I'm so sorry. You must be Nick." She sees me and smiles, slightly. "Hi, Alena," she says. Her hair is in a very messy ponytail and she looks tired. "It's nice to meet you, Nick. I'm Leila. From the office. Sorry to hit you in the face with your own door."

"You just missed," says Nick. He's holding his keys in his hand. "You're from the campaign?"

"Yes. I just brought Danny his things from the office." She tucks some loose strands of hair behind her ear. "I'm sorry about all this. It's just terrible. Jake's very—he's very impulsive, I think, sometimes. I was just saying to Danny. I'm just so sorry. I wish there was something—"

"It's this one who's caused the trouble," Nick says, nodding at me. "She should be apologizing to you."

"No, don't," says Leila. "She doesn't have to. You don't have to, Alena." She looks at me very quickly, and then away, back at Nick. "What those two said in those emails," she says. Realizing she's blocking the doorway, she steps around us into the hallway, and we both have to turn around to face her. "They did this to themselves," she says. "Jake did this to himself. And Will. That's what I think."

"That's one perspective, I suppose," says Nick.

"I'm just so sorry that Danny's the one who—you know."

"I'm sure he appreciates that."

"If there's anything I can do."

"Thanks. That's really—thanks. We appreciate it."

We stand awkwardly for a moment, and it looks like she's about to say something else, but Nick says, "It was nice to meet you, Leila."

"Oh," she says. "Yes. It was nice to meet you too. I've got to get back. See what's happening. Will's got to resign. We've got no campaign manager. It's all falling apart, really. I'm going to go as well, I think. I was just telling Danny. Who'd want to stay now?" She looks at me. "It was nice to meet you, Alena. I liked meeting you. Maybe I'll see you again sometime. I'm so sorry about all this."

"It was nice to meet you too," I say, thinking I will probably never see her again but that I wish I could. I feel like we could have been friends.

She gives me a bright, shaky smile and heads back down the hallway to the elevator.

I hear the television before we step inside. Danny is standing in front of the window, looking out. On the coffee table there's a box of his stuff from the office. On the TV, you can tell it's London news, and some man in a suit is talking to a journalist and saying, *"That's exactly right, Nadia, these kinds of leaks can be extremely damaging to any campaign, particularly at such a late stage, and I would be very surprised if we didn't see—"*

"We're home," says Nick.

Danny turns to look at us. "I'm going out," he says. He picks up the remote from the back of the sofa and turns the television off.

"Where?" says Nick.

"Wherever I like."

"I was going to make dinner."

"Danny," I say. "I just want to say that I didn't know—"

"I still don't want to hear it. Have you been following the news all afternoon?"

"We were at the coffee shop," I say in a small voice.

"Have a look. I'm sure you'll be very pleased with yourself."

"I was just going to say that I honestly didn't know that you would lose your job. Honestly."

"Well, I did lose my job, and I'm sure you're both thrilled about it."

"Danny, where are you going?" says Nick.

"I'm going to try and see Will, my *friend*, who also lost his job today, thanks to my baby sister."

Nick clears his throat, puts his keys down on the counter. "There's an extent to which he did this to himself," he says.

Danny's face is blank, exhausted. "There's an extent to which I don't care," he says. "All I ever wanted—"

He breaks off, doesn't finish. He lets the door slam when he leaves.

39

A cutting for the family scrapbook:

Jacob Carlisle has apologized after the publication of an email exchange in which his campaign manager refers to the death of thirty-one-year-old Eduardo Capello as "great timing" for the Carlisle campaign.

Also published was Mr. Carlisle's reply to the email, which reads: "Have to agree."

Mr. Capello was killed in the bombing of a Liverpool Street branch of Tesco in March.

"I am truly sorry for the impression that these private emails do seem to give," said Mr. Carlisle, speaking to BBC Radio 2 on Sunday evening. "The suggestion that Mr. Capello's death is anything other than an enormous tragedy is abhorrent to me."

The initial email came from Will Rofofsky, Jacob Carlisle's thirty-three-year-old campaign manager. Pressed about his own reply, Mr. Carlisle said:

"I have to be honest here and say that I don't remember seeing the email. It may be that I read it very quickly, I dashed off a reply without thinking, without having read it properly. These things can happen in the pressure of a campaign. But I deeply regret if I have given the impression that Mr. Capello's death was anything other than a devastating tragedy for his family."

He went on to reveal that Mr. Rofofsky had resigned.

"These remarks clearly demonstrated a very serious error of judgment. Will's comments, though made in a private email, were highly inappropriate in light of this recent tragedy, and warrant condemnation. I have therefore accepted his resignation this afternoon."

Another member of Carlisle's campaign staff is also said to have resigned this weekend, for undisclosed reasons.

The emails, which first appeared on the website of local newspaper *The Hackney Standard*, will likely be damaging to the Carlisle campaign, which has appealed to voters with a focus on safety and security in the wake of the recent East End bombs.

Hackney Standard editor Mike Feghali commented: "These emails are going to be absolutely devastating for the Carlisle campaign, with just under three weeks to go until election day. There had already been talk that Jacob Carlisle has been trying to use the East End bombs for his own gain, and this will confirm people's worst suspicions about him. Londoners won't stand for this kind of thing."

Briony McIntosh, independent mayoral candidate and former Green Party MP, described the leaked emails as "evidence of the cynical co-option of tragedy that has too often characterized modern politics," commenting that it is "about time this sort of underlying cynicism is exposed and rooted out."

By the middle of the week, none of us can stand the news anymore. It pours with rain for three days and the sky is solid gray. At school, I try to talk to Ollie about how he shouldn't go to Swansea, but my heart's not really in it, and he just gets weird with me, goes moody and sullen like he wishes he had never told me. Teagan is stressed, trying to learn a piece for a recital, and spends every break and lunchtime in the music room.

It turns cold, too, but Danny won't let us put the heating on because he's wound up about paying the bills, so in the evenings when I get home I end up dragging the old space heater that we keep in the bottom of the boiler cupboard into my bedroom and sitting next to it while it blasts hot, dry air that makes my eyes tingle. It smells like burning dust and makes a rattling sound and any time I leave my room I switch it off in case it catches fire.

I try not to leave my room anyway. I sit on the floor next to the heater in thick socks and jeans and multiple sweaters, trying not to listen in on the murmured conversations from the rest of the apartment. Nick talks very quietly and carefully to Danny, like you'd talk to a wild animal or something. I hear my name a few times. I try not to listen. I listen to the rain drumming against the windows and pretend to do homework.

My brother has never been this angry with me before.

There was one time late last spring when I walked to the park after school to try and get a suntan and I forgot to tell anybody where I was and my phone battery died, and when I got home two hours later than usual Danny had called the police and Nick and Nick's parents, and he was so busy yelling at me when I got home that he forgot to call any of those people to tell them that he'd found me. And the time a bunch of stupid boys at elementary school made all these jokes about my brother that I won't bother to repeat and I deliberately tripped one of them over with a jump rope and he broke his arm and Danny got called to the school and he was furious and he said I should always, always, always just walk away from conflict. Which I thought was bad advice even then, and I think that boy just had fragile bones.

Those times were bad, but this is worse.

It's Wednesday evening before they come up with a list of punishments, and they start reeling them off over dinner, which at least gives us all something to talk about, since every other meal this week has happened in silence.

They're confiscating my laptop for two weeks, except when I need it for homework, when I have to use it in the living room so they can see what I'm doing.

I'm not allowed to go to Teagan's house for a month, and I have to come straight home from school every day; I can't stop off anywhere, except the coffee shop if Nick's there.

I have to do the dishes every night for two weeks.

And I have to write an apology letter.

"To who?" I say.

"To whoever you want to apologize to," says Nick.

"What if I don't want to apologize to anybody?"

"Then write a letter explaining that."

"But to who?"

"It's up to you."

This is clearly some weird activity that Nick has found in a parenting book, and anyway, I say, how am I supposed to write a letter without my laptop?

"How about with a *pen*?" says Danny, as if that makes it a totally reasonable idea.

That's about all he says during the whole meal. When he's finished he gets up and clears his plate and goes into his bedroom.

"How about you write the letter to Danny?" says Nick quietly, once Danny has shut the bedroom door.

"I've already said I'm sorry to his face," I point out.

"You could write it in a letter and explain why you did it," he says. "You could tell him what you said to me about your mum."

Mentioning anything to do with her will only make him angrier, and it's amazing to me that Nick doesn't know this.

x x x x x

The same evening, Mike calls.

"You put me in a really difficult position, Lena," he says when I answer the phone. "I sort of wish you hadn't done that."

Back at you, I think about saying.

"Who was your second source?" I say.

"I can't tell you that."

Danny won't speak to him. Mike sighs. "I'll try calling again tomorrow," he says. "You know, I never connected either of you to the leak. All I did was give Danny a head start on it. As a favor. He didn't have to tell everybody at the campaign that it came from you. Losing his job, that's on him as much as anything. I hate to say it. He could have kept his mouth shut and waited this out. I always knew he was too honest to work in politics."

"Mike reckons Danny should've kept his mouth shut," I say to Nick when I hang up.

"Good advice all around," says Nick.

Nobody bothers to say anything about the fact that Nick moved out for a week and has now come back, which, truthfully, makes me kind of angry with him, with both of them, that they can just do these things and then change their minds and not even acknowledge it, like I have nothing to do with any of it.

x x x x x

I have everything to do with all of this. With Nick moving back; with my brother losing his job; with Mike and Danny not speaking; with Jacob Carlisle on the radio, trying to save himself.

I don't think he will be able to save himself.

It makes me wonder what else I could do. What else I'm capable of.

In three years I will be able to vote and I will still have less power than I did at the moment that I saw that email, which was such a tiny thing but look what happened. Maybe I never planned it but it was still something that I did: I did one thing, and then I did another, and then another, and here we are. Here I am. I've screwed a lot of things up but I've still done a thing: I've changed something in the world.

I wonder if this is how she used to feel. Small and sad and angry and powerful all at the same time.

PART FOUR

40

"Is it over yet?" I say.

Zahra snorts. "It may as well be. I just came to get teabags." She looks around the room. "Are you sure you don't want to come upstairs?"

"I'm doing homework."

"You can do homework upstairs. We're not that busy anymore."

"Have they ruled you-know-who out, yet?"

"Voldemort?"

"You know."

"Sister, they ruled him out hours ago. The whole vote counting thing is just a formality. We all know it's Chris Buckley again. Come upstairs. It's nearly eleven."

"I have to pick a poem about London and write an analysis of it." I hold my book up. It's called *London Poems*.

"When's it due?"

"Tomorrow."

"Ouch." She starts scanning the labels of all the boxes stacked up against the walls. We are in the basement of the coffee shop, where Nick keeps stock and the safe and there's one giant fridge for milk. I like it down here. It's clean and quiet and there's a table and chairs which are supposedly for staff meetings, although I happen to know there has never been a staff meeting in all the time the shop has been open. I like it because nobody is allowed down here apart from staff, but I am, because I'm me. "Can you tell your teacher you stayed up late to watch election coverage?" says Zahra. "That's a worthwhile educational thing to have been doing."

"Maybe. She set this two weeks ago, though."

"*Alena*," says Zahra, mock disapproval. "Bad girl." To herself, she murmurs, "Peppermint, peppermint, chamomile, redbush, obviously we can't stock any *normal* tea, oh no . . ."

"Did Danny come in? He said he might."

"Haven't seen him."

"He said he might come for a bit."

"I haven't seen him," says Zahra. "I don't think I'd like watching any of it if I was him."

Upstairs, in the corner of the shop, Nick has hooked up the old television from the back office so people can watch the election coverage if they want. The vote was yesterday but they've only just finished counting, supposedly. Lots of regulars came in and stayed late and drank extra coffee, so Nick will be happy, although he hurt his bad shoulder when he was messing around with the TV and had to go and lie down in the office for half an hour and take a bunch of aspirin.

I put my *London Poems* book down on the table and line it up carefully with my pen and my highlighters. "He's not talking to me. He doesn't want to be around me."

Zahra stops what she's doing and turns, looks at me for a moment. Then she sits down on an upturned crate. She reaches into her pocket and pulls out a packet of chewing gum and offers me a stick. I shake my head.

"I used to fall out with my parents all the time. Especially when I was your age. I can't remember any of it anymore, but we'd all be furious with each other about fifty percent of the time." She makes a face. "God, I wouldn't be fifteen again if you paid me."

"This is different. He's having a breakdown or something. He's grown a beard. He hates beards."

Zahra's face is serious, like she can see I'm trying to be flippant when I don't feel that way at all.

"I heard," she says.

It's true. Since he got fired, Danny hasn't bothered to shave and has hardly left the house—he's just been sitting around at home in silence, reading utility bills and not even listening to any of his *I am seriously depressed* music. He is silent and then will be randomly angry, with me or Nick or anyone who comes near him. I've never seen him like this, and it makes me feel sick and anxious and like I want to fix him but I don't know how. Last night Nick asked if I wanted to spend half-term in Essex with Gerry and Marie, and then, when he saw my face, said, "We just thought you might like to; it's not a command," but it was pretty clear they both would have been happy to get rid of me for a while.

"He hates me."

"That definitely isn't true," says Zahara.

"He lost his job because of me."

"Oh, *whatever*," she says. "He's better off without it. I bet he thanks you for it one day. Jacob Carlisle is a shallow, opportunistic bastard and everybody knows it. He goes whichever way the wind is blowing and he wouldn't know values if you shoved them up his—anyway, he deserved what he got."

"Don't you think Danny's shallow and opportunistic as well, then? He was part of the whole thing. He wrote half of that *strategy for safety* stuff. Don't you think—"

"No," says Zahra. "I don't. I think Danny's probably the most decent person I know."

I stare at her. "Don't you mean Nick?"

"Ha." Zahra starts unwrapping her own stick of gum and laughs. "I love Nick and everything, but he's only Mr. Wonderful because he loves you two so much. He's only good because you two make him that way." She puts her gum in her mouth. "Don't look at me like that," she says. "I know what I'm talking about. Nick was miserable as shit when he was staying with his brother. Danny's got this whole *I'm the lucky one and Nick's been trapped* pathology, and it's bullshit. Nick's the lucky one. He can't get over how lucky he is."

"Nick stands up for things," I say. "Nick has principles. Danny went to work for a politician and he doesn't even care about politics. He doesn't even believe in anything. He just did it because it was a job."

Not totally true. I think Danny did believe some of the *strategy for safety* stuff. All the stuff about fear. It sounded like him.

"So he's not political," Zahra says. "This is not news to anybody. There's more than one way to be a good person, you know?"

I slouch down in my chair, pull the sleeves of my sweater over my hands. I would like to be a good person. I would like to know what this means.

Then Nick's voice calls from the top of the stairs. "Zahra!" He leans his head through the door and looks down at us. "We need teabags up here. I can't lift a whole box right now. Sorry."

She jumps to her feet. "All right, I know," she says. "Teabags are coming."

"Lena. Home time."

"I haven't finished my homework."

"Well, you're out of time. Come on. We're out too late already. Zahra, are you OK to close up?"

She gives him a vague salute as she drags a box out from under two others.

When I go upstairs, there are three people sitting at a corner table and the TV is still on. They are at City Hall, a place I've never been and truthfully, I don't even know where it is. A woman in glasses is standing behind a lectern shuffling papers. Lots of cameras are flashing. Behind her, they are all lined up. Chris Buckley looks relaxed. Briony McIntosh looks cheerful. Jacob Carlisle is standing directly behind the lady at the lectern, so I can't see his face. The others are all men and I can't probably even remember their names.

"As the returning officer," the lady says, "I am able to announce—"

Nick drops a hand on my shoulder. "Home time," he says. So I don't see the rest of it.

× × × × ×

Danny's still up when we get home. He's drinking white wine in front of the TV and the bottle is on the carpet by his feet.

The TV is showing Chris Buckley smiling and shaking hands.

"Happy now?" says Danny when we come in, without looking away from the screen.

Nick drops his keys on the counter, and then he goes and leans over the back of the sofa and kisses Danny on the cheek. Danny doesn't move, eyes fixed on the TV. Nick squeezes the back of his neck as he stands up again.

"We had a lot of people in tonight," Nick says.

"Good for you," Danny says. As Nick goes back to the kitchen to get a glass of water, I see him roll his eyes.

"You should go to bed, Lena," Nick says.

I play with the keyring that's attached to the zipper on my bag. "Can anyone pick me up from school tomorrow?" I say. "I have to bring my art project home and it's really big and I want to keep it flat."

Nick drinks his water slowly. We both know Danny has nowhere to be tomorrow, or any other day.

"I can try," Nick says eventually.

"We've had a few surprises during this election, but there are no surprises at the end of it," says the news presenter on television.

"I can't do it," Danny says, but he's still not looking at either of us.

× × × × ×

The next day, I write the analysis of a London poem on my lunchbreak and hand it in in the afternoon. The poem I choose is called "The Night City." I like the poem but I don't know what to say about it, so I just write that it's *ambiguous*. Half the class is out of school with the flu and Teagan sends me a photo of herself lying in bed with huge dark shadows under her eyes, captioned, *I'm dying*. During afternoon break I phone Ollie, since he's not at school either and who knows if he's run away or been murdered or what.

"I'm at home," he says. "Watching TV. I was throwing up all morning."

"Oh," I say. "All right. Good." I'm standing in the corridor in front of my locker. "Not good, but—"

"I got an email from my dad this morning," Ollie says. His

voice is weird. Maybe he's delirious. I can hear the TV in the background, loud. It sounds like a property show.

"Really?"

"Yeah. He says Aaron was there but he's gone again. He's gone up north or something."

"Oh." A voice on the TV is saying, "*Within the price range but only three bedrooms, which means Jack and Lydia have a decision to make.*" I have to step out of the way as a bunch of sixth graders in their gym clothes come stomping down the hall. "So what are you going to do?" I say.

"I dunno," he says. "Nothing. I can't do anything."

I don't know what to say.

"I've got to go," Ollie says. "Talking makes me feel sick."

Is your mum looking after you? I almost ask, but I stop myself because I'm certain she isn't.

He hangs up before I can say anything else.

× × × × ×

When I get home, there are boxes all over the living room, and for one awful moment I think that somebody is moving out, or that I am moving out and all my stuff has been packed up for me. But it turns out that during the day Danny drove out to the storage locker and came back with all these old boxes of stuff that used to be his. The stuff I always ignore whenever we go there. Piled up around the living room is stuff like his old school reports, and essays he wrote at university, and stupid souvenirs from vacations, like shot glasses from Mexico and other places that I never even knew he'd been to, stuff that he must have gotten during the tiny part of his life in between finishing college and getting me.

"What are you doing with all of this?" I say.

"I'm doing whatever I like with it," he says. "It's mine."

And so that is the end of that conversation.

When Nick gets home, Danny packs it all up again and hauls all the boxes into the bedroom, and Nick watches him with a kind of dread on his face that Danny might be going to keep it all, but he doesn't say anything.

We get Chinese takeout for dinner, sit on the floor with cartons spread out on the coffee table.

"I could do with some help next week," Nick says. "Zahra's going on vacation and we've been getting busy."

Danny doesn't answer.

"I'm asking if you can give me a hand."

"I can't," says Danny. I don't know how he's allowed to get away with saying things as completely untrue as this.

"I can give you a hand," I say, half a vegetable spring roll in my mouth.

"*Please* don't talk with your mouth full," says Nick. "For all our sakes."

I swallow my food and say again, "I can help you."

"Isn't there something you have to do during the week? Some kind of educational thing or something? I forget."

"I meant I can help in the evenings."

"Oh, that's right, *school*. You have to go to *school*."

"I said in the evenings."

"Danny can help."

"Wow," says Danny. "That's amazing how you just completely ignored what I said. Thank you."

"You're welcome."

"It's your business," says Danny. "I don't think I'm obliged to work for you for free."

"Technically you're a partner in it," Nick says. "It's

registered in both our names. And the debt is in both our names too. So. Bad luck."

"Why don't you go and do a law course?" I say to Danny, and immediately regret it. Nick continues eating, looking intently at his fried rice, but Danny stops and looks at me.

"What?" he says.

"I thought—" I clear my throat. "I thought you said you wanted to do that once. When you finished college. Do a law course."

You'd think I'd just said *Why don't you become a drug dealer.* "That was a long time ago," says Danny. "A really, really, really long time ago."

"But couldn't you still—"

"No. I couldn't. For about a hundred reasons."

"Like what?"

"Like we can't afford it. I wouldn't be any good at it and we can't afford it."

"I just thought you wanted to do that one day."

"Yeah, well, there's a lot of things I wanted to do, but life's not like that, as you'll probably find out."

"Danny," says Nick, and Danny doesn't look at him.

For a while there's just the sound of forks scraping plates. I try and change the subject. "There's a big thing at school because the head of French is pregnant and she's not married but everybody says she's having a fling with the head of drama," I say.

"How do they know that?" says Nick.

"It's just a rumor."

"Maybe you should leak it to the press," says Danny.

Nick almost laughs at this, but he chokes it back and coughs for a while. We all finish eating in silence.

41

Sirens keep waking me up that night, and I'll sit up for a moment, confused, and then fall back asleep. There are always sirens around here but most of the time you can't hear them that loud from the fourth floor, and you get used to it anyway.

The sky is gray when I wake up for the last time, half past five and too early for anything, but I can hear voices and movement and I realize that what woke me up was the phone ringing.

I get out of bed and pull on my hoodie over my pajamas and go into the living room.

"What's going on?"

Nick is dressed already but his hair's a mess and his eyes are creased like he just woke up. Danny is barefoot in jeans and still buttoning up his shirt and saying, "For god's sake, just wait a minute."

"I'm going," Nick says.

"*Wait*," says Danny.

"What's going on?" I say again.

"There was a break-in at the shop," Danny says, as Nick is tying his shoelaces.

"How do you know?"

"The police just phoned us."

"What happened?"

"Nick, would you just *wait*," says Danny, grabbing his own shoes from next to the door. He has buttoned his shirt on the wrong buttonholes. "You realize you're too late to actually apprehend anybody, don't you?"

"Do what you like, but I'm going right now."

"I'm *coming*; just let me get *dressed*."

Nick is at the door now, with his hand on the doorknob, looking at Danny impatiently.

"Lena, we're just going to go and see what the damage is," Danny says to me. "We'll be back before breakfast. Or I will, anyway."

Nick has opened the door and is standing in the hallway. "I'm going," he says.

"OK, OK," says Danny. He looks at me. "OK?"

"What am I supposed to do?"

"Don't do anything. Stay here. Go back to bed." Danny follows Nick into the hallway. He is still barefoot and is holding his shoes in his hands.

"Maybe I should go with—"

The door closes before I finish the sentence.

I don't go back to bed. I go back into my room and look out at the gray morning, wishing I'd gone with them and also not, because if it's anything like the last times when the windows got smashed, it'll just make me want to cry, looking at it. Then I go back into the living room and make some tea and put the TV on, early morning cartoons, and curl up under the blanket from the back of the sofa to watch.

I send a message to Nick: *Is the shop OK?* But I hear his phone buzz and see that he's left it lying on the kitchen counter.

Danny gets back before breakfast. He's bought a bottle of milk. Nick isn't with him. "It's bad," he tells me, rubbing his eyes. He sits down next to me, still holding the milk. "It's really bad. They wrecked the place."

My stomach twists. "What does *wrecked* mean?"

"Like." He looks too tired to answer the question. "Just, wrecked."

It could mean anything. Danny calls my room a wreck a lot of the time.

"Where's Nick?"

"He's still talking to the police."

"Is he going to open today?"

"Lena, it's really bad. It's wrecked. He's not going to be able to open for a while."

"A week?"

"Longer than that."

"Why? What did they do?"

"Broke the windows, smashed up both the fridges, ripped up some of the flooring. Then it looks like something caught fire." He shakes his head. "A couple of other shops on the street got broken into too last night. The newsagent and the photocopy place. Ours is the worst. Looks like a bomb hit it." I see him flinch after he says this.

Why would you smash the fridges? I think. *That Nick carefully cleans every morning. Why would you do it?*

"Were they trying to steal something?" I say.

"Like what?" says Danny. "Soy milk?"

"The coffee machines or something. Whatever's in the safe."

"They didn't steal anything. They just trashed it for the sake of it."

I bite my lip. "So it's worse than the other times."

"Yes," Danny says. "It's worse than the other times."

"Oh." I want to ask if I can go and see it but I know Danny will say that no, I have to go to school. "Nick left his phone on the counter," I say, because I don't know what else to say.

"I know. I'm going to go back. I'll take it with me."

We both look at the TV screen for a minute, where there's a cartoon dog dressed as a policeman.

"Why does this keep happening?" I say.

"I don't know, Alena. It's a bad area. We should move."

He always says this. We should move because of the East End Bomber, we should move because of the traffic, because of kids smashing the windows. But we never do. Maybe he's just saying it but he knows there's no point. He thinks bad luck would follow us.

"When I was little and Nick got hit by a car," I say, "Marie told me that he'd used up all our family's bad luck and we wouldn't have any more. Do you remember that?"

He is silent for a while. Then he says, "She was lying."

"Yeah. I'm working that out."

Then he puts the milk down, and puts his elbows on his knees and his head in his hands for a long time, staring at the carpet.

× × × × ×

The sun breaks through the gray morning and then it's warm all day, and at school everyone is lazy and distracted. At lunchtime I sit in the quad and try to read a book, but my mind is empty and loud at the same time, like radio static, and I can't concentrate on anything.

I get off the bus early on the way home and walk to the coffee shop. You can tell from up the street that something's wrong. The windows are boarded up and there's yellow tape across them. The glass from the door is gone but hasn't been boarded so there's just the frame hanging there like a skeleton. It looks like some abandoned place that no one cares about, which makes me feel sick because I care about it more than any other place I know.

I take a picture on my phone anyway, since that's what people do, and then I send it to Teagan, who was still out sick all day. *Coffee shop got smashed up last night*, I write, and then a sad face, and then I delete the sad face because a sad face is for when you fail your homework or something, and this isn't like that. I can't think of anything else to say, but I feel like she should know. The coffee shop is her place too.

Someone has propped the skeleton-door open and when I get close I hesitate, not sure if I should go in, if it's a crime scene or something, but I do. It's very dark inside.

"Lena, you shouldn't really come in here," says Nick from out of the gloom, and I nearly jump out of my skin.

"Oh my *god*," I say. "Don't do that."

He's sitting in the corner of one of the booths, a pen in his mouth and a folder and a bunch of papers on the dusty, blackened table in front of him. I put my bag down on the floor. I got a bunch of horror novels out from the library in the afternoon and my bag is weighed down with them. "Nick," I say. "Nick, this looks horrible."

He doesn't answer. He takes the pen out of his mouth, puts it down, rubs his face with both hands.

"Can you even see what you're doing in here?" I say. "Is it even safe in here?"

I look at the floor. All the broken glass has been swept into neat piles. It makes you realize how much glass there is in a place like this.

"No. It's not. There's glass and nails and god-knows-what everywhere. You should go home."

There's a weird smell, as well, like burned plastic. I look at the counter where the register is and I can see that someone has smashed the blender, which was just new last week.

I wait for Nick to say something reassuring but he doesn't say anything.

"Do you need any help?" I ask him. "Do you want me to do something?"

"No. We can't do anything right now."

"Are you getting people in to fix it? How long do you think it'll be closed?"

I can hear sirens again, somewhere far away. But it's still a warm afternoon, and it's quiet. The brightness outside makes it seem darker in here.

He looks down at the papers in front of him. "The insurance company is only offering a limited payout," he says in a dull voice. "They say we didn't take adequate security precautions."

"Oh." I scuff the toe of my shoe against the floor. "What does that mean?"

"What does it sound like it means? It means I have no idea what I'm going to do."

I don't know what I'm supposed to say to this.

The map of the world that was on the wall has been torn down and I can see a few charred pieces of it on the floor.

I pick up my bag again, twist the strap around my hand. "Maybe I could help with something," I say.

"No. Come on, go home. I'll be back in a while. Go home. Please."

"Nick—"

"*Alena*," he says. "Go home. Please."

I don't recognize the tone in his voice and it makes me take a step back, stare at him, and wait for him to apologize for snapping at me. But he doesn't, so I go.

x x x x x

I walk as slowly as I can toward home, and look at the afternoon sun glinting off all the cars parked down the street. There's a cat sitting on the roof of someone's old Ford and I watch it for a while as it cleans its paws.

For a moment I feel a little bit like breaking something myself, a car window or something, just smashing something that doesn't belong to me so someone else can see how it feels.

It passes through me and then it's gone, that feeling, and then I just feel very tired.

I check my phone. Teagan hasn't replied. Then, scrolling back, I realize I never replied to her last message either, that I haven't bothered to text or call her all day even though she's ill, except to tell her about the shop, to tell her something about me. *I'm a bad friend*, I think. I've turned into a bad friend. I send her a message, *Hope you're feeling better xxx*, and then I remember that I even called Ollie yesterday afternoon, but not her.

We haven't said anything about the fight we had. It's nice to pretend you don't have to, but now I think maybe Teagan is still unhappy with me. It's like being friends with Ollie has thrown us off balance. *The two of you have so much in common all of a sudden*, she said to me. But we don't have anything in common compared to me and her, to all the hundreds of hours we've spent together, sitting around the coffee shop doing nothing.

Opposite our building there's a little communal garden that nobody ever uses unless it's a really hot weekend, when all the art students suddenly turn up and lie in the grass smoking and drinking cheap wine in plastic picnic cups. It's supposed to have a lock where only the residents have the key, but it's been broken for ages, and when I push the gate it swings open. I cross over to the corner that gets all the sun at this time of day and I lie down and put my bag under my head and close my eyes and feel the long grass prickling the backs of my legs, probably staining my white school shirt.

There's a bench in the garden which has a little plaque that says, *In loving memory, Kathleen Clay, 1936-1998. She loved this garden.* Sometimes I think about Kathleen Clay, whoever she was. I think it's nice that somebody would put her name on a bench. I think it would be nice if somebody had done that for my mother. I don't think she's the kind of person who would have gotten sentimental about a garden, but it could say something else. If there was a bench somewhere that said *Heather Kennedy, 1961-2004, ¡Viva la revolución!* or something. If there was some evidence that she existed.

If I don't go home, I wonder how long it will be before somebody notices. Not long, based on previous experience. But I let myself imagine, for a moment, that nobody realizes for hours, and then they can't find me and they have to call the school and then the police, and then they will be sitting in the living room thinking, *How could we not have noticed?* And then I will come through the door and they will both be so happy to see me.

× × × × ×

Maybe I fall asleep, but when I open my eyes, there's a shadow, a black silhouette of a person standing in front of the sun and looking down at me.

"What are you doing out here?" Danny says.

I sit up.

"I wanted to sit in the sun for a while."

"I called you three times. You're supposed to come straight home. Grounded, remember?"

"I went to the coffee shop. I wanted to see what it was like."

"And then?"

"And then I wanted to sit in the sun for a while."

He shakes his head. "You know you can see this garden from our apartment? If you're trying to hide out, you need a better plan." I don't answer. Danny sighs. He steps around me and goes and sits down on the bench, presumably to wait for me to get up. Slowly, I stand up and dust the grass off my school uniform.

"I wasn't trying to hide."

"Whatever, Alena. It's not safe out here on your own, OK? In case you've forgotten, there's still some guy running around leaving bombs all over East London."

It's nearly a month since the last explosion. A lot of people *have* forgotten, it seems like. But not Danny.

"He's not leaving them in parks," I say.

"Not yet," says Danny.

"And it's four o'clock in the afternoon. There's like a hundred people around."

There's actually nobody else around. But there are windows open in all the houses, and you can hear somebody's radio playing.

Danny looks past me across the overgrown grass. There are black shadows under his eyes. He is pale, like me. We will both probably burn in the sun.

I go and sit down next to him.

"The shop looks awful," I say.

"I know. I know. It's really bad."

"Something's wrong with Nick."

"What do you mean?"

"I just saw him in the shop. He's just sitting there in the dark. There's something wrong with him."

"Well, he's upset about it."

"So what are you going to do?"

Don't go back home, I think. *Don't sit on the sofa and watch TV. Don't have a cigarette. Don't open a bottle of wine.*

"What am I going to do? What do you want me to do?"

"He wasn't being like Nick," I say. "He didn't even want to talk to me."

"His business just got trashed. He's entitled to be upset."

"But he doesn't get upset about stuff like this. He just gets on with it. He's supposed to be, like, *Hey, what a great opportunity to get new windows.*"

"He's not indestructible, Lena."

"I know that. I'm not stupid. He got hit by a car, remember? I'm just saying."

"He didn't get hit by a car. He was beaten up."

Danny's not looking at me. He's staring out toward the road, his hands clasped together.

I think that I haven't heard him properly.

"What?" I say.

"He wasn't hit by a car. That was a lie. We lied to you."

"What?" I say again, in a very small voice.

"He got beaten up walking home from work. We lied to you."

I think, *Nick got hit by a car. I remember it happening. I remember everybody saying,* These roads are so dangerous. "What are you talking about?"

"It was just something we said at the time and then it just stuck and we never got around to telling you the truth. We didn't want to upset you."

"So you told me he'd been hit by a car."

"Yeah. I don't know. It seemed better at the time. You were seven years old. It wasn't like—it was hard to explain things to you."

"But that was years ago and you've still never told me."

"Yeah," Danny says. "Well. I'm a terrible parent."

"Why did he get beaten up?" I whisper.

"Because like every other person in my life he's an *idiot* who can't keep his head down and stay out of trouble and stay safe like a normal person. Because he has to have five thousand *stop the war gay pride save the whales* posters in the window of the shop when it's not like *that's* going to attract any unwanted attention when he's locking up in the middle of the night. Because the world is a nasty, careless, randomly violent place. All right?"

He looks at me then, and probably he can see that I'm about to cry or something: there's a painful, hard lump in my throat. *Everybody must have known this but me*, I think. Nick's whole family and Zahra and everybody. That somebody beat him up, which is such an easy thing to say but which I don't even want to think about, except obviously I start imagining it.

"Who was it?" I say. "Who beat him up?"

"It doesn't matter," he says.

"It matters to me. Did they get arrested?"

"No."

"But who—"

"It was three drunk guys coming home from the pub on the corner. They said something to Nick and he couldn't just leave it alone, he couldn't just walk away. He had to stand up for himself, and so they punched him in the face, and they hit his head against a wall and pulled his shoulder out of its socket, and then when he was lying on the ground they stamped on the same shoulder and shattered it. And if you think I should have told you all of that when you were seven years old, then I'm sorry, but I didn't. We were trying to protect you."

There's a weird taste in the back of my mouth like I'm going to be sick. I swallow it back. "And what," I say, hating myself for the way my voice is shaking, "you just now decided you don't want to protect me anymore?"

He looks back at the road, shaking his head again. "Alena," he says, but he doesn't say anything after that.

I wonder if tomorrow I should tell the school counselor that I think I'm living in a *hostile home environment*. We all had to have an interview with her when we first started at the school, and she talked very gently and spoke to us as if she'd known us forever. "Now, Alena," she said, "is everything all right at home? How do you get along with your parents?" I could see she had a form in front of her that told her who my parents were.

I probably sounded defensive when I told her that I got along with them great and that there were no problems and that I wasn't sure this meeting was necessary.

She said, "You were very young when you lost your mother," and I said, "I don't remember it." As if that made it OK.

If she was here, I think, but I don't know what to think after that. For years and years I hardly thought about her at all, and now that's all I can think sometimes. *If she was here.*

42

I come out of my room when Nick gets home later in the evening. It's nearly eight o'clock. Danny is working on his laptop and the kitchen smells of something burning.

I am not supposed to tell Nick that I know he was beaten up until Danny talks to him about it. I hope Danny never talks to him about it. I'd rather pretend not to know.

"Have you been at the shop this whole time?" I say to Nick. I am in my pajamas already, and I've washed my hair so it's hanging damp around my shoulders.

"I had to wait for someone to come and fix the door," he says. He hangs up his jacket and stops and stares at it for a few seconds like he's too tired to move any further. Then he crosses the room and drops his keys on the counter. He picks an apple out of the fruit bowl, turns it around in his hand a few times but doesn't eat it. "Just to warn you, Danny, there's three massive crates of coffee in the back of the car."

"So what else is new?" says Danny.

"Is there any hot chocolate in the car?" I say. The shop gets this powdered hot chocolate with bits of mint in it, and it's good and sometimes Nick will bring some home.

Nick looks at me blankly for a moment. "No. All that stuff's still in the basement."

"I'm looking at the insurance policy again," says Danny. "We might have a better claim if we try and—"

"I really don't have the energy, OK?" Nick says. "Stuff like this keeps happening and there's nothing I can do to stop it. Why even bother?" He puts the apple back in the bowl and leans on the counter next to Danny, rubbing his temples.

I sit on the back of the sofa. What's burning is something in the oven.

"Something's burning," I say.

"What are you talking about?" Danny says.

"Whatever you're cooking. I think it's burning."

Nick says, "I'm talking about the fact that I work at that place seventy hours a week and get nothing in return except for it getting trashed now and again and the police lecturing me about security gates."

I say, "Can't anyone else smell that?"

Danny says, "I burned a lasagne about half an hour ago. It's in the garbage. The oven's off. It's fine."

"Then what are we having for dinner?"

"Nothing. Dinner's in the garbage. We'll all starve."

"We can eat dried coffee grounds if you want," says Nick.

Danny frowns. "Look, if we write to the insurance company and tell them—"

"No," says Nick. "I'm done. I don't want to. I'm sick of it. I'm going to close it down."

I hear myself make an indignant sort of gasping sound, and they both look up at me and I say, in a voice that comes out too high, "You can't do that."

"Yes, I can," says Nick.

"You actually can't," says Danny. "In case you hadn't noticed, the coffee shop is our only source of income."

"I had noticed, funnily enough. And given that most weeks the coffee shop is barely breaking even, maybe it's not the most sustainable—"

"Oh, I'm glad you've finally noticed *that*," says Danny.

"We literally can't *afford* to fix it up. All right? So what do you want me to do? You're not working, we're about two months from the rent going up. Have you seen this letter Alena's got from school about a class trip to Mongolia or some godforsaken place—"

"It's Russia," I say. "It's to Russia. It's to learn about Catherine the Great. It's not till next year."

"Well, wherever." Nick breaks off, glances in my direction, and then gives Danny a pointed look. "We can talk about this later."

"You can talk about it in front of me," I say.

"I don't want to talk about it anymore today. I'm tired. It's been a really long day. I'm tired."

"You can't close it down," I say "You can't. Please. That's not fair."

"It's not *fair*?" says Nick, incredulously. "Not fair to who?"

"I don't know. But you can't. Nick, please."

Nick is shaking his head. "I had to write a check for two hundred pounds this evening to get the door *temporarily* secured. Two hundred pounds. For the *door*. So what do you want me to do? Do you mind not eating for the rest of the month? Do you mind if we sell the car? Do you mind if I get rid of Zahra?"

"I don't mind if you sell the car."

"Who the hell did you get that charged you two hundred pounds?" says Danny. "Did they replace it with a door made of gold?"

Nick glares at him and starts banging around the kitchen making a drink.

I have never once in my life heard Nick talk about money. Danny does, but I never pay any attention because Danny is just worried about everything, all the time. So if Nick is angry with us and angry about writing checks, I know that this is bad, bad, bad. And I think why it's different from the last time the shop got broken into, and I think it's because Danny doesn't have a job. And then, as I'm thinking that, Nick says, as he's cracking ice into a glass, "And maybe if you hadn't gone snooping around other people's emails and getting Danny fired, Lena, by the way, maybe he'd have found another job by now and we'd all be in a better position to deal with this."

He's not looking at me. I can feel my wet hair making the back of my t-shirt wet and I feel cold.

Danny says quietly, "All right, that's enough."

"I don't even want to go on the Russia trip," I say. "I just brought the letter home because I had to. I never even said I wanted to go."

Nick says in a dull voice, "If you want to go, you should be able to go."

"I don't want to go."

Danny looks distracted. "Are they really going to take a class of fifteen-year-olds to Russia? Is that safe?"

"It's not till the end of next year," I say. "I'll be sixteen. Nearly seventeen."

Nick knocks back his drink and makes a face. "God. Now I feel really old," he says.

And he looks it, too. They both do. They both look tired and old and unhappy, even though they're not, really. They're not that old.

And I know, then, that I have made them this way. Their lives are not supposed to be like this. And they know it too.

43

By the time I've decided that I should call my aunt, I'm already out of bed and looking for her phone number. It's written on each of the Christmas cards she's sent me. It's the middle of the night and everything is silent. I have been lying awake for hours and hours and hours.

It takes ages to find it because I'm trying to be quiet and because I thought the cards were all tucked inside the *Collins Encyclopaedia of Family Health 1978* that I keep on top of the wardrobe, and that I sometimes use as a place to save letters and cards. And then every time I get the cards out I also learn about lupus or childhood asthma or something. But the cards aren't there. So then I have to tear my room apart until I finally find them in the shoebox under my bed, where I keep the ribbons that I save from birthday and Christmas presents. And then I check my phone but I know I don't have enough credit to call somewhere like Australia. So I will have to use the landline, which doesn't work from my bedroom. So I tiptoe into the living room and sit on the sofa in the dark and listen carefully to the silence for a while, to make sure that everybody's asleep, and then I dial the number and pretend that my hands aren't shaking a little bit.

It's been twelve years since she's seen me, so we either have a lot to talk about or nothing at all.

When my mother's sister answers, she says "Hello-oh" in a sing-song voice, London with a hint of Aussie, and I say, even though I'm sure that it's her, I say, "Can I speak to Niamh Kennedy, please?"

She is silent for a moment. I must sound very British. Very far away. She says, "This is Niamh. Who is this?"

I say, "This is Alena." And then, stupidly: "Alena. In London." I clear my throat. "Kennedy. Your niece."

There's a sort of gasp that makes the line crackle, and then a little high-pitched squeak, and then a man's voice in the background saying, "Who is it?"

"*Alena*," says Niamh.

I say, "Yes, Alena."

"*Alena.*"

"Yeah."

She says, "Alena, yes, Alena, of course, of course it's you, sweetheart, of course it is."

"I'm just calling—" I say. But I can't finish the sentence because my voice breaks on the last word and I have to put my hand over my mouth or I will cry. That thing when you don't know that you're going to start crying but it just happens. Because of things. Because of everything. I screw my eyes shut and that makes a tear spill out, and then another one. And she goes, "Sweetheart, sweetheart, what is it, has something happened, what is it, where are you, it must be the middle of the night, Alena, sweetheart, Alena, I'm so glad you've called us."

And even as she's talking to me, even as she's being so nice, I think, *Why have you never called* me, *if you care so much?*

She says, "Alena, Alena, what is it? Alena, I'm so glad you've called. What is it, sweetheart?"

I try again. "I'm just calling—" I say, but my voice breaks again and I can't finish the sentence, and she says, "What can we do, what's happened, we can call the police for you, Alena, we can call the police."

And I say, "What?"

She says, "Has your brother done something to you? Where are you? Has he done something to you? Has something happened?"

And then I take a breath and wipe my eyes with my sleeve and see my stupid face in the dark mirror above the TV. And I say, "What?"

She says, "I knew something like this would happen one day. I knew this call would come."

I say, "What?"

She says, "What do you need to tell us? It's OK, Alena, sweetheart. What do you need to tell us? You're so far away. It's going to be OK. What can we do? What has he done?"

"No, it's just—I'm just calling because—"

I don't know why I'm calling. I had thought that I might say to her, *I don't think my brother wants me here anymore.* I had thought that she might say, *Of course he does.* But I know, abruptly, that this is not what she will say, and whatever she will say, I don't want to hear.

She says, "Just what? What is it? Alena, talk to me. I'm your family. What's going on? What has he done?"

But before I can answer, Nick and Danny's bedroom door is opening and Danny is coming out rubbing his eyes, saying, "Lena, it's the middle of the night. Who the hell are you—" And Niamh is saying, "Is that him? Is that him? Alena, do you need to get away? Are you safe?" And I'm thinking, *OK, Danny was right all along, she really is a basket-case,* and Danny is frowning at my tearstained face, and I say, "I'm sorry, I don't think I should have called."

Her voice gets loud and a little hysterical, which means that Danny can hear her perfectly well when she says, "You've done the right thing, Alena, we can get you away, you've done the right thing, let me talk to him, let me talk to him right now, we can get you away, we can call the police."

At the sound of her voice Danny's expression is so aghast that it would be funny, if I didn't have the feeling that I was right in the middle of making a huge mistake.

I say, to anyone who's listening, "Actually, actually, I'm sorry, I'm not sure I should have called," and Danny says, voice like stone, "Give the phone to me."

"That's him, isn't it?" says Niamh, and I realize, from her perspective, he probably does sound vaguely threatening, but the idea that I might be in danger from him, that she thinks she might need to call the police—that would be funny, too, if anything was funny right now.

"You don't need to call the police," I say. "I'm fine. I'm really fine."

Danny says, "Oh my god. Seriously?" He is holding out his hand for the phone, while I sit cross-legged on the sofa, clutching it with a sweaty hand, Niamh's voice in my ear like a siren. I'm not crying anymore.

"Let me talk to him, then. Let me talk to him. Where are you? What time is it? Let me talk to him."

I hold the phone out. "It's Niamh," I say. "It's Mum's sister. I called Niamh," and he gives me a *no kidding* look. "She wants to talk to you."

He takes the phone and he says, "This is Danny." Pause. "Yeah, it's the middle of the night." Pause. "I don't know why she's crying." Pause. "I don't know why. I'm about to ask her." Pause. "No, I'm not *threatening* her, *Jesus*, Niamh, how can you possibly—"

"He's not threatening me," I say loudly, and Danny glares at me, quite threateningly, as it happens.

"You can talk to her any time you want, but right now it's the middle of the night and whatever it is, I think it should wait—" He breaks off. She says something. "Wow," he says. "I think that's the most spectacularly offensive thing you've said to me in my life and the bar was already set pretty high on that—"

Nick stumbles out of their room then, and switches the light on and we all squint and shield our eyes and I can hear Niamh saying, *"I've been waiting for this call for twelve years, I've been waiting for this whole charade—"* and then Danny just hangs up and throws the phone onto the sofa like it's a grenade.

Nick looks at us both. He says, "What now?"

× × × × ×

Ollie told me a while ago that when his brother lived at home and used to get in trouble a lot, the police would sometimes turn up at their door and ask where he was—ask if they could come in, ask when they'd last seen him. And his mother would block the doorway and not let them in, or she'd accuse them of harassment, or she'd threaten to set the dogs on them, even though their only dog is Brandy, who is not exactly what you'd call menacing.

We are in the middle of a stand-off when they come to our door: Danny is standing there running his hand back and forth over his hair and saying, "Why now? Why tonight? Why did you suddenly feel like you needed to—" and I'm saying, "What's wrong with her? Why did she think I was in danger? She didn't even let me *say* anything—" and Nick is saying, "Do you know how much it costs to call Australia? Did you look it up?" which, admittedly, I didn't. Then Nick says he's going to make some tea, and Danny just stands there shaking his head and looking bewildered, and I'm thinking maybe I should just ask if I can still go and stay with Gerry and Marie in Essex.

The kettle takes a long time to boil and the minutes are ticking by in silence and then there's a knock at the door and I think we must have woken up Mrs. Segal next door, but Nick and Danny give each other a sudden, serious look, like they know.

There are two police officers, and they stand in the doorway and say that they are here because a lady in Australia has just called them and said that there is a girl who might be in danger. I am the girl.

I expect Nick and Danny to say, "This is ridiculous, this is outrageous, no, you can't come in," but they don't. They are quiet and polite, and while I stand there saying, "I'm not, I'm not in danger," Danny says, "Yeah, I'm sorry, this is a mistake, I'm sorry, come in."

The policewoman, whose name is Louise, has to take me outside to sit in her car so that I can talk safely. The policeman, whose name is Simon, stays and talks to Nick and Danny in the apartment.

In the car, Louise says, "Right, Alena, I want you to know that nobody is going to make you go back upstairs if you don't want to."

Louise is nice. You can tell she's specially trained. She uses my name a lot. I am sitting in the front of a police car in my pink elephant pajama bottoms and my Converse sneakers and my coat. I say, "This is a really, really horrible mistake. He's my brother. He's my guardian. He has all the documents. He wouldn't hurt me. He wouldn't do anything to me."

"And what about Nick?"

Like Nick would ever hurt anybody. "Nick's a vegetarian," I say. "He won't even drink non-organic milk. Please. This is, like—this is just a huge mistake. We can go back upstairs. Seriously. This is a total mistake."

She says, "How old are you?"

"I'm fifteen."

She says, "Ah," like that explains everything. She says, "When I was fifteen I ran away from home to try and meet Van Halen."

When we go back upstairs, everyone looks tired and pissed off, and Simon and Louise nod at each other, and Louise says, "We're sorry to have had to have bothered you tonight." Nick and Danny have been practicing their *why can't all parents be like us* routine and they're all, "It's fine, no problem, just doing your job, we totally understand, have a good night now," and when the door closes behind them, we all stand in the brightly lit living room and look at each other.

"This year just keeps getting better and better," says Danny. He looks at me. "What did she ask you?"

"Danny," I say. "I didn't—I would never—Niamh—she's crazy. I didn't say *anything* to her, I literally said, *Hello* and she goes, *You're in danger, you're in danger, I'll call the police.*"

"Yeah." Danny sits down on the sofa and leans his head back and looks at the ceiling, and Nick sits down next to him and puts a hand on his knee. "That sounds about right."

There is a car alarm going off somewhere outside.

"Why did you call her?" says Danny. "Why did you want to speak to her?"

All our voices are scratchy because we're so tired.

I don't answer and he sits up straight and looks at me. "You haven't even asked me about her in years."

"There's no point asking you," I say. I feel like crying again. "You wouldn't tell me anything even if I did. You'd just say, *Yeah, she's crazy, don't worry about it.*"

"I think I've been proved right on that point."

Nick snorts.

"I just wanted to speak to her. I just wanted to see what she would say. She's the only family we have."

"See what she would say about what?"

"I don't know. About you. About our mum. About me."

"What about you?" The shadows under his eyes are very dark. He looks a bit like he's going to cry, as well.

Nick looks like he just wants to sleep forever and pretend he never met us.

"She wanted me to live with her. She wanted to take me. After our mum died. She wanted to take me to Australia."

"And what?" Danny says in a shaky voice. "Do you think that would have been better?"

"Do *you* think that would have been better?"

He opens and closes his mouth but doesn't say anything, like he can't form the words or can't remember how to speak. It feels like all the air has been sucked out of the room suddenly, like a vacuum where it's hard to breathe.

"Guys," says Nick. "Guys. Lena. It's three in the morning. You're supposed to be at school tomorrow. This has not been a good night. None of us are in the right state of mind for this conversation. We all need to go to sleep. Seriously."

"I wouldn't have called her if I'd known. I didn't know what she was like. I didn't know what she would do. I didn't know this would happen."

"We know you didn't," says Nick.

"Well, it did happen," says Danny.

"Niamh has had some bad things happen to her," says Nick. "She's quite a damaged person."

"What does that mean?"

"Well, it was her sister who died, and she—"

"It was my *mum*," I choke out. "It was my *mother*."

Then the car alarm has stopped and there is total silence.

Nick says, quietly, "Of course it was. I know it was."

"*Good*," I say. "Because nobody ever acts like she has anything to do with me."

Danny leans forward and rests his forehead on his arms almost as if he's going to be sick.

"Nobody will talk to me about her. Nobody will talk to me. And you lie to me, you both *lie* to me, you lied to me about Nick—"

"Alena," says Nick.

"If nobody even wants me here—" I say around the hard lump in my throat, but I can't finish the sentence. There is no end to this sentence. Nick is already rising up from the chair and saying, "No, no, no, no, Alena, come on, no, no, no—" and Danny is saying, his voice muffled by his sleeve, "There is literally nothing that I can do that will ever be—" and then I start crying for real and Nick is saying, "Come on, it's OK, we're all just tired," and hugging me so I get snot and tears all over his shirt and I think Danny might even be crying too but I don't want to look—and maybe I'm just tired or maybe it is the worst and loneliest that I have ever felt in my life.

We do all go to bed. Sometimes it's the only thing you can do.

Lying in the dark, I have an imaginary conversation with Niamh in my head.

"Maybe I should live with you after all," I say.

"Sweetheart, no," she says. *"Nick and your brother love you too much. But I'll come and visit and tell you all about your mother. I can tell you're just like her. I heard what you did and it's exactly what she would have done. I can tell you're just like her."*

44

When I wake up the next morning, it's nearly eleven o'clock.

I have four messages from Teagan.

Sorry my phone broke!! the first one says, from early this morning.

Then: *using dad's old nokia. so so so upset about the coffee shop. what can I do? can I help clean up? Dad says he could help too.*

The next one is from an hour ago. *Where are you?? Are you ill now too?? I'm back at school*

Then, finally, ten minutes ago, *where are you?????? Xxxxx*

So maybe she isn't angry with me after all.

Be there soon I think, I text her. *I missed you xxxx*

"We thought we'd let you sleep in," says Nick, when I go into the living room. He is sitting at the kitchen counter with a bunch of paperwork. "I can drop you at school in a bit. I'll write you a note."

"Where's Danny?" I say.

"He's gone for a run."

"Where is he really?"

"He's gone for a run. Really."

My eyes are all swollen and my face is blotchy, so I wash my face with cold water and use some of Nick's really expensive moisturizer that smells nice, where it's so fancy you only need a tiny bit of it at a time. I brush my teeth twice to make up for never doing it last night and comb my hair, which is getting long, long, long, and get dressed for school.

In the car, on the way, Nick says, "Are you feeling OK today?"

"Yes," I say, which is sort of true. I am leaning my forehead on the car window, watching the road rolling by. It's good to sleep late, and Nick is being really nice to me. He has written me a note saying I had to go to the dentist, which means I've missed the first two double lessons.

Mostly I feel the way you feel when you've just gotten over being ill, where you're feeling better than you were but still empty and shaky and not like you.

"Are *you* feeling OK?" I say.

"Yes. I'm feeling OK." He pauses. "Thank you."

"Is Danny feeling OK?"

Nick smiles; his eyes crinkle at the corners. "Danny's feeling OK," he says. "Listen. I think he's going to talk to you later. After school." He glances at me, sees my expression. "Not in a bad way. Just, there's some things I think he'd like to talk to you about."

"All right."

"And look. I'll be home later. After that. And then you can talk to me, as well, if you want."

"What does that mean?"

He's quiet for a minute, and then he says, "Talk to Danny first, all right?"

"Am I being sent away?" I say, and it's meant to be a joke but it doesn't really come out right, and Nick doesn't take it as a joke because he says, "Alena, if you ever went anywhere, it would break our hearts."

I can't look at him. I turn the radio on, and we listen to the London traffic report for the rest of the way.

× × × × ×

When I get home, Danny is sitting on the sofa in some kind of trance, and he jumps when I close the door behind me.

"Sorry," I say. And then: "What are you doing?"

He gets up. "Nothing. I don't know."

"Oh. OK."

It's turned into another warm day and the windows are open. You can hear someone vacuuming on the floor below us. Danny looks different and I can't work out why for a moment but then I realize it's because he's shaved his stupid beard off.

We look at each other. "My keyring just broke," I say. I hold up two bits for him to see. It's a red plastic picture frame with a little cut-out photo of me and Teagan in it. The plastic bit that attaches to the chain snapped when I took it out of my bag.

"Give it here," he says. I put my bag down and go over to him, hand him the broken parts.

He looks at it in his hands for a while, but doesn't do anything with it. "So, listen," he says. "Come and sit down with me for a bit."

Waiting for this all day has made it awful. I don't want to sit down. I want to turn and run, go back to school.

"OK," I say carefully. I kick my shoes off and sit down. He sits down next to me and puts the keyring down on the coffee table.

"Did you have a good afternoon?" he says.

"It was all right." There's a silence. "I got a really good grade on an English essay I wrote a few weeks ago."

"Yeah?"

"Uh huh."

"What was the essay about?"

"It was about the theme of power in *Lord of the Flies*."

"Sounds good."

"I liked the book."

"Good. That's really good."

"What did you do today?" I say.

"We've been cleaning up the shop. It looks better. It's looking OK."

"OK."

"I think it's going to be OK. I think a lot of it we might be able to fix up ourselves."

"Really?"

"Yeah. In another life I think I could have been a carpenter." I make a face at him. "So Nick's not going to close it down."

"No," says Danny. "Of course he's not."

"He said he was."

"This is *Nick*."

"He shouldn't have said it then, if he wasn't serious."

"He was serious at the time," Danny says. "He was just upset. He was upset and he was tired. We all feel like that sometimes and we say things we don't mean."

"I don't."

"Well, you're tougher than us, then."

I tug at the hem of my school skirt. "Do you want to talk about me calling Niamh?"

He takes a deep breath. "Not really. But I think we should."

"I'm sorry I called her."

"Yeah. I wish you hadn't."

"So do I."

"Look. I know that I haven't. I haven't been." He stops and picks a pencil up from the coffee table, starts twirling it through his fingers. "I haven't been looking after you very well recently. I was angry but I was—I didn't deal with it properly."

I don't know what to say to this. Even though I think it's true I don't want him to admit it.

"We're actually doing a play of *Lord of the Flies* in English," I say. "Like we're writing it and acting it ourselves. But there's girls in our version. There aren't any in the book."

"OK. That sounds good. Do the girls restore order and harmony to the island?"

"No, they're just as bad as the boys."

"Sounds about right."

We go quiet for a minute.

"If you wanted to talk to Niamh," Danny says, "you should have asked me. You shouldn't be creeping around in the middle of the night."

"It had to be the middle of the night because of the time difference," I say.

"Right."

"And I thought I wouldn't be allowed."

He is still concentrating on the pencil. "It's not like she called you every week and I wouldn't let her talk to you," he says. "She never called. You never asked me if you could call her."

"If I'd asked, would you have let me?"

He doesn't answer.

"She thinks you're a pedophile or something," I say.

"I know she does."

"I'm sorry."

"What for?"

"I don't know. I'm just sorry."

"OK."

"I felt bad about when I was little and she met me and I just screamed at her and tried to hide."

"What are you talking about?"

"You know. I've told you. It's my first memory. Where she's coming toward me, and you're there, and I just screamed."

"Oh," he says. "That."

"Yeah."

"You shouldn't worry about that."

"I'm not anymore. Now I know what she's like."

"She wasn't always. She was all right when I was younger, when she was living in London. She used to take me to football practice. She just didn't think it was right for you to live with two men. And I guess they wanted children. I don't know."

"I don't care. I don't want to speak to her again."

"Well, that's fine too," says Danny.

"So why didn't you let her?"

"Let her what?"

"Take me to live with her and Drew."

He shakes his head. "Why didn't I *let* her? Why would I let her? She hardly knew you. She wanted to take you to *Australia*. She hadn't even spoken to Mum in about two years. Mum hated—would have hated the idea. She'd have killed me."

"Oh."

There's another silence. The vacuum cleaner has stopped.

"Anyway," he says. He coughs. "I have something to say. A few things. I have a few things to say."

The next silence is so long I start to think he's forgotten what he has to say, but eventually he gets it out. "I got Nick to phone Lynn Wallace this morning. And if you'd like to have lunch with her or something—if you'd like to talk to her—you can. You can have lunch next weekend or something. If you want to. She'd like to. So if you want to do that, then you can."

I'm so shocked that for a minute I'm not even sure who Lynn Wallace is and I'm wondering if he means somebody else, somebody I've forgotten about.

"OK, close your mouth, Alena, it's not that amazing."

"But what about—you said she was a bad influence."

"She is. I think she is. But you can decide that for yourself."

I am still gaping, and he looks half amused, in a tired sort of way. "I'm sure she'll have a lot to say. If there's things you want to know I'm sure that she'll tell you when you meet her. If you still want to."

"Yes. I do want to. Yes, please."

"OK. Good."

I am still trying to get my head around this when, for some reason, Danny says, "Look, not to start this again, and I don't know why it still matters, but I want you to know that Will Rofofsky isn't as bad as you think. Maybe he deserved what he got or maybe he didn't, I don't know. But he grew up on some miserable estate in Tottenham and had to work really hard to get to where he was, and he really loved his job. He was my friend. And for the five minutes he met you he liked you; he thought you were funny. And his career is pretty much dead right now. So. I just want you to try and understand that."

I try to think about this but I can't. I can't imagine him existing outside of the campaign office.

"Do you understand that?" Danny says. "People say stupid things all the time. Mike said the East End Bomber was good for newspaper sales. We joked about it. That's how people talk."

I remember it: Mike coming in late to the coffee shop, Danny asking about circulation. That is how people talk sometimes.

But Mike never asked anybody to vote for him for anything, and anyway, it was never just about a joke that Will made. Even I know that. It was the way they acted the whole campaign: using people's fear to make Jacob Carlisle look strong.

"So, about Jacob Carlisle?" I say.

"What about him?"

"Are you going to say he's not as bad as I think?"

Danny sighs and stops twirling the pencil. "You know what? I think I met him a total of about five times. And one of those was when he came here."

"But did you like him?"

He looks like he's thinking about it for a while. "I don't know. Not really. I had a certain amount of—I guess I felt some sympathy for him. Some of his ideas were OK."

"He's a single parent."

"Yeah."

"That makes him sound like a good guy."

"Yeah. That's why we went on about it all the time."

I pull my legs up on the sofa and tuck them under me, facing him.

"I was raised by a single parent, though," he says. "And nobody ever acted like it was something to be proud of."

"People are more impressed by men raising children."

"Tell me about it."

"She didn't seem like a bad influence," I say. "Lynn Wallace. When I met her. She kept saying she had to respect you as a parent."

Danny doesn't answer. He is arranging and rearranging

the pen and the two broken bits of my keyring on the coffee table, lining them all up and then moving them again.

"She said I looked just like you when you were my age."

"I hope you weren't too offended."

"She wanted to say that I looked like Mum but I know I don't."

"No," he says. "You don't, really." Then he says, in a quiet voice like it's costing him a lot just to even think about it, he says, "You're like her in other ways, though."

I look down at the gray weave of the sofa. We have had this sofa forever. We should probably get a new one. I don't even know where it came from, if it came with the apartment or what. "Nick sometimes says I'm just like you," I say.

"Is that when you've done something to annoy him?"

"Yeah, usually."

Danny grins, and then the grin falters a little bit. "You know what? She said from the minute you were born that you were going to be a troublemaker." He looks at me, tries to smile again. "And so you have proved to be."

I can feel the corners of my mouth tugging downwards like I'm going to cry, *again*. I don't know how far I can push it before he shuts down but I decide to try my luck. "Do you think—if she was still alive, do you think she'd like me?"

He looks at me again. He is very still. "Do I think she'd like you?"

"Like, do you think she'd like me as a person?"

"Lena. She'd be crazy about you. She'd be absolutely crazy about you. She was, already."

I swallow. It hurts, a bit. "I don't remember her at all. I pretend that I do sometimes but I don't."

"I know you don't. It's OK. I know you don't."

"It's not OK."

"I mean it's not your fault."

"It is my fault," I say. "I should remember. I want to remember her. We had this whole life together for three whole years—"

"Alena," Danny says. "There's something I have to tell you."

The tone of his voice shuts me up, turns the room silent. He's turned toward the blank television screen and he's looking at our dark reflections.

"But first." He stops, clears his throat. "First. What I'm about to tell you. I want you to know that Nick never wanted to lie to you. That was my choice. I made him do it and he hates it; he's hated it every single day since it started. You should know that. You shouldn't be angry with him."

I shift a little bit further away from him. My mouth has gone dry. "What are you talking about?" I say.

"There's something I have to tell you. A lot of things. It's time for me to tell you some things."

I see, clearly, that what he is going to tell me is not what I have been waiting to hear. *Don't*, I think, *don't, don't, don't*, and he says, "I don't really know where to start, so I'm just going to start anywhere, all right?"

And I hear myself say, "All right," and then he starts.

PART FIVE

45

He was on the side of the road when she called him, sitting on the car hood waiting for a tow-truck.

She said, "Where are you?" and he said, "I'm on the side of the road waiting for the AA." He told her that he thought it was the hydraulics, not that he even knew what this meant, but he used to try and impress her with things like that. He was in his first year at college and he was driving home for the weekend.

She told him he should get away from the road, that it was dangerous to wait with the car in case a truck lost control and veered into the hard shoulder and crushed him to death. This is what she said to him. She said, "Danny, for god's sake. Put your hazard lights on and get away from the road."

He said, "Why are you calling me?"

She said, "Don't overreact. I've been arrested. Can you call Dionne for me?"

Dionne was one of her friends. She was a lawyer.

He said, "What have you been arrested for now?" because it wasn't the first time, and she said, "Assault." He said, "Mum. Mum. Mum. I thought it was going to be a peaceful protest."

She said, "It escalated. I don't have time to discuss this now, Danny. Sweetheart, can you call Dionne at her office for me, please?"

He said, "What did you do?"

She said, "Look, it shouldn't have happened but they blocked our route and they had horses and god-knows-what. There was a lot of shoving and fighting. There was a policeman. It was the heat of the moment. There was a lot of pushing and shoving and I hit him."

Danny said, "Are they going to charge you with something?"

There was a pause on the line and then she said, "Danny, I had an empty Appletise bottle. It was glass. It broke. I don't even know why I was holding it. I hit him with a glass bottle."

He said, "Please tell me you're joking."

"I don't even know why I was holding it, Danny, honestly."

"Mum."

She said, "I know. I know." She said, "If you put the news on, you'll see what's happening. There's been a lot of arrests."

He said, "I can't put the news on; I'm standing on the side of the road waiting to be hit by a truck."

What he didn't know then but he found out when he managed to see her later was that she also got pushed to the ground and hit her head on the pavement. A doctor had seen her at the police station. He said that she should be OK but if she had any headaches or dizziness or sickness she should go to the hospital and have an MRI. But she didn't, so she didn't.

Four years later, Danny says, nobody remembered this detail but him, that she'd hit her head, and when he brought it up, people looked at him with pity and said, *I'm sure that had nothing to do with—*

But she had seemed wrong, he remembers, just a little out of it for a few days after. A strange, glassy look in her eyes.

It had been Lynn's march. She'd organized it, drawn up the route, notified the press, invited all the big anti-war groups. "So why didn't *you* get arrested?" Danny asked her, when he saw her.

"I was marching in a different section," she said. "There's no point blaming me for this, Danny."

But he did, he did, he does. Heather had been telling him for months that she was going to stop going on demonstrations. She was going to start lobbying her local representative, campaigning from home. She was getting too old for demonstrations, she said. But it had been Lynn's march, and Lynn was her best friend. Lynn, who was marching in a different section.

After Heather was bailed out and came home, he took two weeks off college to stay with her, told his friends he was sick with the flu, sat around watching TV while she and Lynn coordinated a letter-writing campaign from the kitchen table. Danny and Lynn weren't talking, but Heather found a lawyer who everyone said specialized in this kind of thing, and said to Danny, "Everything will be fine, everything will be fine," over and over again, light as air, like an incantation. But he overheard her talking to Lynn, saying, "I don't have the heart for this fight; I'm too old for this. I have a grown-up son; that's how old I am." Lynn saying, "The fight's here whether you've got the heart for it or not."

Presumably, Danny thought, he was supposed to be the grown-up son.

Still, she made him dinner every evening and read all the essays he'd written that semester, kept telling him how wonderful they were.

When they set a date for her court case it seemed so far away that for a while Danny managed to pretend the whole thing had never happened. There was a whole spring and summer in between, and after he'd finished his exams Danny came home and got a summer job in the local cinema and Heather went back to work at the university library, started going out a lot in the evenings wearing her favorite silver earrings, obviously seeing somebody who she didn't want to introduce, which was fine with Danny because he was still attached to her last boyfriend, Simon the gardener, who'd been a reassuringly boring person with a huge collection of early Bob Dylan bootlegs that he'd make Danny copies of on tape. "Your mother's a bit of a free spirit, isn't she?" Simon used to say admiringly, which Danny would agree with while privately thinking that this was a bit of a cliché. And while Simon was essentially a gentle, melancholy hippie kind of guy, Heather was an altogether tougher person: flintier, more resilient, more joyful. Goodbye, Simon.

"Does whoever you're going out with know about your life of crime?" Danny said to her one evening in May as she was on her way out.

"No, and he doesn't know about my smart-aleck son either, thank god," she said, kissing him on the cheek as she passed him on the way to the door.

× × × × ×

It was almost a normal summer. Up until the night that Heather told Danny over dinner that the lawyer had told her to prepare for the worst. Her court date was coming up.

He said, "What does 'prepare for the worst' mean?"

"It means she says I should prepare for a prison sentence."

He put down his knife and fork and stared at her. She looked back at him. She was very composed. He was not. He said, "They can't do that. Mum, they can't do that. Come on."

She said, "And there's something else I have to tell you."

"They can't do that. Are you serious?"

"Danny."

"A prison sentence for, like, a couple of months?"

She said, "Danny, there's something else I have to tell you."

× × × × ×

At first Danny thought she might have done it on purpose, some wild scheme to keep her out of prison, like maybe she thought they wouldn't lock up a pregnant woman. And even if in his heart he knew this couldn't be true, he heard himself saying over and over again, "How could you be so irresponsible? How could you be so irresponsible? How could you be so irresponsible?" like he was the parent and not her.

He said, "How could this have happened? How did this happen?" and she raised an eyebrow and said, "Well, the usual way, I suppose," and he said, "But who—" and she said, "I'm not going to tell you that. It doesn't matter. He's not going to be involved."

The fact that she was pregnant and wouldn't tell him who the father was and wouldn't tell him anything except to say that it was an accident—a surprise—and that she'd decided to keep it—the fact that she was going to have a *baby* at least gave some kind of clarity to his new and permanent state of anger and anxiety, and saying, "How could you do this to a baby?" stopped him from saying, "How could you do this to me?" which is what he really felt when he thought about her going to prison, but which he thought sounded childish and selfish and petulant. He was struck with wild and desperate ideas about maybe she should flee the country, go and join her sister in Australia, and he called the lawyer himself one evening and said, "Can they really send somebody to prison if they're pregnant?" and the lawyer said *Yes, they can, they do it all the time.*

× × × × ×

Heather was an organized person, gritty and essentially optimistic, and she already had lists and plans and *ways-this-will-work*. She told him that if she was still in prison when she had the baby she would apply for a place in a mother-and-baby unit where they'd let her keep it for eighteen months and by that time she'd probably be released anyway.

Danny said, "For god's sake, Mum, you can't raise a baby in a prison. It'll end with some kind of serious psychological—"

She said, "Danny, this is what I'm going to do," and that was the end of it. Danny's friends had always thought he was lucky, that his mum was some kind of flake who would let him do what he wanted: a single mother with wild, curly hair and right-on politics who wore ethically-made boots and charity-shop skirts to work. *I bet she'd let you get high at home*, his friend Toby said to him once, *I bet she'd buy you beer*, but Toby was kind of an idiot, and wrong. She was more serious than people realized, and stricter, and ever since Danny could remember, she'd always insisted on knowing where he was at all times, even if where *she* was was chained to a soon-to-be-demolished school, or something. It was the seriousness that used to make him nervous, the way she regarded the world as a thing that could be changed, and had to be.

Still, privately, he thought that they wouldn't really send her to prison, that they couldn't, and that even if they did, it would be for a couple of months and she'd be released before the baby was even born and they'd all look back on the experience as character-forming.

She went to prison. She got six years. It was the maximum possible sentence. They said she would serve half of it. She had a lot of friends in the courtroom and everybody cried, apart from Danny, who says he remembered it like he was having an out-of-body experience; he had tunnel vision and he couldn't feel his hands. The policeman was there with his scarred face and Danny couldn't look at him.

× × × × ×

As soon as she got to prison they told her that because of the length of her sentence she would have to arrange for the baby to be taken care of on the outside, or it would be placed in foster care. She told him this in a phone call from the prison. She sounded far away and tearful. There was a weird clicking on the line, the calls being monitored.

"They'll send us to a mother-and-baby unit," she said. "But that's only for eighteen months and they might not even let me keep her that long. They might take her away sooner."

Danny was at home alone, eating soup at the kitchen table. The day before, knowing she was going to prison, she'd made a vegetable soup and left it in the fridge so he'd have something to eat when he came home without her.

Danny said, "Mum, they won't. They can't do that."

She said, "Somebody needs to be ready to take care of her. Once eighteen months is up. Maybe even less than that. Do you understand? Somebody needs to be ready to take care of her until I'm released."

He didn't know what to say. He said, "How do you know it's a girl?"

She said, "I just have a feeling."

"You thought that I was going to be a girl as well, though," he said.

She said, "Well, I'm sure I can't be wrong twice," and then an automated voice on the prison phone told them they had thirty seconds left.

× × × × ×

She wasn't wrong twice.

Four and a half months later Danny got a phone call on a Wednesday afternoon from a prison officer to tell him that his sister had been born. Three weeks premature, but she was fine. He was waiting to go into a lecture. He ditched the lecture and borrowed gas money from his friend Lisa and drove to the hospital where she'd been taken. It was in central London and he got stuck in rush-hour traffic and couldn't find anywhere to park and ended up leaving the car on a side road where he was probably going to get ticketed, and when he got there and found the right ward he had to argue with a prison officer before anyone would let him into the room and when they did she had one wrist handcuffed to the bed and he said, "Are you fucking joking?"

Heather said, "Danny, behave." She looked terrible, her hair scraped back and a hospital gown that didn't fit.

He said, "Where's the baby? Where's the baby? Where have they taken her?"

"They're doing some tests," said the prison officer, and Danny ignored him.

Heather said, "They should have brought her back by now. Can you go and find her? They took her an hour ago—"

And Danny ran, actually ran, out of the room and down

the corridor because he had a vision of his new baby sister being taken away by strangers before he'd even seen her, and when he found a nurse, he could hear the panic in his voice as he tried to explain and the nurse eventually realized who he was and took his hand and led him to a room with four or five babies and pointed at the one that was his sister and said, "Here you go, she's absolutely fine, she's right as rain, this one," which was a phrase that stuck with him and he still thinks it sometimes: when he looks at me, he thinks *right as rain, this one*, and remembers that nurse.

× × × × ×

"They're sending us back to the mother-and-baby unit at Holloway," Heather said later. "But I'm getting a bad feeling. The things they've been saying. I don't know how long they'll let me keep her. I don't think they'll let me keep her for the full eighteen months. That's the feeling I get."

Uncuffed, finally, she was holding the baby, who was asleep. A prison officer was sitting on the other side of the bed, reading a newspaper. They were talking in quiet voices, like he wouldn't be able to hear.

He didn't want to say it, but Danny didn't think the baby should be in prison all that time anyway—more than a year— not that she'd know any better, but it seemed wrong; it seemed like a bad start to a person's life.

"So somebody needs to be ready to look after her until I get home," Heather said, her voice a little shaky but steel in her eyes. "Just until I get home. If they take her into foster care they might never give her back. Do you understand what I'm saying, Danny? Somebody needs to be ready. It might be only a few months she can stay with me."

"I could do it," he heard himself saying. "Do you think I could do it?"

"Yes," she said. "I think you could do it."

× × × × ×

They agreed that he could do it. He didn't think that he could do it.

Eventually they told him he had to leave. Walking out of the hospital at nearly eleven o'clock, exhausted but wide awake, he started to feel like he was having a panic attack. His heart was racing and he was wheezing slightly, like his childhood asthma was kicking back in. It was a cold night but his palms were sweating. His eyes felt sandblasted open. He couldn't remember where he'd left the car. He walked endlessly around the side streets that surrounded the hospital and couldn't find it, started to feel like he was going crazy, like he couldn't breathe properly. He walked past the same half-deserted bar three times until a woman standing outside smoking asked him if he was lost and for some reason he didn't understand her and she had to repeat the question until he said, "No, no, I'm fine," and then he walked into the bar, thinking maybe he just needed a drink.

Inside, it was very hot and bright and he realized in an instant that he didn't have any money; he'd left his wallet in the car. He was stopped in the doorway and a bartender came up to him and said something, and he didn't understand him either, and so he sat down in the nearest chair and knew, in an abstract kind of way, that he was hyperventilating. Gray spots were starting to drift in front of his vision and he could tell that people were staring at him.

Then somebody was sitting next to him, the bartender,

and they had their hand on his back, between his shoulders, and they pushed his head down toward his knees and said, "All right, just breathe," and held him there for a few seconds. Then they pressed a glass of water into his hand and he downed the whole glass in a few seconds, put his head down again, waited for the gray spots to recede. The guy's voice was distant but reassuring. He was saying to somebody, "No, I think he's fine. Let's give him another glass of water."

"Are you with someone?" said the guy. "Do you want me to call someone for you?"

Danny did: he wanted to say, *Yes, call my mum, my dad, my brother, my grandma*, but there wasn't anybody, anywhere, who would come. He just shook his head and drank the second glass of water when it came, and put his elbows on his knees and his face in his hands and when he was able to speak he said, "Sorry. This is weird. I'm sorry."

"Don't worry," said the guy mildly. "No problem. You're fine."

"God. Sorry."

"Do you want a drink or something? An actual drink?"

"I don't have any money."

"You weren't just mugged or something, were you?"

"No, I just—"

"It's all right. I just finished my shift. You can have one of my free drinks."

The guy got him a whiskey and Coke and had one himself. Danny was too exhausted to be embarrassed. The guy said, "So are you just having a bad day or what?"

"My mum had a baby today," Danny said. "I have a baby sister."

And the guy said, "Really? Congratulations."

Danny said, "Yeah. No. It's complicated."

The guy said, "In what way?"

And he had that kind of manner—that kind of vibe some people have where you just kind of want to tell them everything—so Danny told him everything, and the guy just listened and nodded, and at the end he said, "That does sound complicated." And then he said, "I guess the good way to look at it is that your sister probably won't remember any of it. This probably won't be part of her life at all."

And Danny realized that yes, that was true. He could make that be true.

He could look after the baby until Heather got out, and by the time she was four or five she probably wouldn't remember anything about it.

He'd done a year and a half of college. He could still finish his second year. Then he could take a year off. Three years, if necessary. And then as soon as Heather was home he would go back and finish. And then he'd go on to law school, like he'd been planning.

It was possible that things would be OK. The baby didn't even have to know.

The guy finished his drink. They were about the same age, Danny guessed, except he had that kind of zen-like maturity some people have, which was fine, because Danny felt like he'd aged about ten years in the last few months and other people his own age now mostly seemed impossibly young.

The guy was wearing a white shirt, Danny remembers, with sharp lines like it was freshly ironed, even though he'd been working in a hot bar all night. There was a cleanness about him. He finished his drink and said, "I'm Nick, by the way."

Danny never finished his second year of college. He lasted six more weeks and then he dropped out.

They let her keep the baby for nearly five months in the end, but in that time he spent every weekend either visiting them in prison or trying to find an apartment to rent that the social worker would think was an appropriate place for a baby, which was a nightmare, even though Danny was pretty much like, anywhere is still more appropriate than a *prison*, but the social worker didn't see it that way. So he didn't turn in any of his spring semester essays and his advisor told him there was no point taking any of his summer exams because he was so far behind.

Lynn, by her own admission, knew nothing about babies either, but Heather begged her to help and so Danny and Lynn called a temporary truce to the fight they'd been in ever since the first arrest, and she helped him buy baby things and set up the apartment and was relatively cheerful while Danny snapped at her about everything.

Danny's heart sank a little when Lynn was introduced to Nick and the two of them hit it off and started talking about viable alternatives to capitalism and the future of nuclear disarmament, but he didn't say anything because he was still thinking that any minute Nick was going to realize what he'd gotten himself into and leave.

Nick was useful because he hit it off with everybody, including the social worker who—until that point—had seemed less than convinced that Danny was going to be an appropriate caregiver for baby Alena. They'd only been seeing each other a few months but Nick seemed happy enough to be presented to various parties as a sensible guy with a savings account and a straightforward manner, all of which Danny felt reflected back on him in some useful way. It turned out Nick only worked in the bar in the evenings, and the rest of the time he was manager of an organic food shop in Camden. He had a second job because he was saving money; he wanted to start his own business. He thought maybe a coffee shop.

Nick had two younger brothers and was good with kids, he said, and he'd talk about Heather being in prison like she was Nelson Mandela or something, which was nice, because most of the time Danny was still so angry with her he could hardly think about it. When Nick talked about police brutality and the right to protest, Danny felt something loosen in his chest, felt like he could breathe more easily. Nick had a way of casting out the shame of it all, of finding the good in things.

× × × × ×

"You met me at a very strange time in my life," Danny used to say to him sometimes. It was the last line from *Fight Club* and they both thought it was funny. But every now and then, Nick would say, "I met you exactly when I was supposed to meet you," or something totally straightfaced and serious like that, and Danny would roll his eyes because he wasn't the romantic one in the relationship, but secretly he'd think, *Yes, yes, yes* and *exactly* and think that maybe there was a pretty good chance that they were going to be together for a really long time—although, honestly, they were young enough that a *really long time* was like a year or two, and it was hard to ever think much beyond that. It was hard to really get his head around the fact that one night he'd walked into a bar having a panic attack and six months later he was living with his boyfriend and was totally one hundred percent responsible for a baby. He was twenty years old. Sometimes he'd wake up in the middle of the night and hear me crying and not know where he was.

× × × × ×

The first time Niamh showed up was right after Danny brought me home from the prison where I spent the first five months of my life. Danny hadn't seen her in years and Nick was suspicious right away, but she bought me presents and was mostly polite and Danny thought maybe she just wanted to help.

Danny had loved Niamh when he was a little boy. But when he was a teenager, she'd apparently said to Heather one day, while they were drinking coffee and Danny was at school, "Do you think Danny's sort of normal, Heather? With girls I mean?" and Heather had laughed and said that no, she did not think that Danny was normal with girls, and Niamh had retreated, after that, from both of them.

But Danny had tried to forgive her and to remember that Niamh was screwed up because she'd had a husband who'd left her three weeks after they got married, and when she moved to Australia with her new husband, Drew—"A fascist," Heather said at the time, "that's all I have to say about him"—Danny had continued to send polite Christmas and birthday cards, and occasionally he'd get one back.

But Heather, calling him on the prison phone, sounded genuinely panicked for almost the first time when he told her that Niamh was visiting. She said, "Danny, be careful. Find out what she wants. She'll want to take Alena back with her. I know she will."

Danny said, "I don't know, she seems like she just kind of wants to help out—"

"She thinks I was a bad mother to you. That's why she thinks she can do this."

"Since when does she think you were a bad mother?" said Danny. Only he was allowed to think that she'd been a bad mother, and even then he was capable of admitting that she'd plainly adored him every day of his life and there had always been breakfasts, lunches, dinners, and birthday parties and clean clothes, so really.

"Just please tell me that you'll be careful, Danny. Find out what she's doing here."

"I honestly think she just wants to help," said Danny.

× × × × ×

She did not just want to help.

Danny still doesn't want to talk about everything that happened, other than to say that before she finally went home, there were lawyers and fights and tears and calls to the police and Nick losing his cool for the first time Danny had ever seen, and if Danny had maybe had a couple of doubts himself about looking after me, he was at least convinced that he'd be a better parent than Niamh or Drew, which was reassuring, in a weird way.

She never visited Heather in prison. She sent Danny an email before she got on a plane back to Australia: "*I hope neither of you ever tell Alena that she started her life in a prison,*" it said. "*I hope she never knows.*"

It was the only thing they ever agreed on. The conviction had been in the local newspaper but it never showed up online— he searched at the time, every couple of weeks, but nothing ever appeared, and he figured that as soon as Heather got out she'd want to forget it ever happened. Niamh was right about that one thing: there was no reason I ever needed to know.

Mike had given him a job at the *Hackney Standard* and a lot of the time Danny was able to work from home, and he got me a place in a pretty good day care and at some point he moved out of the apartment he'd rented and Nick and him rented an apartment together. Nick's parents made it clear that they thought the whole arrangement was crazy and that neither of them was remotely qualified to be looking after a baby, but in the end, they were distracted and charmed by the sudden introduction of a de facto grandchild into their lives and they were always making excuses to come into London to visit. And there would be invitations to family barbecues, and Nick's brothers would be there with their girlfriends, and cousins and aunts and uncles and grandparents, and Danny would watch them all, feeling like he was behind a glass screen, and he'd be thinking, *This must be what a family looks like*, and then he'd miss his mum so much he could hardly breathe and he'd think, *Two years, one year, six months*, or however long it was until she was coming home.

× × × × ×

Except.

When it got closer. Once she started to talk about it. When, in the visitors' room, she said to Danny, "I've been thinking about where Alena and I are going to live." Some treacherous, dark part of him thought, *Maybe she should stay with me*. Because I was happy, after all: a happy little kid who liked stickers and coloring and was fiercely attached to Nick, and it was hard to see how it was going to work, just passing me over to somebody else. They'd already tried to introduce the idea to me—that, at some point, my mum was coming back for me and I'd live with her. But they'd realized they were just scaring me, that I understood it as some kind of threat, that I'd have nightmares about somebody coming to take me away, so they'd mostly shut up about it because they didn't know what else to do.

But how could he say that to Heather, whose guiding light for the last three years had been getting home to her daughter? And, anyway, Danny had plans. One night a few weeks before, while Nick was asleep, he'd dug out his first-year college transcripts and emailed his old advisor to ask whether he could come back in and finish his second year or if maybe he should start again from scratch, and was there maybe any funding that he could apply for? And the email his advisor sent back had been so warm and enthusiastic that Danny had read it three times a day for like a week, and then felt guilty every time he saw me and told himself he wouldn't do it, he wouldn't go, he'd stay with me and he'd tell Heather that it wasn't fair to uproot me at this age. Then he'd read the email again and see himself in the campus library, in the campus bar, going to lectures, coming home on weekends and staying out late with Nick in Soho bars, with nobody waiting for them to get home, not that Nick ever went to Soho bars but still, but still.

The most he could bring himself to say to her was that he thought they needed to take it slowly. Because I hardly knew her. I knew Nick and Danny, and I cried pretty much every time I was taken to visit her in prison, even though there was a family-friendly visitors' center with toys and pictures on the wall. I still screamed, every time, Danny tells me, like I just had a bad vibe about the whole place, and he totally sympathized. The visits all ended with everybody fraught and upset and close to tears.

"As long as it takes, Danny," Heather said. "I know it's not going to happen right away. I've got my own life to rebuild, anyway. I know I can't take her back right away."

Danny nodded, couldn't speak. He couldn't see a way through it that wasn't going to hurt somebody.

In less than four months it wouldn't matter.

x x x x x

It was three o'clock in the afternoon and Danny was at work. My day care called him to say that nobody had come to pick me up. I was three. He could hear me talking in the background. And Danny was furious because they'd arranged it so carefully: that Heather would pick me up and take me back to her house for a few hours, and Danny would come later to collect me, and if it went well, then maybe she could start to do it once, twice, maybe three times a week, slowly, slowly, just to see how I reacted. She'd been out of prison for three and a half weeks.

Her cell phone just went to voicemail because she'd probably forgotten to charge it, and Danny honestly felt like she'd forgotten how to live in the real world while she was in prison. So he had to leave work early to come and get me. Which he did. Then he took me to her house to see if she was there.

Then he went into the kitchen and she was lying on the floor.

He took me to the neighbors' house and they called an ambulance. He went back into the kitchen. Then he went out again and went into the back yard and sat down on the grass, thinking he was going to be sick. He went back inside. An ambulance came. It was Wednesday afternoon. He called Nick. Nick did everything else that day, as far as Danny can remember. He remembers that there was still a pot of tea on the kitchen counter and nobody thought to pour it out until a week later.

x x x x x

There's no way to prove that it was because she hit her head on the ground four years before at an anti-war protest, but Danny says it was. He says to me, "I know that it was, so don't ask me to explain it to you; I just know that it was."

x x x x x

Niamh and Drew came to the funeral. Made a scene. Standing outside the funeral home, they said they were going to start legal proceedings, that they wanted to take me to Australia. Then Nick threatened to call the police and they left. Lynn was there and said she could help, that she knew a lot of lawyers herself, and Danny said he didn't want her help; said none of this would have happened without her, and soon they were shouting at each other, both in tears, and someone from the funeral home had to come and intervene.

x x x x x

Niamh wrote to Danny, afterwards, saying they would consider relocating to London if Danny would give custody of me to her and Drew. He never replied.

x x x x x

I'd still have the nightmares, sometimes, after she died. Somebody was going to take me away. *No, no, no*, they'd say. *Nobody's going to take you away.*

And by that time it was true. She wasn't coming back for me.

And I had that feeling for years, for ages even after she was gone, that fear.

It was her I was afraid of. It was her I was screaming at, not Niamh. My only memory, stubborn as a weed, her coming toward me, me screaming. My mother, who loved me.

I was with her in prison for five months. I never lived with her again.

46

He tells me the whole story without looking at me. It's probably the longest he's ever spoken for, and when he stops, the clock is still ticking; our reflections in the TV are exactly the same, the sun is still bright outside, and everything about my life is different because what I thought I'd lost it turns out I never had.

"Alena," Danny says, in the new silence. His voice has gotten hoarse. "Do you want to say something?"

Take it back, I want to say. *Take the whole thing back. This is not what I was waiting for.*

I thought I was getting closer and now she is further away than ever.

"No," I say. "I don't want to say anything." I get up and go to my room, close the door. I lie down in bed, pull the covers over my head, lie there, just breathing, until it starts to feel like I'm suffocating.

Nick comes home later, and knocks on my door. I'm still in bed.

"Lena," he says gently, opening the door just a little. "Do you want to talk?"

I tell him no.

"OK," he says, and goes again.

It unfolds in my mind in little pieces, the meaning of it, all the people who have lied. Not just Danny, but Nick, who I always thought never lied to anyone, and Nick's parents, too, and Mike, and Mike's wife, and Zahra, maybe, as well. The effort of it all, just so I wouldn't know—what? What a troublemaker she was? What a bad person?

I roll over, take my Greenham Common postcard from where it's tucked into a book next to my bed, the four pieces stuck back together with Scotch tape. I look at her face. Nineteen, fist raised, shouting at the sky. She would never even know me. Not even for a few years. We would never know each other.

× × × × ×

After a while, I get out of bed, change into jeans and a shirt and flip-flops, leave my rumpled school uniform lying in a pile on the floor. I tie my hair in a ponytail and go into the living room. Nick is doing paperwork at the kitchen counter and Danny is leaning next to him with a cup of coffee. My room, the apartment, the three of us: everything feels small and claustrophobic, locked-in.

They both look up, look guilty, look at me like I've caught them doing something wrong.

I tell them that I'm going out.

They glance at each other, back at me, not sure what's going on. "Where are you going?" Danny says.

"The cinema," I say, improvising, and they look at each other again, and back at me again, hesitant, uncertain, and then say OK and Nick gives me a twenty-pound note from his wallet.

"That's for the cinema," Danny says. "That's like—don't go and buy junk food in the supermarket. Buy it at the cinema. All right? No supermarkets."

In the elevator on the way down I call Teagan, but the phone goes straight to voicemail and I wonder if her dad's crappy Nokia phone has died now too. I send her a message anyway, *call me asap?* but then I remember she was supposed to be going to a recital with her parents this evening.

There's no reply, so as I step out onto the street into the warm evening, I text Ollie: *Cinema or something? I have money.*

47

YES, he texts back. *Come here first?*

I get the bus to his house. I am noticing weird details: the scratches on the windows and the lining of the woman's coat in front of me, like I can only concentrate on little things. I need to get my hair cut. One of my flip-flops is nearly broken.

They've made me a liar as well, is one of the things in my head. All the times I've had to explain my family to people and I've said, *My mother died when I was three and then I went to live with my brother.* And in fact that sentence should go the other way around.

When I get to Ollie's house he is halfway out the door—he tells me he has to take the dog out quickly, so he leaves me sitting alone in his living room. No one's home. In the empty house I have the sudden thought that maybe Ollie is lying too: maybe his mum has gone as well. Maybe he lives here alone and nobody knows.

Danny texts me. *Forgot to ask what time you'll be home x*, it says. I send a reply. *Don't know.* This will worry him.

Everything worries him.

Ollie's sketchbook is lying open on the coffee table and I pick it up. You'd think his art might be all black paint and death symbols, but it's actually really pretty. Intricate little sketches of leaves and birds and beetles that he's colored in strange, unexpected pinks and yellows and oranges. It's hard to tell if he's used ink or paint or crayon or what and I trace my finger over one of the pictures, trying to feel the texture of the colors—and then I hear the front door open and I close the sketchbook, put it back on the table. A woman wearing work clothes walks into the room and we both startle when we see each other.

I start trying to explain who I am, and she interrupts and says, "Fine. Where's Ollie?"

"He took Brandy out. Your dog. The dog. He's walking her around the block. He'll be back in a minute."

She nods, putting her handbag on the coffee table. Not knowing what to do, I stand up awkwardly and say, "I guess he didn't know that you'd be home soon."

"What did you say your name was?"

"Oh. I'm Alena. Kennedy."

"You're the one lives with her brother."

"Yes."

She nods again, and then walks through to the kitchen and I hear cupboards opening and the clink of ice. She comes back out with a glass in her hand. "It's good of you to be friends with Ollie." She looks exhausted, I think. Even her clothes look tired. She looks older than she probably is. She doesn't smile at all.

"Oh," I say. "Yeah. We have a lot of classes together. So."

She takes a long drink, emptying the glass, and then goes back into the kitchen and refills it. I sit down again and try to start discreetly texting Ollie to tell him to come back but she walks back in and says, "He's been a miserable little sod since his brother went traveling." She sits down in one of the wicker chairs opposite the sofa. "And that dog. Sick to death of it."

I don't know how to respond. "I didn't know Aaron had

gone traveling," I say, which to me means backpacking around Thailand and not leaving town after getting busted for dealing pot to teenagers.

"He's gone traveling," she says, and for a moment we look at each other and I can see that she knows that I know this isn't true and it's like she's daring me to contradict her.

Parents are all such liars, I think.

"He's gone traveling," she repeats. "It was a good idea for him. Aaron's very ambitious. Very bright. He wants to see the world. But now Ollie just mopes around, hangs around like bad weather. So I thought at least he's finally found a friend or two to put up with him."

I try to nod politely. She finishes her second drink, seems to relax a little. I get the idea that she might offer me a drink and I wonder what I'd say.

"So you're the one lives with her brother."

"Yes."

"I remember him at parents' evening. Last year, maybe, something like that. Everyone was pointing him out."

My skin prickles. I don't like this idea, my brother at my school without me there, people talking about him. He hates parents' evenings but he always goes to them. Nick too, usually. They wear ties.

"Ollie's had this idea he'd go and live with his brother. Aaron was always talking about an apartment and Ollie had this idea Aaron was going to take him with him. Aaron's obviously ditched that plan, taking off." She gives me a long look. "I expect Ollie's jealous of you."

I stare at her. This has obviously been some sort of national announcement that I've missed, that Ollie is jealous of me, and it still seems ridiculous, so I say, "I really doubt that."

She does smile then, bright and brittle. "I expect he is. I expect it all seems very glamorous to him."

And I am sick of this, remembering Danny saying that I'd find Lynn Wallace glamorous: this stupid word they use when they want to make us sound childish and naïve and like we aren't equipped to see the world correctly: *Oh, it's because we think it's glamorous*—turning anything new or bright or interesting into some cheap trick we've fallen for. Like we are really that easily impressed.

"I really doubt that," I say again.

Then again, maybe he is messed up enough to be jealous of me. But not because my brother is glamorous. I see it for a moment, through Ollie's eyes: it's just that my brother hasn't abandoned me, whereas Ollie's been ditched by pretty much his entire family and the last one standing doesn't seem to like him very much.

Danny never abandoned me. This is true. And he had at least two chances.

I hear Brandy barking right outside the door and I know Ollie's home, so when I hear the front door open I stand up and get my bag and say, "By the way, Ollie's a really amazing artist; you should be really proud," just as he walks in to the room.

They both look surprised, so I say, feeling my blood rising, "And Aaron's a drug-dealing sociopath, from what I remember." Then I turn and walk out, pushing past Ollie and bending, very quickly, to scratch Brandy's ears on my way to the door.

I have to stand outside for five minutes waiting for Ollie, who eventually comes out with his arms spread like, *What the hell?*

"I'm sorry," I say, not particularly sorry, but with my heart still thumping, a little exhilarated. "She was telling me how great Aaron is."

"So?"

"So I just think you're a much better person than he is, and you should both know that."

For a minute I think he'll be angry but he just shakes his head slowly and says, "You've lost it."

"Maybe," I say. I don't feel like I've lost it. I feel like I've found the right words for a change. "It's true, though."

And he stares at me, not looking pissed off, just a little stunned, like I've introduced him to an idea he's never heard before.

× × × × ×

The movie Ollie wants to see is called *The Last Atrocity*. It's the final movie in the *Atrocity* trilogy. I haven't seen the first two. It doesn't matter. There's noise and blood and explosions, and all the sound and light clears my brain out, wakes me up.

"Can I tell you something?" I say, as the credits are rolling and Ollie's still staring, rapt, at the screen as he scrapes the bottom of a box of popcorn for the last bits.

"Huh?"

"I found something out today."

He turns to me. "What?"

The house lights go up and the music gets turned down. The cinema's almost empty so we can stay in our seats without having to get up to let anyone out.

"When I was born," I say, and then I have to lower my voice, realizing how quiet it's gone. I say it all, in a rush. "When I was born, my mum was in prison. She hit a policeman in the face at an anti-war protest."

Ollie's eyebrows go up and his mouth drops open a little bit, clearly impressed.

"Apart from a few months in prison, I never lived with her at all," I say. "I've lived with Danny the whole time. She died almost as soon as she got out of prison."

That's it. The whole story. It took Danny twelve years to get it out but I can tell it in five sentences.

I feel light-headed for a moment, almost giddy, maybe just from the sugar in the popcorn.

"Are you serious?" he says.

"Yeah."

"Wow," he says.

"Yeah."

"How'd you find out?"

"Danny told me. This evening."

"Wow."

"Yeah."

"So it really wasn't your fault, then."

"What?"

"That you don't remember her."

And something turns over inside me then, like a stone in the dirt, and on the other side of it is the truth of this, that it isn't my fault after all.

"No," I say, "it's not," and I'm about to say, *It's Danny's fault for lying to me*, but of course this isn't true either.

It's her fault, I suppose. She did this to both of us.

× × × × ×

It's late when I get home, and Danny is waiting up. He's sitting at the kitchen counter with his laptop. The apartment is dark apart from the lamp in the corner and the blue light from the computer screen.

"Hey, kid," he says, gently.

"Hey."

He picks something up. "Here," he says. "Fixed your keyring." He holds it out to me.

I pause for a moment, and then go and take it. I turn it over in my hand. He's removed the broken link and reattached the chain so you can't even see where it snapped.

"What movie did you see?"

"*The Last Atrocity.*"

"Oh," he says. "Any good?"

"Pretty good."

"What was the first atrocity?"

"It didn't really say."

"Who'd you go with?"

"Ollie."

"Ollie who likes art."

"Yeah."

"You didn't have any dinner," he says. "Nick made stir-fry. We saved you some. Are you hungry?"

I realize that I am.

I sit down. He gets a bowl out of the fridge, takes the tin foil off the top, microwaves it, and puts it down in front of me with a fork.

"Did she really make you soup?" I say. "The day before she went to prison. So you'd have something to eat."

He sits down again. "Yes."

The food is too hot to eat and I poke at it with my fork, waiting for it to cool.

"I know you're probably angry with me," Danny says.

I don't answer.

"It's OK if you are."

I don't answer.

"There's something I forgot to say," Danny says. "The main thing I meant to say earlier. I forgot to say it. I think I might have told you that story wrong."

"What?" Honestly I'm not sure I want to hear anything else. I'm tired. I feel like I could sleep for days.

"It's just that there's something I want to make clear to you," he says. "Which I obviously should have told you earlier but I always just assumed you already knew."

"All right," I say. I sit and wait.

"It's just that I know I say things sometimes that I shouldn't say, especially lately, and I act as though—I act as though I didn't, but I did have a choice. I did have a choice, Alena. Nobody ever forced me to do anything. People were fighting over you. I did have a choice about whether or not I took you, and I wanted to, I really wanted to, and so did Nick, and it was literally the best thing we ever did, ever. I've never once regretted it for even, like, a second. So. I just wanted to make sure you know that."

My face feels hot.

"That's all," he says.

"Literally the best thing ever?" I say.

"Literally."

"And you still think that even now?"

"Yes. God, yes, of course, Lena. Yes. Jesus."

"Even though you never got to go back to college."

"Yes."

"Or hang out in Soho bars with Nick."

He smiles, a little bit. "I could still hang out in Soho bars with Nick."

"You could still go back to college."

He shakes his head like he can't think about this. Then he

says, "I keep trying—I swear to god, I've tried really hard not to screw this up, every day. I promised I would always—but there's so much *stuff*, there's so much—school, and the dentist, and sign this bit of paper and clothes that fit and crossing the road, and whole *books* about, like, your emotional development. And then you do this crazy thing with Will and Mike and my job and I'm thinking, *What is this about?* Is this like your political awakening or is this because Nick and I have screwed up or is this just because you hate me for something or what?"

"I don't hate you," I say.

"And then I'm thinking, when I'm talking to you, Is she turning into this grown-up person I don't even know? Does she have enough friends? Is she using humor as a defense mechanism? Is she trying to defend herself from this awful unloving world and you're never going to be happy, you're going to buy a gun or write angry poetry—"

"I would never—"

"It's just that the world is this randomly violent place and you're supposed to be my responsibility. And everyone in my life wants to start the revolution or something. It's different now than when you were little." He looks at me. "I don't want you to be like her," he says. "I don't want you to be like Nick. I want you to be safe."

"I am safe," I say.

We look at each other for a long time, until it feels weird. Then he says, "I miss her a lot. I really miss her a lot. That's why I can't talk about her. It's not because—it's not just because of what I told you earlier. It's because I miss her. I wish she was still here."

I wish that as well but not in the same way he does. I will never miss her in the same way he does.

"I have this dream all the time," he says. "I've had it for years and years. Where she's standing outside the apartment and she's knocking at the door and she's calling for me, she's saying, *Danny, Danny,* and I'm inside but I can't find the key. The door's locked and I can't find the key to open it, and I know that if I can't find it she's going to go again. And I'm always shouting to her, I'm saying, *Mum, please, wait, I'm looking for the key.* But I can never find it."

"That sounds horrible."

"Yeah."

"Am I ever in the dream?"

"No. In my dream about you, you're swimming in the sea and I'm on this boat, and you're waving at me and I'm telling you to swim back to the boat because there's this massive storm—"

"Danny," I say, "did it hurt her feelings that I cried when I was taken to visit her?"

He blinks a few times. "No," he says. "No. She understood. It didn't hurt her feelings."

I can see that he's lying. I guess he doesn't know how to stop.

We don't say anything else. He waits up with me until I finish eating.

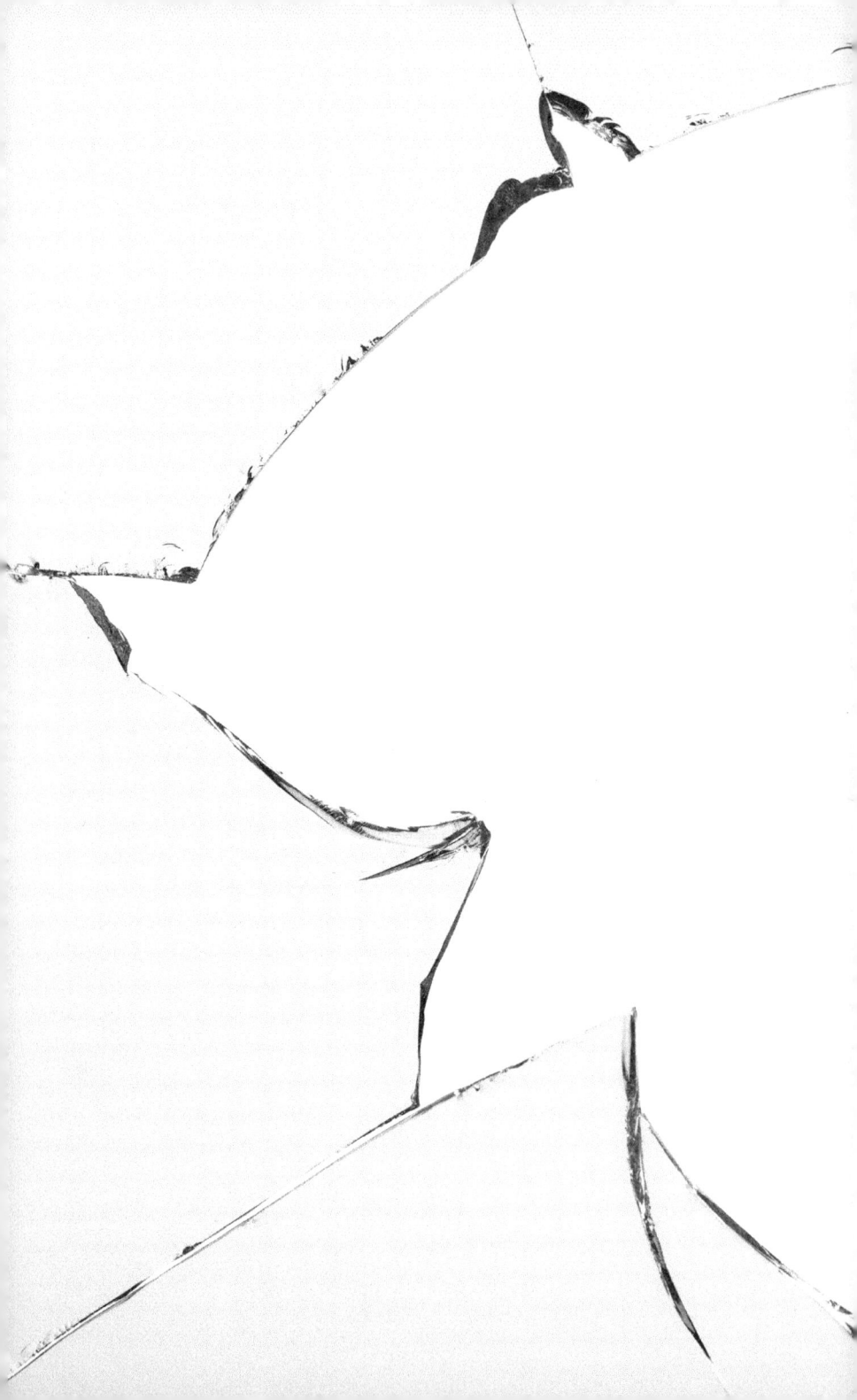

PART SIX

48

Teagan's just gotten a third piercing in her left ear. It's red, still—inflamed and raw-looking around the silver stud. Any day now a teacher will make her take it out.

She keeps touching it, carefully, as we sit on the steps outside the music block, our sweaters tied around our waists and our legs stretched out in the sun. It's gotten hot early this year.

It's Friday, a week after Danny told me everything. Teagan called me that same night: it was nearly one a.m. and she was on the landline in her kitchen, whispering.

"Are you OK?" she said, after I told her the story. I was whispering too, lying in my dark bedroom.

"I don't know," I said. "I just feel sad right now."

"Me too," she said. "I feel sad for everybody in that story."

To us it's a story, I thought. *To Danny it's something that actually happened.*

We've talked about it a lot, now. All week, every breaktime, turning it over till we've looked at every possible angle. Right now, Teagan is musing over whether it's ever OK to hit a policeman in the face with a glass bottle.

"No," I tell her, because I've been thinking about this too. "I don't think it ever is."

"What if instead of a policeman, it's Jacob Carlisle and he's trying to close down the coffee shop?"

I make a face. "No. Even then."

"But you have to stand up for what's right."

"Not by smashing someone's face in. Anyway, she didn't do it on purpose. It was an accident."

Or she said it was an accident. She told Danny it was. But you would say that, wouldn't you? I'd like to ask her: Was it really? Or were you so angry in that second—so furious about everything—that you did something you regretted forever but you still meant to do it in that second?

I wish I could ask her. I could say, *That policeman is probably still walking around with his scarred face. How does that make you feel?*

Teagan sighs and fiddles with her ear stud again, wincing. "I never used to feel this boring," she says. "With my normal mum and dad and their dinner parties."

"Since when do your parents have dinner parties?"

"I don't know. They talk about it sometimes. You know what I mean."

I look at our feet, next to each other on the step. We are wearing the same shoes, flat black sandals with ankle straps. They don't really fit the school regulations but no one's noticed yet. We bought them separately, last spring, and turned up after half-term with no idea that we had the same shoes.

"Yes," I say. "I suppose I know what you mean."

"Not that boring is completely bad," says Teagan. "I mean, I'm obviously glad my brother isn't Aaron Cohen."

"Right?"

"Seriously."

"You were right, though," I say, carefully. "When we had that fight. When you said my family was nothing like Ollie's." I look at her, checking that bringing up the fight isn't a bad idea, but she's just twisting her earring, listening to me. "I was thinking about it. My family's probably a lot more like yours, honestly," I say. "I mean, my actual family. Now."

"Right, with a few more prison sentences and massive feuds."

"Right."

We go quiet for a minute, listening to the distant shouting and yelling from the football field.

"It's good that we're friends with Ollie," Teagan says. "I think it's good."

"So do I."

She nods. I can hear a teacher blowing a whistle, then shouting at the football players to wrap it up.

"Speaking of feuds," says Teagan, "have you worked out what you're going to say to this Lynn Wallace person tomorrow?"

Then the bell goes for the end of lunch and I stand up, brush my skirt down with my hands, and reach out a hand to pull Teagan up. "No," I say. "I have no idea."

49

So Saturday morning, Danny buys me and Lynn Wallace a coffee and a tea and then he says to me that I should call him and he'll come and pick me up when we're finished. Then he leaves. He doesn't really look at Lynn or talk to her except to ask her what kind of coffee she wants. When he's gone Lynn says, for some reason, "That poor boy."

We're in a café near Brick Lane, sandwiched in between a hairdressers' and a vintage clothes shop. The café serves tea and coffee and wine, and square pizza on a board instead of a plate. Lynn is wearing a bright necklace with multicolored gems. I can't tell if it's worth five hundred pounds or if it's from a charity shop but I like it, and it gives me something to look at because she is studying me very intently and it's hard to meet her eye. Some part of me is still a little angry with her.

"Can I buy you something to eat?" she says.

"I'm fine," I say. "Thank you."

I can tell that this will be the end of small talk. I can tell that Lynn is not the kind of person to sit around and talk about the weather.

Before we left the house, Danny said to me, "Look, if she says anything bad about me, please remember that there's two sides to every story."

Lynn stares and stares at me until I get awkward and I can feel my face start to go warm, and she says, "Well, this is quite emotional for me. To have not seen you since you were such a little girl."

"You saw me a few weeks ago."

"Well. That's true."

"You got me in a lot of trouble."

"I can imagine."

She clearly isn't going to apologize, so I say, "When was the last time you saw me before that?"

She looks into her coffee for a few moments. "I'd have to say it was about two days after Heather's funeral," she says. "I came to see you when it was just Nick there. I came to say goodbye to you. And it seems like yesterday. It's hard for me to believe you could be fifteen already."

I don't know how to answer, so she carries on. "But I used to look after you all the time when you were a baby. Your brother had the apartment with the blue carpet. I'd take hundreds of photos of you to bring to your mother. You were always happy. Always had a huge smile. You were really very sweet."

"I don't think I am anymore."

"Well, that's all right," she says. "There's better things to be."

"Danny thinks you're going to say all kinds of terrible things about him."

"I've no idea why he thinks that. He's wrong."

"He's said some bad things about you."

She smiles slightly, but it doesn't reach her eyes. "Yes. I'm sure he has."

"But mostly he's never said anything about you. I never even heard of you until this year."

"Yes. Well. That was the way he wanted it."

"And you went along with it."

"And I went along with it, and I can see that you're angry about that."

I don't answer.

"I always had it in mind that when you were eighteen I would try and look you up," she says. "That I would send you a letter. I can't tell you how often I've thought about you. And then suddenly here was an email from you, saying I might remember you, I might remember your brother. As if I could have forgotten."

I think about that stupid email and still feel a twist of hurt that she didn't reply, that she phoned Danny instead.

"You know, don't you," she says, "that your mother was my best friend? When she died it was the worst thing that ever happened to me. I think about her every day."

"Oh," I say.

She picks up her coffee but doesn't take a sip, just holds it in her hands for a while. We've gotten serious really quickly. I almost wish she would ask me about school and what I want to do when I'm older, give us both space to breathe before we get into the worst things that have ever happened to us.

At the next table a couple are arguing about what kind of pizza to order.

"Part of me thought that Danny would come around. After he'd given himself some time to recover, he'd realize he still had a child to look after and he'd want help, he'd want to get in touch with Heather's friends, he'd want a community around you. But he only accepted my help when she was in prison because Heather forced him. Once she was gone—"

"He only just told me about her being in prison. I only just found out about it."

"I hope he told you it was a terrible injustice."

"He said she hit someone in the face with a glass bottle."

"In self-defense."

"He didn't really say it was in self-defense. He said she didn't mean to do it."

"It was in defense of a larger principle."

"Oh." I fiddle with a hairband that's around my wrist. "Because I don't really agree with violence," I say. "I don't think."

"Good," says Lynn. "Your mother believed in nonviolent resistance and so do I."

"Oh."

"But chaos finds a way. Things go wrong. We're all fallible. It's hard to commit to nonviolence when there's a police horse coming at you. The prison sentence was ludicrous. Really, Alena. All out of proportion." She shakes her head, like she doesn't want to get angry all over again. I don't want to argue about it either, really, or not today, but part of me thinks *things go wrong* isn't an excuse.

Part of me understands how angry Danny must have been with her back then.

"Anyway," says Lynn. "If she hadn't died so soon after, we'd all have forgotten about prison by now. We'd be laughing about it. But for your brother it was all the same thing in his mind, just one terrible thing after another. And there he was after the funeral, under siege for the second time from your aunt and uncle—who are appalling people, by the way; she was trying to physically pry you from his arms and saying the most appalling things—and I could have helped, Alena. I only wanted to help him, and he told me he never wanted to see me again, that he didn't want me to have anything to do with you."

She looks at me almost pleadingly, as if I might be able to explain this terrible decision he made or to undo it, somehow. But I can't and it does seem like a terrible decision but at the same time I think how he must have felt, how awful everything must have seemed right then, and how easy it would have been for him just to let me go, just to let Niamh take me and for him to go away and get better and carry on with his life.

"Don't get me wrong," she says. "I know what he thinks of me, but Danny's a good boy. He always was. He did the right thing to take you and he did it without hesitation. It never crossed my mind that you wouldn't be all right with him. It never crossed my mind. And your mum was smitten with Nick. I can tell you that. He used to visit her a lot. She really thought Danny had hit the jackpot, there."

"Yeah. Everyone thinks that."

"It's not that I blame him for what he did," she says. "He had to make his own decisions. And he was still young. And he was very close to Heather, despite all his moaning and theatrics about her behavior." Then she is quiet for a while, and then she says, "No, I *do* blame him. Whatever he thinks of me, it's hard for me not to be angry with him for wanting to keep you away from Heather's friends and from her community and from everything she did. As if there was something to be ashamed of. You know she founded the London Women's Anti-Militarization Coalition? It's still going. It has hundreds of members. We have a plaque for her on the wall in the committee room. I'd like you to come and see it."

"OK," I say. And then: "I've never heard of it."

"He's really never mentioned it to you?" she says, sounding a little bit like she might cry. "She used to bring him to the meetings when she couldn't find a babysitter. He used to make us tea."

"Danny doesn't talk about anything like that," I say. "Ever."

"No? Well. I suppose he was never very political. Had a conservative streak, if anything. That's Heather's fault, probably. She never really wanted him to get caught up in it all. She was happy for him to read his books and play football and go to school and come home safe and that was it. She didn't want him getting in trouble."

"That's what he's like with me."

She smiles. "Well, and Heather was young when she had him. She was more protective, more nervous. By the time you came along—she might have brought you up differently. I don't know."

She can't have been that nervous, I think, *if she would take him to a women's anti-nuclear protest camp when he was one year old*, but I don't mention this.

Lynn sips her coffee, puts it down, drops another sugar cube into it. "She was just thrilled with you, Alena," she says. "Thrilled to have a little girl. She couldn't wait to come home to you."

She is wearing black mascara and it's smudged a little bit at the corners of her eyes. She is looking at me very directly.

"She never even really knew me," I say.

"Not to sound overly sentimental, Alena, but she knew you in her heart."

That doesn't mean anything, I think. *That's just one of those things people say.* I feel disappointed for a moment.

Lynn says, "Before Danny was born she was convinced he was going to be a girl. And then just after he was born she said she still thought she'd have a daughter one day. And you know, there was a German girl at our school when we were teenagers. Her name was Alena. She was a prefect, I think. She was very beautiful and political. We were both rather in love with her. So I think she had your name picked out for years."

This was a thing I thought I'd never know.

I take a deep breath. "My brother says she died because she hit her head at the protest. It caused a hemorrhage or something and she didn't even know."

Lynn doesn't answer.

"Do you think that's true?" I say.

She is quiet for a long time. Then she says, "He was desperate for someone to blame. Really desperate. He should have blamed the police if anyone but instead he blamed her and then once she wasn't there anymore he blamed me. Blamed me for that day at the protest, for the arrest, for prison, for her death, the lot. Blames me for world poverty and the sinking of the *Titanic*, too, I expect."

"But do you think that's what happened?"

"I have no idea. There's no way to know. It was Danny who came up with that idea and once he thought it, it just stuck. But knowing why it happened won't mean that it didn't happen, will it, so what's the point? It happened. She's gone. Blaming me won't bring her back."

"It's not just you," I say. "It's her. It's like he's still angry with her. When I mention her, it's like he's still angry with her for what she did and for going to prison and for dying and for everything."

"Well, he thought she abandoned him. That's what he felt like. He was a teenager when she went to prison. He was nineteen. I can't say that I think he's right but you have to understand how young he was, Alena. And then she was pregnant and there was another child she was abandoning. That's how he saw it. And he thought if she'd just stayed at home in an apron—well. We all like to imagine the ways our parents could have been better, don't we?" She sighs. "He thought she and I were going around causing trouble when all Heather should have been doing was looking after her children. But she was, Alena. Listen to me. I said this to him and he wouldn't listen, but she was looking after you just like she was looking after him. She was looking after the world you were going to inherit. She didn't want you to grow up in a world of endless warfare and she knew that's the way we were heading. And she was right, wasn't she? Look at the world we have now. We all went out shouting and fighting because we wanted it to be better than that for our children. The same when Danny was a baby and she took him to Greenham. We wanted a less dangerous world for you."

I wrap my hands around my mug of tea, feel the warmth seep into my palms.

"I don't know any of this," I say.

"Then it's about time you did."

"So you really knew her since you were at school?"

"Alena. Yes. We were ten years old when we met. We were best friends for thirty years. Since we were children. Mine was the first Caribbean family on the street when we moved in and Heather's parents didn't even want us to play together but she ignored them. We were inseparable." She stops stirring her coffee and lays the spoon carefully on the saucer, looks at me with clear, dark eyes. "What is it that you want to know?"

When I was a kid Nick and Danny once took me to Hamley's on my birthday and said I could choose three toys. But

I spent like four hours going around the shop and I couldn't choose a single thing, couldn't even start to imagine what to pick, and in the end I just sat down in the middle of the floor and said that I didn't want anything, that I just wanted to go home. There was too much. I wanted everything.

Suddenly, in a café on Brick Lane on a Saturday afternoon, I run out of questions. I can't think of a single thing to ask.

We are quiet for a moment, and then Lynn nods, sits up straight. "Well," she says. "We don't have to do this all at once. We've got time. And your brother will be back for you soon."

She gives me her phone number and says next Saturday we should go and see my mother's plaque in the London Women's Anti-Militerization Coalition committee room. Then, just before she leaves, she takes something out of her handbag, an envelope, and hands it to me.

"Here," she says. "I've got all kinds of letters and photographs you'd probably like to see, but I wanted to find something to give you today. I had a search and found a note your mother sent me the day that Danny took you home from prison. I thought you might like to have it."

I don't have time to answer before she snaps the clasp on her handbag shut, smiles brightly, and leaves.

I wait a few minutes, alone, before I open the envelope. Inside there's another copy of the Greenham Common postcard, undamaged, and then a piece of notepaper with a date scrawled at the top—five months after I was born.

Lynn,
Not enough tears in the world here since saying goodbye to my beautiful baby girl this morning but

I know she's all right with my beautiful baby (grown-up) boy (and the terribly handsome new bartender boyfriend who we adore). Feeling very sad and reflective and responsible as to how we all ended up in this less-than-perfect situation. But! Everything I've done has been with the best of hopes and intentions and so I hope stubborn aforementioned baby boy will start to forgive me soon. What do you think?

Another q—what will Alena think when she's old enough to understand all this?

I think she'll be a forgiving human with an open heart.

But who knows? I suppose I'll have to wait to find out.

Lots of love to you, Lynn, out there in the world. I'll be joining you all again soon.

H.

I don't notice, at first, when my brother comes back for me. But when I look up he's standing opposite me.

I fold up the note and put it back in the envelope with the postcard, put them both in my bag underneath the table.

"So she just left you sitting here alone, then," says Danny. "That's great. What, did she have to go and picket an embassy?" He pulls out a chair and sits down. I notice the woman at the table next to ours give us both a long, curious look, like trying to work out our relationship.

"Yes," I say. "American."

"Naturally."

A waitress appears and asks if we'd like anything else. "Yeah," says Danny. "Please. A black coffee. Lena?"

"Can I have a chai latte?"

"A black coffee and a chai latte."

The waitress scribbles it down and leaves. Danny glances at the prices on the menu on the table and flinches. Then he looks at me and says, half nervous, "Well?"

"Well what?"

"Has she signed you up for the revolution? Are you going to drop out of school to go and fight in Spain?"

"I don't think they're fighting in Spain anymore."

He slouches in his chair. His clothes are covered in paint, again. They've been working every day at the coffee shop, trying to put it back together, and coming home every evening probably high off paint fumes, both a little manic. I think they're waiting for me to run away from home or have a breakdown or start screaming and crying but I don't feel like that anymore.

"So what did you talk about?" he says, and then, quickly, "I mean, you don't have to tell me if you don't want to. I respect your right to—you know, whatever."

He's trying so hard. I start to wonder if he's been reading Nick's parenting books.

"Next week she's invited me to go with her to the London Anti-Military Women's Committee," I say. "She says there's a plaque, for Mum."

Danny looks at the edge of the table, is silent for a minute. "London Women's Anti-Militarization Coalition," he says.

"Right. You remember it?"

"Yeah. I used to make them tea."

"So I'm going to go."

He doesn't answer.

"If that's OK," I say.

"Did she say anything about me?" he asks.

The waitress brings our drinks, in mismatched ceramic mugs, stands by the table for a while arranging the sugar and sprinkling cinnamon on top of my drink. When she's gone, I say, "She didn't say anything bad." And then, "Actually I think she misses you."

He doesn't respond to this.

"Maybe you could come too," I say. "Next week. We could all go. We could—"

"I don't think so."

"If you spoke to her, if you sat down and properly—"

"Don't, Alena. Don't try and do this. It's not going to happen. Letting you spend time with her is the absolute limit of what I'm going to do."

"You're just going to avoid her for the rest of your life."

"Yep."

"Danny—"

"Are you going to stop avoiding Nick?"

I go blank for a second, confused by the subject change. "I'm not avoiding him," I say.

"Lena. Come on. You haven't been to the coffee shop all week. You don't speak to him at dinner."

"The coffee shop's closed."

"Yeah, but you can come and hang out with us, come and help us fix it up. It's fun. We're laying new flooring."

"That doesn't sound fun."

"He'd really like it if you helped out." He pauses. "It belongs to you, as well."

I scrape my spoon across the foam on the top of my drink, make a little pattern in the cinnamon dust. I already know it won't taste as good as the coffee shop's.

"I thought it was me you were going to be mad at," Danny says. "I thought it would be me you wouldn't talk to."

What can I say? *I had higher expectations of Nick*, or, *Yeah, but you clearly have massive psychological issues whereas Nick has no excuse.*

It's been easier to talk to Danny this last week than any time I can remember. I can tell he feels the same. Like suddenly we are free of this stupid secret that he thought was so terrible, and it's OK to talk again. Her name isn't a curse.

"I told you that he never wanted to lie to you," Danny is saying. "It was me that told him—"

"People are responsible for their own behavior," I say. "What you told him to do isn't an excuse."

Danny looks at me, raises an eyebrow. He is smiling. "You sounded *exactly* like Nick just then, you know that?"

I scowl.

"I think he's even coming around to maybe letting you work there," Danny says. "On weekends. If you still want to. Maybe share the Saturday afternoon shift with Zahra."

I sit up. "For money?"

"Well, yeah. Nick's got this thing against slave labor. You know what he's like. Me, personally, I'd make you do it for free, but—"

"I thought you didn't want me to work there either."

"I've been persuaded."

"How come?"

"I just have."

"Danny," I say, "did Jacob Carlisle really try and close it down that time?"

He looks away from me. It's a very dangerous thing to bring up Jacob Carlisle's name. I am feeling wild. "Not directly," he says.

"But—"

"He was involved in it. Sort of. It was part of a wider thing."

"Then how could you possibly—"

"It was a long time ago."

"But how could you—"

"I wanted it to close down," he says. He looks back at me, straight in the eye. I realize he's confessing something, something he hasn't even told Nick. "Honestly. Back then. That's the truth. There were all these groups that used to meet there and put up their posters and plan their demonstrations and honestly, Alena, some of them *were* breaking the law, and the whole thing just used to—" He breaks off, looks at his coffee. Clears his throat. "It used to scare me, honestly. I was scared Nick would get in trouble. And then after he got beaten up."

"But it's still just a coffee shop. He sells lattes. It's not exactly—"

"That's what she used to say to me. *It's just this, it's just that, you don't need to worry.* And I used to lie awake waiting for her to come home because I always thought she was going to get in trouble. And people said, *Don't worry, don't worry, you're being stupid,* and look what happened. She's not here, is she?"

This is true. She's not here.

I let that fact sit for a moment, her absence at the table gather weight, until, for a strange moment, it feels like she *is* here.

"All right," I say. "I'm sorry."

"You don't have to be sorry. I just get sick of being told not to worry. There's a lot to worry about."

"You really shouldn't have gotten together with Nick, then," I tell him. "You should've gotten together with some boring guy who worked in a bank."

"I know. I realized that about three days after we met," says Danny. "But I liked him, though. I couldn't help it."

This is sweet. It seems like a sweet thing to say. I decide to try and remember it.

"I like him too," I say.

"Good."

"Some of the time."

"Some of the time is all we need right now," he says.

50

So I get talked into going to the coffee shop that afternoon. Since I saw it last it looks a lot better, but it still makes me feel upset to look at it, like how Danny probably felt looking at Nick after he got beaten up that time. Something you love that someone has smashed up for no reason.

Nick looks up from what he's doing when we walk in, and when he sees me I can tell he's surprised, and pleased.

"Hey," he says. "My two favorite people."

"I've come to help," I say to him. "Danny says you need help."

"I do need help."

Danny flicks one of the light switches by the door but nothing happens.

"I think the fuse has blown," says Nick. "I was just going to check."

"I'll do it," says Danny, and circles around Nick, touching his shoulder as he passes, before disappearing down the stairs to the basement.

Nick looks at me. "How was it?" he says.

I sit down at one of the tables, which is white with paint-dust, and put my bag down on the floor. "It was OK," I say. "It was nice." There's a silence. "She invited me to meet up with her again next week. To go and see a plaque. She says there's a plaque for our mum in this London Women place."

"The Anti-Militarization Coalition?" says Nick, because apparently everybody knows about it but me.

"Yes."

"Good. That's a good thing for you to do."

It's another thing I should have been able to do years ago, I think, but then I look at Nick's serious face, and I remember that my mother thought that I would be a forgiving human, with an open heart.

Danny and Nick shouldn't have lied to me. And my mum should never have picked up that glass bottle. But those things won't change, even if I carry all my anger around inside for years and years the way Danny has. I don't want to be like that.

"You could come too, maybe," I say. "If you want."

I see relief in his face. "I'd really like that," he says.

I nod, and look around the coffee shop, at the exposed wires and bits of ripped-up flooring. The way that the sun is slanting through the windows shows all the dust sparkling in the air. "It still looks pretty bad in here," I say.

"Yeah," he says. "But it can all be fixed."

It was Nick who finally fixed the fire alarm in our apartment, that time when it was broken. He got the manual out and read the whole thing, and then he fixed it properly, rather than just forcing it back into place and hoping for the best.

He's probably right. He can probably fix this too.

× × × × ×

I don't end up helping all that much.

Later, Nick is lying on his back underneath the counter where the pipes for the soft drinks and everything are and trying to tighten something with a wrench. Danny is leaning on top of the counter, spinning a screwdriver around in his hand, like they do with guns in westerns. He's not doing anything with the screwdriver; he's just carrying it around.

"If you could only listen to one Bob Dylan song for the rest of your life," I say, "what would you pick?" I'm still sitting at one of the tables, drinking a warm can of lemonade that I found downstairs.

Danny looks appalled. "I'd kill myself," he says. "Don't ask me things like that. It's upsetting."

"I'd have 'Subterranean Homesick Blues,'" says Nick.

"How original," says Danny.

"Do you want to know what I'd have?"

"Lena, you're not old enough to even start to be able to make a decision like that, OK? That is like a profound, philosophical question and you're not ready to tackle it, so don't even try."

"I'd have the one from the album with him and the girl on it."

"'The Freewheelin'.'"

"Yeah."

"Which song?"

"The one you used to play all the time."

"That narrows it down," says Nick.

"You know the one. Something something north country way. That one."

"'Girl from the North Country,'" says Danny. "I'm depressed now. How can you not know the name of that song?"

"It was written about a hundred years before I was born."

"Thirty years."

"Well, that's the one I'd have."

"OK, good choice."

Then the guy who delivers the free local newspaper leans in through the open door. "Hi!" he says. "When are you lot opening up again?"

Danny holds up two fingers. "Two weeks," he says.

"Maybe," says Nick, but nobody can see him.

"Nice!" says the paper-man. "Good work!"

"Thank you!" says Danny, not that he's doing any work.

"Are you Nick? You look different."

"I'm Danny."

"You're Danny. Nice to meet you, Danny. I'm Keith! I deliver the paper!"

"I can see that!" says Danny. "Nice to meet you, Keith!"

"Have you heard?" says Keith.

"Heard what?"

"They've got him."

"Got who?"

"East End Bomber. Got him this morning. Apartment in Tower Hamlets."

"Seriously?" says Danny, and I say, "Really?" at the same time, and Nick sits up and smacks his head against the underside of the counter, so then there's a long pause while Danny checks to see if he has a concussion and Keith offers advice about putting ice on his head and checking his vision, before I actually get to ask.

"So who is he?" I say. "Who did they arrest? Is he a white supremacist?"

"Nah," says Keith. "They think it's some guy who got fired from Tesco's."

"What?" I say, and Nick, getting to his feet and rubbing his head, says, "What?" and Danny says, "Are you joking?"

"Yeah," says Keith. "Some guy who got fired from Tesco's. One of those revenge things. You know. Just some nutter, basically." Keith shrugs like it happens all the time.

"It wasn't—" Nick shakes his head, blinks a few times. "He's not an eco-activist, or something? Or a neo-Nazi or—"

"Nah," says Keith authoritatively. "It was a nutter. Got fired from Tesco's." He shrugs again. "Anyway! Good work you're doing here! Keep it up!"

"Thanks," says Nick vaguely. "But, listen, do they actually *know*—"

But Keith has already gone.

We are all quiet for a few moments. I'm feeling something a bit like disappointment that there isn't a better explanation, like that he isn't a fascist or a neo-Nazi or whatever, or something. Something that we could have talked about over dinner and Nick could have told us how it could have been prevented.

You can try and stop nuclear weapons, maybe, or wars, but it's hard to think how you could have stopped someone getting fired from Tesco's.

"Well, good," Danny says. "They've got him. I mean, thank god, right?"

"Right," says Nick. "Definitely," but he's frowning and looking at the spot where Keith was standing, like maybe he feels the same as me.

"Is your head all right?" says Danny.

"It's fine." Nick scratches his eyebrow and says, "It's fine. I'm going to wait and watch the news. There must be more to it than that."

"Who cares?" says Danny. "They've got him."

"Yeah," says Nick. "But there must be more to it."

I've already got my phone out of my pocket and have loaded up the news. There's a picture of him on the front page, probably from his Facebook profile or something. *Face of a killer*, it says underneath. But he just looks like anybody. It's just a normal photo of a man.

It's not enough. It's not a good enough reason for somebody to have died.

"Do you want me to try turning on the water again?" Danny is saying.

Nick sighs and says, "Yeah, all right. Try the water again."

Danny leans across and turns the tap. Water gushes out.

"Jesus," he says. "I can't believe it. We actually got something to work."

"What do you mean 'we'?" says Nick. "I'm the one who fixed it."

"Yeah," says Danny. "And I turned the tap on. Teamwork."

"I helped too," I say, looking up from my phone where, inevitably, they've put up the photo of Eduardo Capello and his baby daughter again. Now that they've caught the bomber they'll probably stop printing this photo all the time. In a few months nobody will be able to remember his face.

"Lena helped too," Danny confirms. "Is it time for a break or what?"

× × × × ×

Later, probably, Nick will still find some way that it's political. Like it'll be about housing or mental health care provision. And Danny will be like, *The world is just like that. The world is just violent.*

We should all just lock the doors and stay inside, he'll say.

And he'll probably be right, except you could be inside and a plane could crash into your house, or someone on the floor below could leave the stove on and start a fire, or you could be making a cup of tea and a blood vessel in your brain could explode. So.

Maybe you just have to concentrate on the things you can change. Try and find the pieces that could be better, and then fight, the way Lynn and my mother did.

This is what I want to do. This is how I want to live. Like she did.

51

It's two weeks later, the Friday before spring break, and me and Teagan and Ollie are lying on our backs on the school field while the cross-country runners do their lunchtime practice, wheezing their way past us every couple of minutes as they lap the field. The sky is very blue. I think it's going to be a hot summer. I close my eyes and the sun makes orange blobs behind my eyelids. The grass underneath our bare arms and legs is dry and brittle, yellowing already.

"When you say *party*," Teagan is saying, "is it like cakes and balloons, or live music and cocaine, or what?"

"It's like Nick's going to open the door and turn the cappuccino machine on."

"So not a *huge* party, then."

"*Party* is probably the wrong word," I admit. "It's more of an *evening*. A reopening evening. Zahra's boyfriend is going to play his guitar and depress everybody. There'll be vegan brownies. Nick'll probably make a speech about community solidarity and fair-trade bananas."

"Oh, OK," says Teagan. "I'll definitely be there for that, then."

"Good."

"Ollie, you have to come as well," says Teagan.

He doesn't answer. "Does the coffee shop actually have a name?" he says. "Or is it just the coffee shop?"

"Oh," I say. "Yeah." For a second I can't remember. "It's called Ground."

"*Ground.*"

"I know. It's stupid. No one calls it that."

"Like coffee grounds, or the ground we stand on?"

"I don't know. Coffee grounds, I guess. Maybe both."

"But who cares," Teagan says. "It's special. And it nearly got shut down. So we have to go to the reopening party."

"Evening," I say.

"The reopening evening."

"Fine," says Ollie. "Yeah. All right."

"Something else I was going to say." I sit up on my elbows, glance at Teagan, who nods. "Nick's got this idea about having art from local artists on the wall. I was thinking maybe you could bring some of your stuff. Some of your sketches, for the wall. I think they'd work really well."

It was Teagan's idea but she doesn't say anything, just tilts her head sideways and looks at him.

Ollie blinks a few times, then sits up as well, pushes his hair out of his eyes.

"What do you think?" I say.

He frowns. "Isn't it supposed to be all political stuff in there? Isn't it supposed to be, like, fair-trade organic-milk art?"

"No," I say. "It can be anything."

"Although," says Teagan, "now I really want to see some fair-trade organic-milk art."

"Your stuff would be perfect," I say. "It would be really good."

"I dunno," he says. "All right. I dunno. Maybe."

Teagan catches my eye, looking exasperated, and makes me laugh.

The runners complete another lap, breathing hard, still going.

× × × × ×

I heard Jacob Carlisle again last night, on local radio. There was no one else home and I was doing my homework with the volume turned down low. It turns out he's been writing a book this whole time. It's called *Independent Man*. It's about the experience of being an independent in an era of party politics, apparently.

It sounded bad. I felt sort of embarrassed for him, giving this interview where he kept saying the name of the book over and over.

"What do you say to the critics who say you exploited the death of a young man for political gain?" the interviewer said, but then I heard the key in the front door and I switched the radio off.

It's still dangerous to mention Jacob Carlisle's name at home. Sometimes you can and Danny will make jokes about him, and sometimes he'll get all moody and silent about it. He's totally weirdly unpredictable sometimes. I've complained about this to Nick, and like always he just says, "I know he is," in this fond voice as if I've just said, "Oh my god, Danny is amazing."

Thank god they met each other because I don't think anyone else would put up with their weirdness.

Nick can get a little moody too, sometimes. He never used to, or at least he never used to in front of me. I think maybe now that I'm getting older he's starting to feel like he doesn't have to try so hard to be some superhero from a parenting book all the time. He can just be a person, sometimes.

Nobody seems to remember exactly what it was that the drunk guys from The Eagle pub said to Nick that night while he was locking up, but I suppose it's not hard to imagine. There's a rainbow flag in the window of the coffee shop, and it's not one of those streets where there's a rainbow flag in every window.

I've heard a lot of stuff myself, but usually from stupid boys in the playground. It would be different when it's three drunk men, when it's night, when you're on your own. It would be frightening. Nick would've been scared.

"I wasn't scared," Nick says, when I ask him. "I was angry."

I don't believe him. I think he was scared as well, but he still turned around and defended himself.

I think Danny's probably right. He should have ignored them, and come home safe. Not because it's the right thing to do. Just because we love him.

If I had been there, though, I don't think I'd have ignored them, either.

× × × × ×

I don't know what Danny's going to do now that they've finished the shop. This is something else it's not really safe to mention. He says he doesn't want to work for Mike anymore, and he says no one else will hire him because of what happened at his last job.

Some nights I hear them start talking about money, but I turn the radio up and drown them out. I've spent a lot of time listening to other people's conversations lately. I am trying to start thinking about the things that I want to say, instead.

52

It's not even summer yet but I always start thinking about Christmas at strange times of year. I don't know what we'll do this year, but usually when it gets near December Nick gets Zahra to string fairy lights up around the windows and along the counter. Sometimes I help her. The lights are really cheap and every year half of them aren't working but when it's dark in the evening and he switches them on and people are walking past on their way home from work—that's when I start to get excited. And I don't even know why because what's the big deal about Christmas, anyway? But I like it because we go to Nick's parents' house and sometimes his brothers are there as well and his parents have all these traditions about when you're supposed to open presents and what you have to eat and they start with champagne and orange juice, of which Danny drinks about four glasses within five minutes of getting to the house, until Nick glares at him. Nick's dad asks me about what books I've read and his mum has gotten me all different kinds of presents and wrapped them in red and gold foil paper and signed them *from Santa* which she's always done and it's like a long-running joke just between us.

And they have fairy lights too, except theirs are more expensive and all of them work properly, and before we go home at about six or seven o'clock they switch them on and they blink on and off in rainbow colors and everyone drinks coffee and it feels exactly like the coffee shop. It feels exactly like home.

And sometimes I think, *What if we didn't have this anymore? What would we do? What if Nick moved out or the coffee shop closed down or somebody was standing in the street and a bomb went off?*

That's what it's like inside my brother's head all the time, I've realized: he's thinking, *what if, what if, what if.* He can't see anything good without thinking that he'll lose it.

I don't want to be like this. I don't think she would want me to be.

× × × × ×

Supposedly grief happens in stages, but Danny says it's more like a tide, that it comes in, recedes, comes in again. His is different than mine but I know what he means and when I decide that I'm allowed to grieve too, that I can do it whenever I like, even now; even though I didn't know her, I recognize that feeling. I've stopped imagining all the things we might have done together since I know they never happened, but instead, lately, what comes in like a wave is the thought of all the places she will not be but should have been: if I go to college, if I get married, if I have children, if next week I get an A on my latest piece of homework, she will not be waiting for me when I get home to clap her hands and beam, delighted. She would have been.

If she'd been different. If she'd stayed at home that day. If she hadn't read the news or been angry about the war. If she hadn't picked up a glass bottle.

It's like a second life, at the edges of this one, that comes into focus sometimes, and then fades away. Comes in like a tide and then goes out again.

I try not to think about my mother lying on the kitchen floor waiting for somebody to find her, and a pot of tea going cold, and how she probably loved me so much but it didn't matter because by the time I was four years old I had already forgotten her except as somebody that I was afraid of, once.

There are a lot of things I could still ask. I could ask when was the last time Danny spoke to her. What kind of food did she cook. What was her favorite film. What did she think I would be when I grew up. There are a lot of things I could ask. Like if I am really anything like her or if I am more like my brother. Even if I'm more like Nick. Or if I'm like none of those people, if I'm only like myself.

Or here's what I could ask: I could ask if, maybe, when me and Danny are together, when Danny is picking me up from school, or picking my coat off the floor, or asking what time I'll be home, or leaning over the kitchen counter with a cup of coffee and asking if I had a good day, if maybe she is really there as well. If maybe she's been there all along, just waiting for me to see her.

ACKNOWLEDGMENTS

Thanks to:

My family, immediate and extended, for all their support and enthusiasm, but especially my mum and dad, for their utter magnificence, and Stu, for all kinds of inspiration.

The wonderful Caroline Ambrose, and everyone involved with the Bath Novel Award.

Stephen Foster, who offered the first enthusiastic words about this book. And everyone on his short course at Writers' Centre Norwich in 2011, but especially Katy Carr and Susie Lockwood.

Sarah Bower and Ashley Stokes at the Unthank School of Writing, and the fantastic group who did the novel writing class in 2013, especially Jon Curran and Carey Denton.

Chloe Sackur and Charlie Sheppard at Andersen Press, and my brilliant and tremendously patient agent Laura Williams.

Duncan Smith, for agreeing not to comment; Nick Cleaver, for lizard suggestions; and Richard Tahmasebi, who really, truly understands themes.

The Greenham Common postcard that Alena finds is inspired by a real photograph, taken by Cynthia Cockburn, of women protesting at Greenham in 1983. It was published by Sheffield Women Against Pit Closures and Hackney Greenham Women as part of a series of postcards distributed by Housmans Bookshop.

ABOUT THE AUTHOR

Catherine Barter grew up in Warwickshire, and then lived in Norwich for ten years, where she worked in a library, a bookshop, and for an organization campaigning for the rights of garment workers. After gaining a PhD in American literature, she ditched academia for the lucrative world of independent bookselling. Currently she lives in East London and co-manages Housmans, a radical independent bookshop in King's Cross.

UNEXPECTED.
ECLECTIC.
ADVENTUROUS.

For more distinctive and award-winning YA titles, reader guides, book excerpts, and more, visit *CarolrhodaLab.com*.